Relative Vacations

Patricia Sands Schultz

RoseDog❦Books

PITTSBURGH, PENNSYLVANIA 15222

For additional information or to order additional books,
please write:
RoseDog Publishing
701 Smithfield Street
Pittsburgh, Pennsylvania 15222
U.S.A.
1-800-834-1803
Or visit our web site and on-line bookstore at www.rosedogbookstore.com

My thanks to the Computer Lab staff of the Charleston Library, South Carolina, for their technical assistance, encouragement, and patience.

Contents

Prologue

FIVE YEARS HAVE GONE BY, and Lisa was graduating from high school. She had continued with the school newspaper writing, an after-school swim club, and a French Club with an emphasis on literature. These had given her a busy schedule, but she thrived on it.

The four years in high school included interviews with rock stars that came to her town or a neighboring town. She also participated in several water shows for the public. The French literature she did on her own, giving her quite a bit of quiet time. Since she now had a boisterous five-year old stepbrother in the house, quiet time was much appreciated. Her father had fixed up a corner of the attic with an old carpet, a desk and chair, an old easy chair, and two walls of plywood that ensured privacy. The third wall included the attic peak and a window, giving Lisa many hours of pleasure over the four years of habitation. She used her "triangle" for reading, studying, doing homework, and writing stories for the newspaper. She asked for an attic swimming lane to be installed! Her father said no. They both laughed. She asked for a telephone. Her father said no again. She settled into her precious "triangle" a few hours every day and let the rest of the world scatter itself around. Some of her friends were jealous. Some were in awe. Some were happy she could escape the little boisterous one and still be at home. They were the good friends.

Barbara, her stepmother, prettied up the "triangle" a bit. She also kept a list of phone calls that Lisa received downstairs. If there were an important call which needed an immediate response, she would tap three times on the kitchen ceiling, Lisa's floor, with the broom handle.

When Lisa graduated high school with honors, especially in French and swimming, her family was proud and felt rewarded for its many contributions.

During these five years, Lisa did not return to any of her relatives for more summer vacations. Sadly, her Florida grandmother passed away last year. Her grandfather came up and lived with Lisa and her family for a few months, but he missed his friends and the warm weather. While he was up north, though, he and Lisa had a good time talking about her trip to Florida nine years earlier.

Her maternal grandmother, Isobel, had never visited during their intervening eight years, so it was a great and pleasant surprise to have her come out west for her graduation. They also talked about Lisa's excursion to Long Island. Isobel described her new shop which was on a side street now, but nevertheless drew many customers. She told her about the friendship she now enjoyed with Abigail who still owned the Southampton Guest House with Howard.

Her cousin, Suzanne, from California, came once, but it wasn't a happy reunion. Suzanne was determined to be boy-crazy. Lisa was determined to be educated.

Mary Joan, her aunt in Charleston, sent lots of pictures of the new addition to the family, so Lisa felt very close to their adopted boy, now seven. The child and Lisa even wrote to each other.

Aunt Sally in New York was about to retire but did manage to come west for the graduation.

Lisa's re-acquaintance with her grandmother and her aunt proved more than successful. They were both pleased with Lisa's growth into adulthood. Isobel and Aunt Sally were more than interested in her education and her future plans for collecting college degrees. Lisa wasn't sure which direction she should take. She thought she would like to write, especially as a reporter. But maybe she would major in French literature. That seemed to lead nowhere, unless, of course, she became a professor. She leaned toward writing. Undecided for now, she would go to a small local college for a year or two and take some liberal arts courses. Aunt Sally and Isobel agreed. She could always transfer to a larger college when her goals became clearer, provided her grades were satisfactory. Both her relatives stayed around for a few days after the graduation, talking and planning.

Francesca, her friend from Long Island, was already in college, a college which gave her everything her family wanted: rich friends. Princeton was going to teach her economics and keep her far enough away from her mother, which was a relief for everyone concerned. Francesca and Lisa still enjoyed each other's letters. And probably always would.

While she had her aunt with her, Lisa finally pulled up her courage and asked Aunt Sally if she ever saw Herbie. Her aunt hesitated.

"You know Rosie got married," said Aunt Sally.

"Yes, she sent me an invitation. That was last year. What about Herbie? We exchanged a few letters, but then he just stopped writing. Is he okay?"

"He left New York. Still keeps in touch with his family to let them know he's alive but that's about it. He's somewhere in California. Works on a farm. Artichokes, I think. Told them he still loved them and New York, but wanted to live in New York by choice. Not just because he was born there. Been gone for about three years now. Didn't even come back for his sister's wedding," commented Aunt Sally with a raised eyebrow.

"Maybe he didn't have the money," Lisa softly said. "That's a long way, from coast to coast. I hope he's okay. I still use the same address occasionally, but he doesn't answer. Herbie was a nice guy. I liked him."

Aunt Sally left the graduation festivities first. She was traveling to Europe in a few weeks and needed to get organized. Isobel had a shop to take care of, so she followed soon after. It was great seeing both of them, and Lisa spent the next few days alone in her "triangle", thinking about her childhood, her teenage years, her scary approach into womanhood. She was sad, she was happy, remembering all her relatives. She wondered why life couldn't just freeze and keep all the good times and good people just as they were. Herself included. She would choose to freeze a bit from each relative vacation. She laughed to herself when she thought how the food that went into the freezer stayed the same. Take it out and you have the same food you put in. Couldn't do that to people though. The only way to keep the delicious moments would be to write about them. She wiped a few tears from her cheek when she remembered Gram, her paternal grandmother. She decided she would write her first story about Gram! But before she pushed the mouse into action, she heard the top of the broom handle on the floor beneath her. Someone wanted her on the telephone. She hadn't left the message "Not to be disturbed" on the kitchen wall so the call could be from anyone. She decided to go down, take the call, and then leave her message on the wall. It was from Janice who suggested they walk over to the college that they both would be attending and investigate more of its interiors.

Lisa put Gram's story on hold.

• • •

THE CLOSING DAYS OF AUGUST proved exciting and exhausting. Lisa's classes were just what she almost wanted: Introduction to American Literature; Introduction to European History; Introduction to Russian Art; Introduction to Biology; and Introduction to Trigonometry. The last two introductions were not her favorites. The first three filled every minute of her thinking hours.

There were no openings on the newspaper staff. She decided to write anyway. She started to write some criticisms of the literature she had been given for homework. When the teacher was not interested in reading her work, she slacked off and concentrated on the specific questions assigned for each essay and poem. She wasn't disappointed as she soon found out that her homework alone took most of her time. And her social life took up the rest.

During the first two weeks, her social life consisted of the girls in the dorm where she lived. She knew a few of them from high school, but it was the girls from across the state and some neighboring states that interested her the most. Many of them came from farm families and added a whole new dimension to Lisa's frame of reference. She started to write short stories about their experiences on a farm.

It was while she was thinking and writing about one of them that she met a young man in the library. She smiled when she first saw him because he resembled Michael, her California friend, whom she had also met in a library. He asked her why she was smiling.

"You remind me of someone," she quietly answered.

"Who?"

"Someone I met in California. Carmel, California."

"Is that where you're from?

"No, I was born here and grew up here. I went out to Carmel to visit an uncle and his family. And you?"

"Me? What?"

"Were you born here?"

"No. The next town over. You could say I came to college to see the world." He gave her a huge smile.

"Freshman?" Lisa asked him.

"Sophomore."

"Seems like a nice college. Teachers seem okay. The books are new and the classrooms are clean and airy."

"Been to the cafeteria yet? That could use more air. And less kids. On the noisy side."

"No, not yet. I don't even know where it is. I go back to the dorm for lunch."

Indicating the surrounding bookshelves, he asked, "Have you been here long? Time for a soda or cup of coffee? I'll show it to you."

"I just got here and I do have some research to do on the kings of England."

He laughed. "Introduction to European History. Right? Does Olsen still teach it?"

"Yes. Is he good?"

"Does he still tell those awful jokes?"

"You mean he does that all the time? I thought he was just nervous meeting a new class. He spent most of these two weeks telling terrible jokes."

"And filthy, right? He went right to the bottom of the barrel with us. Some were funny but most were not."

"I don't like them. And the few friends I've met so far in the class agree with me. Do you learn anything?"

"A little bit. But let me warn you. Don't report him or even tell another teacher. I was so angry last year at the waste of time that I went to the Guidance Office. And I got a C for the year even though I did all the work, passed all the tests, was never absent, and even got into class discussions. Whenever he held any. She probably told him about my remarks, giving my name. He kept on telling those jokes, and I got my only C. So don't complain."

"Thanks for the warning. I wasn't planning to, but who knows how I'll feel after a few weeks Did you complain to anybody about the C?"

"No. I learned a great lesson. Take the nonsense if it comes your way and no reporting it. Look, I've got a little research myself. When you've got all you need on the kings, let's go to the cafeteria."

"Okay. My name's Lisa."

"Kevin."

• • •

AFTER A FEW MONTHS, Lisa and her classmates were asked to write a 500-word autobiography. This was a fun and easy assignment for Lisa. She wrote about her five vacations visiting her relatives around the country. Giving each locality some 50 words, she filled out the assignment with stories about her father and stepmother. Of course she spoke about her mother, too, although her memory here was vague. She wrote about her five-year old stepbrother, Freddie, who received so many small gifts from Aunt Sally, (usually one a month), that whenever he saw the mailman coming up the driveway, he would run across the room yelling "Aunt Sally sent me something." Maybe it was because Aunt Sally didn't have any children, but it didn't have to be an occasion for her to send something. Lisa didn't remember if her aunt had sent her gifts when she was little. But she always liked her. And more so when she met her five years ago.

A week after handing in her paper, she got called down to the Guidance Office.

The counselor, Ms. Lambert, asked her to sit down and then very seriously leaned over to her and asked, "Don't you have any friends, Lisa?" Taken back, she answered a bit curtly, "Of course I do."

"But you only write about your family. What you say about them is lovely but not a word about any friends. Don't you think that's strange in an autobiography?"

"I don't know…. I can do it over. I have lots of friends. And more now that I'm in college. I really don't know why I didn't write about them."

"No, it's all right. But do think about that, won't you," said Ms. Lambert, so sweetly. Lisa wanted to throw up!

The rest of that day was not easy. But Lisa decided to watch her writing more carefully. She would include some of her friends in her stories, if appropriate. Learning how life worked is not always easy.

The rest of Lisa's freshman year went as smoothly as did Kevin's sophomore attendance at a mid-west college that graduated more than a thousand happy and well-adjusted students every year. There was a war on the other side of the world, and it involved a lot of Americans in combat. But there was no draft. Therefore every soldier, sailor, and airman in battle had volunteered and most of them were glad they had.

There were a few demonstrations on campus, of course, and several teachers talked about the pros and cons of having such a war. The professor of European History I led quite a few discussions about it. He always tied them in with the assignment of the day and was clever enough to try to keep his opinions out of them. Lisa could never figure out his politics and was happy about that. He would only take sides with justice, and prove, or try to prove, to the class that wrong was always wrong no matter what flag was carried. There would always be a few students who argued that wrong was sometimes right. The professor, Dr. Mahoney, would then enhance his argument with specific examples. Lisa enjoyed listening to some of the agitators as they fell to the common sense of the professor. She did not get involved in the heated discussions, but did ask a question now and then.

The discussion that got her most excited was about a college campus in a neighboring state during the Vietnam War. Dr. Mahoney explained that there were many people, mostly young, who were opposed to the war. As he began to describe what happened, he jumped up and sat on the edge of his desk. This meant he would be taking the whole period to tell the story and its effects.

"On a particular day, about thirty years ago, some of the students gathered into an angry mob. Most of the students were carrying signs, screaming anti-war slogans, and marching in and out of buildings around the large green. But some of them broke away and set fire to one of the smaller buildings. This seemed to have excited the emotions of even some of the more peaceful ones and before the riot had a chance to simmer down, the National Guard was called. The soldiers assembled themselves on the green, lining up with one knee on the ground and positioning their guns to fire. Someone yelled for the students to stop marching, but the sight of guns pointed at them had the opposite effect. Most of them screamed the anti-war slogans even more violently and began marching right toward the soldiers. Someone then yelled, "Fire" and the soldiers, trained to follow orders, fired their guns!"

The professor stopped, took a deep breath, and quietly announced that four students were killed. "The guns had real bullets, and they were aimed to destroy what was considered an approaching enemy."

Lisa froze. Was Dr. Mahoney telling the truth? Were there really college students killed on campus? "For marching? For screaming? For carrying anti-war placards?" someone shouted.

"Don't forget the burning building. This was not considered a rally. At least not by the government. They saw it as a dangerous mob becoming even more dangerous," he quietly said. "But.....was it right to kill anybody?"

"No. No!" several students yelled out. Others stood up and screamed.

The professor held up his hand to quiet them down. "No, it was not right," he gently added. "It was wrong to set the fire, but it wasn't wrong to march and sing anti-war songs. And it was wrong to point guns with live bullets at the students. And to fire was insane."

The class quieted down. The professor went on.

"Of course the whole country was up in arms. The media quickly surrounded the college, and photos of dead and wounded students and screaming young men and women were taken and distributed around the world.

"One foolish man, an important man in the country, made the statement that "violence breeds violence." That did not go over very well. We had a popular magazine in those days that printed the photograph of one of the dead students on its cover. Now, this was all many years ago. The pain is gone, but we can learn many lessons."

"Why didn't they use rubber bullets?" asked the boy next to Lisa.

"Don't know. Why didn't they use common sense?" asked the professor.

"Who? The students or the soldiers?" asked another young man.

"Both. When you have emotions running your decisions, awful things can happen."

"Were the soldiers punished? Or at least the commander who yelled "Fire", a young woman in the front quietly asked.

"What about the governor who ordered the National Guard to the campus? What about the man who ordered real bullets to be used?" asked Dr. Mahoney. "The whole situation held this country at a standstill, a standpoint. And I believe became one of the main causes of ending that awful war. I bring all this up now because many people do not know about it. Thirty years is a long time, and many who were angry about what happened are either gone or too old to continue protesting. Do you agree that this tragedy and that war in general should be discussed in a history class, even if not European history? All countries, all groups of people, large and small, make mistakes. Some because of the greed of their leaders for power, some because of ideologies. Mistakes are made and people suffer. We do learn from our past, however. And so over the years, over the centuries, we do improve."

"Why does it take so long to improve?" asked the same girl in the front.

"Think about how long it takes you to improve in certain areas of your life. A long time in some cases. Well, groups, countries, take longer. There are a lot of people in those groups, those countries. It takes time and effort to mature. I recently took out the famous movie, "Lawrence of Arabia", which was made in the sixties. So much of what was said on the film could be said today. And the story it told was about events of eighty years ago!"

"Could we see it here in class and then discuss what was said?" asked Lisa.

"Good idea. I can easily tie it in with our assignments. Another film we should see is "The Paths of Glory." Also about the First World War. And "The Story of Emile Zola." About the French army commanders and a man called Dreyfus."

"How about discussing what is going on today?" asked the boy next to Lisa.

"Absolutely. But we have to remember to keep our emotions out of what we say. And that brings us to 10:50. See you all tomorrow."

• • •

"THAT'S WHY WE CALL HIM HONEY," said Lisa with a big grin.

"I don't get it," Kevin said with just as big a grin as Lisa's.

"Dr. Mahoney without the first two letters. And most of us think he is super sweet. Of course, some of the students don't."

"Sweet!? He's great. I remember. But I don't think he would enjoy being called 'sweet.' That's awful. Who are the ones who don't think he's 'sweet'?"

"The trouble makers. Don't know why they're attending college. Life must be very boring for them. I don't have enough hours in the day. No time to get bored. I wish each day had five more hours to its name."

"They would fill up quickly, and you'd be asking for five more hours. You're a thinker and a doer, Lisa. That's a good combination."

As they got to the corner of the parking lot, Kevin leaned over and kissed Lisa on the nose, of all places.

"See you at 8:30. What color is your dress?"

"Pink."

"Well, I ordered white, okay? Mom said they would go with almost any dress you'd wear."

"We went through this last week, Kevin. My dress is still pink, and your flowers will still be white. Are you nervous?"

"Being King of the Spring Dance is not all that easy. Especially taking the Queen. Guess I am kind of nervous. Sorry. Wish tomorrow was now."

"Not me. See you at 8:30."

It was a wonderful dance. Both Lisa and Kevin had a few dances with other boys and girls, but both were happier when they had each other as partners.

During one of the slow dances, Lisa told Kevin that she and her friend, Ruth, were thinking about backpacking through Europe that summer. Summer would be upon them in another six weeks, and plans were being made all over the campus.

Kevin was going to work with his father on the farm. Picking fruit and, later, corn. He would be paid a little, but he did it mainly because he enjoyed working with his arms and legs. Like up and down ladders, bending over, tossing good fruit into baskets and throwing away rotten lettuce and peaches. All under the sun and in the rain sometimes. He liked books and studying but really enjoyed the outdoor work. At one time he had considered becoming a farmer, but his dad talked him out of it, pointing out the poor income as well as the hard work. So he tested these activities each summer against his academic life. He also enjoyed sports and thought perhaps he would become a high school coach. Now he was beginning to enjoy history and thought maybe he would teach history. Maybe do some coaching on the side. Time would tell. He wasn't pushing for an answer right away.

But now he was surprised at Lisa's possible plans to be away for the summer. He had hoped she would stay in town, maybe get a summer job, and he would see her on weekends. But Europe? That's a long way.

"How long would you be gone? The whole summer?"

"Don't know yet. We just thought about it last week. We both have some money saved up from graduation and from Christmas. We're going to the travel agency next week."

"Well, don't go for the whole summer, okay? A month, six weeks the most, okay?" stammered Kevin.

"We'll see," replied Lisa, laughing at herself using that adult expression of postponing decisions. How many times did she hear her relatives use that excuse! "You'll be busy working on the farm. Or.... you could come with us."

"No, not this summer. Money. But maybe next summer."

They finished the dance, returned to their table for a drink and some snacks. And more talk. Kevin liked Ruth being Lisa's friend. Ruth was a good kid.

"Did you tell Ms. Lambert that you have a friend?"

"No, silly. She probably doesn't even remember me."

"Send her a postcard from London telling her about your *friend.*"

"How did you know we were going to go to London?" asked Lisa.

"Everybody goes to London sometime during their European trip."

"Is that because they speak our language? That's why we decided to start our trip there. Put our feet down on foreign soil where we can be understood. At first, anyway. Then we can go across the channel and investigate the rest of Europe."

"Here comes your traveling buddy. With Steve of all people."

"Hi, Ruth. Steve. Didn't see you before."

"Hi. You did a great job on the speech, Kevin. It will probably get you the presidency next year. If you want it. Steve's going to run for Treasurer. Right, Steve?" asked Ruth.

Steve smiled slowly as he spoke to Kevin, "Want me on your team?"

"The Junior class needs a strong team. What with all the projects we have in mind."

"You have to win first, Kevin," said Lisa.

"What are some of the projects?" asked Ruth.

"Helping the kids in town with their homework. Teaching them how to study. Organizing some sport days for them."

"What age?" asked Ruth again.

"I don't know yet. Probably from ten to sixteen. There are lots of kids that have their afternoons with nothing to do, most parents working. And some of the kids are getting into trouble."

"Boredom," added Lisa.

"Won't some of the teachers have something to say about that?" asked Steve. "I mean about the schoolwork. They'll want to know what we're doing, right?"

"Look, he's already involved. Of course you don't have to be Treasurer to help with homework. Unless you're charging them," challenged Ruth.

"Funny! Strictly volunteer. But I could do both. Collect students' fees and take on a kid or two for some reading help," answered Steve.

Turning to Lisa, Kevin asked, "Another dance? Music sounds good."

"Excuse us, Ruth and Steve. See you later," said Lisa as she moved to the dance floor.

The hip-hop turned into a slow number, and Lisa and Kevin continued to dance.

"I'm not so sure about Steve." said Kevin in a low voice.

"I know. But a lot of that was rumor, wasn't it? Maybe none of it was true."

"He never came out and denied it. Strongly. He said he didn't do it. But then he laughed about it a lot."

"Wanting to be Treasurer again is claiming his innocence, isn't it? How much was actually missing, Kevin?"

"Not much. A little less than a hundred. He was handling over a thousand, what with dues, pictures, dance decorations, gifts for teachers. I just wish he would have stood up and followed it through, proving he had nothing to do with it. He just laughed it off. Thought it was funny. A lot of the kids still believe he took it. Right out of the safe. His fingerprints were all over the box, but so were lots of others.

Including mine."

"I trust Ruth and don't believe she would date him if she had any suspicion. We never talked about it too much, but her brother really believes the money just got lost traveling around so much between the bank and the safe and the merchants. He feels it was carelessness on someone's part, not thievery. I hope so, for her sake. She likes him," said Lisa as she placed her head gently on Kevin's shoulder.

"Like I said, he should have fought the rumors. Written an article for the school paper, even the paper in town. Fight for his innocence. The school sure didn't help him. They should have done more than just hold a few meetings. And closed meetings at that! We don't have any idea what was said at them. I don't know what to believe now. Wanting to run for Treasurer next year is either scary or funny. I'm not sure I'd want him on the team if I become President. I like him enough. But I have to trust him."

"Why don't you have a serious talk with him?" asked Lisa.

"I did. You know I did, but he just laughed. Said he had no idea what could have happened. None of the merchants were of any help. Only a few of them had kept records of the stuff we bought. It's over now and maybe by running again, he's telling people that he was completely innocent. Like you said."

"Let's forget about it now and just enjoy the dance," Lisa softly said.

"Right. But I want to hear more about your trip to Europe."

"Later."

• • •

LISA AND RUTH POURED OVER MANY MAPS during the following weeks. Their travel agent helped them with passports, foreign currency, railroad reservations. They decided to visit France after a week in England, then on to Italy, up to Germany and Switzerland, up again to Denmark, over to Holland, and back to England again. Like a circle tour. They also wanted to take a peek at Scotland and Ireland before returning home.

The more they read, the more excited they became. The agent was concerned that they didn't want to book hotel reservations in each country. Even cheap hotels took reservations. But Lisa, considering herself quite a traveler, thought they could take a chance on finding rooms in every large city. Aunt Sally told her that she had seen several young people in railroad stations, asking and receiving accommodations. Of course, Aunt Sally had excellent reservations, but she did say that the kids seem to be having such a good time standing on line and discussing various hotels and their prices. She thought Lisa might enjoy that. And the countries she was visiting all seemed safe enough for inexperienced travelers. In Lucerne, Switzerland, Aunt Sally heard three girls delightfully accept a room at a convent. Lisa was amazed at her aunt's frivolous attitude but latched on to the idea of not being tied down so far in advance. Aunt Sally enjoyed the luxury, while Lisa would enjoy the excitement.

Kevin got in on some of the decisions as he was concerned that Lisa was so loose about her accommodations. Lisa tried to convince him she was perfectly safe. The two of them went over all the possible cities and the tours she and Ruth could take. The planning was great fun. But Kevin was strangely quiet.

"Going to ride in a gondola?" asked Kevin.

"Absolutely."

"And go up the Eiffel Tower?"

"Of course. And in Germany we want to take a boat up the Rhine River. Oh, Kevin, I can hardly stand it. Thinking about all these things. I wish you were going to be with us. I know. You're all set for the farm. It'll be fun, Kevin. You'll get a good tan and be so healthy. And have a little more money. And I'll have none!"

"What has your father been saying about all this?"

"He thinks it's great. He and Barbara went over there a few years ago, and they want to go back as soon as Freddie is old enough to enjoy the sights and sounds of traveling."

"He's not worried?"

"No. He sent me all over the country five years ago and never worried. And I was just a child then. He knows I won't do stupid things. And I won't. I had such wonderful times visiting my relatives without doing dumb things. He trusts me."

"I trust you but I still don't want you to go," Kevin softly said.

"Oh, Kevin, please don't say that. I want you to be happy about my going."

"Lisa, could you possibly wait till next summer? I know I could make it then. I'd have the money and could give plenty of notice for my father to get extra help. I would never be a controlling kind of guy. I have to let you do what you want. But we've meant so much to each other these past few months. It just doesn't seem right for us to be separated for such a long time."

"Six weeks isn't that long. We could make it four weeks. Let me talk to Ruth."

"You know how much I love you. And I know you love me. We're still young and probably shouldn't get married for a couple of years. But I just don't want to be away from you."

"I feel that way, too. I really don't want to be away from you. Oh, I don't know what to do! I suppose I could wait till next summer. It certainly would be more fun seeing Europe with you. What would Ruth say? I don't think I can do this to her. We've already made so many plans. Oh, Kevin, what should I do?"

"Take it easy, Lisa." Kevin took a deep breath. "Let's talk to Ruth. And invite her with us next summer. Then let me talk to Dad. Lisa, we could have a wonderful summer this year. You could get a part-time job and start your writing. And we'd have every weekend together. I'm sorry, Lisa, I shouldn't have waited this long. Should have spoken up the minute you mentioned it at the dance.

"You seemed so happy about the idea."

"I was in a way. I was shocked, really. Didn't know what to say. The more I think about it, the more I don't want you to go. Talk to Ruth."

Still shaken but clearer about wanting to stay with Kevin, Lisa went over to Ruth's dorm.

"Ruth, got a minute? Could we go for a cup of coffee?"

"Boy, you look serious. Sure, let me find some money."

They walked to the Eatery in silence. Ruth made a few remarks about school exams coming up soon. "Plenty of studying to do," she murmured. They got cokes instead of coffee and brought them over to a corner table. Lisa took a deep breath.

"Ruth, do you think it's possible we could go to Europe next summer instead of now? Just a thought. What do you think?"

"I can't believe this!" Ruth exclaimed with her eyes stretched wide open. "I was trying to find a way to ask you the same thing. My family is a little tight on money right now. And since I was going to borrow some from them, I thought how much easier it would be for me to go next summer when I would have all my own money. But I didn't know how I could tell you. I can't believe you want the same thing."

"Guess it's always better to speak up. Kevin did."

"Oh, Lisa, this is great. My parents will be thrilled. They didn't want to spoil anything so they were going to borrow from the bank. Now they won't have to. I can even get a summer job."

"Next summer, right? For sure."

"Sure! Why do you want to wait till then? Am I allowed to ask?"

"Do you mind that Kevin wants to go with us next summer?"

"No, I guess. Oh, I see. He doesn't want you to be away for so long. This is really serious, isn't it? You and Kevin. Nice to have someone wanting you with him all the time. You feel the same way? I guess you do, or you wouldn't be asking to postpone our trip. Ah, love, isn't it *grand*?

"Yes," Lisa whispered, self-consciously. "I think it's also *grand* that you wanted to cancel it for this summer. Wouldn't it have been awful if neither of us found the courage to speak up? We would have had a terrible time over there. Now we can plan for next summer. You will come with us, won't you? asked Lisa.

"Maybe. That's a long way off. But, yes, it would be great to have a man along. Protect us from those amorous Italians."

"And he can carry our luggage!" screamed Lisa. She looked around and covered her mouth as she apologized to the few kids sitting around.

"Lisa, I'm glad we're such good friends. And to think, only two towns away, and we never even knew each other till this year."

"Guess that's what college does. What I'm happy about is that I went to a small college nearby. Meeting people I might never have known, even though they live so close."

"Kevin." Ruth gave her a big smile.

"Yes, Kevin. Wait till I call him!"

• • •

THE EXAMS CAME AND WENT. Lisa, Kevin, and Ruth took them with lighter hearts and clearer minds.

The summer started with Lisa and Ruth finding ideal part-time jobs: Lisa in a flower shop where she could work while thinking about the writing she would do that evening; Ruth in a travel bureau where she could dream about next summer without interfering with her work.

Kevin happily picked peaches and lettuce.

Lisa and Kevin saw each other every weekend and by the end of the summer, Lisa finished her five stories: one for each vacation she took with a relative. She edited and edited again and finally put them all in one package and called it RELATIVE VACATIONS.

The lines are fallen unto me in pleasant places; yea, I have a goodly heritage.

Psalms 16:6

Book One
Lisa in Florida

Chapter One

The flight attendant approached the nine-year-old sitting next to the window in Row 4.

"You are Lisa?" he asked as he checked the papers in his hand.

"Yes," she answered as she turned her head toward him. Tears were streaming down her cheeks. Then a deep sob.

"Can I help?" the attendant kindly and quickly asked.

Lisa turned her face away and shook her head. She took out a tissue from her backpack sitting on the floor in front of her.

"How about a soda? And some pretzels?" he asked.

"No, thank you," was what she said, but she was thinking he should go away and leave her alone. This put a scowl on her face.

"Lisa, ring that buzzer over your head if you want something. You'll have to undo your seat belt and stand up to reach it. Do you know how to unhook it, then hook it again when you sit down?"

Lisa nodded as she wiped her face again.

"I'll check with you in a few minutes." And he left.

Lisa was mad at herself for crying. She didn't want anybody to know she missed her father already. How could she be away from him for two months? No, she decided it would only be a month. But even a month was too long. She hadn't meant to complain so much about going back to day camp this summer. Last summer she had loved the swimming in the morning, but she did not like the arts and crafts in the afternoon, the whole afternoon! Making cards and envelopes out of colored paper for hours and hours was a bit much. She went along with it last year but was determined not to do it again. Of course, they probably would have a different activity this summer, but she didn't like cutting paper or using that white paste either. It smelled and made her fingers all sticky. But she had decided too late that she would have done all that rather than go down to Florida to visit people she didn't even know. And leaving Daddy alone! That was terrible. Sure he had Mitzi when he came home from work. But even Mitzi shouldn't have to be in an old kennel all day. Oh, it was all wrong.

If her father had just let her stay home in the afternoons, she could have read a lot of books or looked at television until 5 when her friends came home from arts and crafts. When he said she was too young to be alone, she told him she had Mitzi; but he insisted that if she didn't go to camp, she had to go to his parents in St. Petersburg, Florida. Sadly, they had a terrible argument and said mean things to each other. She loved him very much and knew he loved her. So why did they fight so much? And now she had to leave him for such a long time. Was he punishing her? When she had pleaded with him, he threw up his hands and went in to watch the news.

Patience was not one of Josh's finer character traits. She knew he was a kind man, generous, and loving, if things went his way. He worried about this growing impatience. He couldn't remember if he had been this impatient when Joanna, his wife, was living. She was gone now almost two years, and he thought that he was over the pain and was becoming calmer, both in the office and with Lisa. But whenever Lisa got stubborn and willful, he simply lost it. He tried talking with her when she was quiet about the difficulties they were having without Joanna. Most of the time Lisa went along with his wishes, after the explanations, although there were times when she absolutely refused to cooperate. And this had been one of those times.

He simply couldn't leave her alone in the house. He couldn't take any time from work. His parents seemed to be the perfect solution if she refused to go to camp. In fact, he thought that he and Lisa were getting too close, depending on each other too much. She even resented his seeing Barbara, the new secretary in his office. When she came to their house for dinner, Lisa was not very friendly. Sometimes rude. But he was sure that would soon work out.

Nevertheless, he had to take care of Lisa's summer schedule first. His parents were delighted with the idea though they were a little concerned about the two-month plan, both for Lisa and for themselves. His father, Carl, was having problems sleeping at night and was resorting to naps during the day. Finally, they all decided to try a month and see what happened. Finally Lisa gave in. She had some good talks with her grandparents on the phone, and they did seem to be nice and even had some fun ideas. Okay, she'd go.

So here she was 30,000 feet in the sky, her heart breaking with the thought that she wouldn't see her father for such a long time. She still missed her mother. At the time she had almost decided never to love anyone else ever again. It was too awful to say goodbye forever. But her Dad was so good to her that she couldn't stop loving him.

The first year, of course, was the hardest. Even now she thought about her mother every day—in school, going to a friend's house after school and biking around the neighborhood, and even when Daddy came home for supper and the evening. Where did her mother go? Why did she go? In the beginning she almost felt like looking for her. That wore off, and she accepted that she wouldn't ever see her again. But why? No one had an answer. No one.

She teared up again. She hadn't cried like this for a long time. She didn't like crying. Her eyes got all red and swollen. She was feeling sorry for herself; she knew that. But not to be able to see her father for a month. Oh, she loved him so! She didn't want him to be lonely either. Of course, he had Barbara. That thought made her rather angry, but at least it stopped her sobbing.

She wiped her face again, blew her nose, and decided it was time for a soda.

Chapter Two

The attendant returned with the soda and pretzels. "Nice to have you aboard, Lisa. It says here your grandparents are going to meet you when we land in St. Petersburg."

Lisa only smiled. She didn't want to tell him the whole story as to why she was flying down to Florida. She would simply get off the plane and walk over to them, though she really didn't remember what they looked like. She hadn't seen them since her mother's funeral. Her father did give her some pictures of them so she wouldn't go off with strangers. She smiled to herself and thought how silly to think she would go off with strangers. She reached down into her backpack and took out the pictures and smiled again. Her grandfather looked a little like her father. He was tall and had a thin face. Her grandmother was short and fat. Both had gray hair and both were smiling, but most people smile when their pictures are being taken.

Lisa didn't remember anything about them from the funeral. She did remember her other grandmother, her mother's mother, who lived in Southampton, New York, who never stopped crying. Not big sobs, just continuous tears rolling down her cheeks. Lisa hadn't cried, and she didn't know why. She loved her mother just as she loved her father. He didn't cry either.

The attendant returned an hour later, after lunch had been served and eaten. "Did you enjoy your lunch, Lisa? Pretzels didn't fill you up?"

"Yes….No."

"Is there anything I can do for you? I see you have a book with you. Is it a mystery?"

"No," she answered, wondering why adults ask so many questions.

He smiled, again. As he moved down the aisle, he reminded her to ring the buzzer if she wanted anything. Now they both smiled. He left, and she was alone again. She looked out the window at the clouds, big mountains of them, and down at blobs of green earth. Islands, maybe.

Would her grandparents like her? What would she call them? Daddy called them Mom and Dad. When they wrote to her, they signed Gramma and Grandpa, but those were old-fashioned words. Maybe she could call them by their first names, Alice and Carl. Her friend, Betty, did that with her grandparents.

Oh, why had she agreed to go on this trip? Her father kept pushing the idea. Was it really because he didn't like some of the friends she was making at the Center where she went every day after school to do her homework and talk? A little "wild" he said. She didn't think so, but he was the boss. Unfortunately. He worried too much. Not like Betty's father, who never came to the Center. Betty told her that he didn't care what she did—"Just have a good time."

She closed her eyes and missed her father. Who would read to her before she went to sleep? Who would take her for pizza? To the movies? Let her read to him? That she liked the best. Who would….. She drifted into sleep.

Suddenly she woke up. Her book had fallen off her lap, and she had to unbuckle the strap to lean over and pick it up. She got herself settled again, opened her book, and then heard someone tell her they were going to land. That nice lady, who gave her lunch and didn't ask any questions, was talking to her.

Then the regular attendant appeared and told her he would take her to the terminal and help her find her grandparents. He started to ask a question.

"Here are their pictures if that will help," she quickly said.

"You hold on to them, Lisa. We'll just look around until you see them and they see you. How long has it been since you've seen them?"

"Couple of years. They have lots of pictures of me. They'll know me."

The plane started to bump along the runway, and some voice from a box in the ceiling was telling them to "stay in your seats" until the sign went off. What sign? The plane stopped. Everyone got up. She followed them along the aisle, ducking suitcases as people took them down from the bin above the seats. Finally, she was out of the plane, and accompanied by the attendant, she walked into a large room that had lots of people standing around.

"Lisa!" someone yelled. She looked across the room and saw two gray-haired people coming toward her. This was them.

"Hi." they all said to each other. Watching her grandfather sign some papers, she smiled at the woman with him, her grandmother. She had wonderful blue eyes that danced all over. She whispered softly to Lisa, "We're so glad to have you here." Then to her husband, she said, "Carl, let's go and get this young lady into more comfortable clothes. Unless she's hungry."

"No, I ate on the plane."

"Okay, let's go!" said her grandfather. "First, we'll pick up your suitcase. Then we'll show you St. Petersburg on the way home, especially the Gulf where we can go swimming whenever you wish. And fishing! Fair enough?"

"That's what Daddy always says, 'Fair enough?'"

"Let's go," he said smiling at his wife. And they went—through the terminal, to the baggage claim, and then to the car.

Chapter Three

Lisa woke up, rolled over, and wondered where Mitzi was. She sat up. Where was she? Hearing dishes in the kitchen, she remembered she was in Florida. She carefully got out of what her grandparents called a sofa bed and crossed the living room to the doorway of a large kitchen, larger than the one at home. She liked hers better.

"Good morning, Lisa," said her grandmother.

"Morning." She felt funny about being here but didn't know what to do about it. They seemed like nice people, her grandparents, so she'd be nice.

"How did you sleep?"

"Okay." After a few seconds of silence, she added, "I didn't know where I was when I woke up." More silence. "I started looking for Mitzi."

"Your dog, of course. Well, your father is taking good care of him."

"Her."

"Of course, her. Believe she's going to some kind of a dog camp for a few hours a day. Not overnight."

"From 8:30 in the morning until 6 at night! That's a long time to be alone."

"But think of all the new friends she'll meet," her grandmother added.

"Other dogs you mean."

"Yes. She'll have lots of fun. She's a friendly dog as I remember her."

"You hardly know her. Just that once at Mom's funeral."

"No, we were up there when you were real small, three or four."

"I don't remember." There was a slight pout on her lips.

"Now what will you have for breakfast? Orange juice? Pancakes? Toast and jelly?"

"Do you have any cereal? And bananas?" Lisa wished she were home where she could get her own breakfast.

"No bananas, but we have corn flakes," her grandmother said as she got some dishes and a box of cereal out of the closet. "We'll get some bananas when we go shopping. You might want to make a list of foods you would like to have."

"Fair enough!" Lisa giggled. "What am I supposed to call you? Daddy said Gramma. I don't like that, do you? How about just Gram?"

"Well, it's nice of you to ask what I would like. I've been writing Gramma to you, but I do like Gram. What will you call your grandfather? He's been signing Grandpa, but I guess he could go along with a new name."

"I thought about Grandy. You like that?"

"Yes, I do. Better check it with him though."

"I could use your real names. Alice and Carl."

"Hmm. I think I like Gram and Grandy better. Here comes your grandfather now with the newspaper."

Lisa's grandfather opened the front door and walked in with a big smile. "Hi, hi, hi," he said. "It's a beautiful day. Great day for the beach. How about a swim, young lady?"

"Can I call you Grandy instead of Grandpa?"

He looked just like her Daddy, except for the gray hair. And a bigger stomach.

"Sure you can. Grandy sounds good," he said. "How'd you sleep? Sofa bed comfortable?"

"Okay," Lisa answered through her last spoonful of corn flakes. "Can we buy a box of Froot Loops when we shop? Should I get my suit on now?"

Her grandmother gave Grandy a bit of a look. "Little early for swimming, Carl. I thought we'd drive downtown and show her a little of St. Pete. Maybe even lunch out."

"Sure thing," said Grandy. "An early lunch and then the whole afternoon on the beach. How's that, Lisa?"

"I'm not hungry for lunch. Just had some cereal."

"Oh, he doesn't mean this minute. Why don't you take a shower? Do you take showers at home? Good!" as she saw Lisa nod. "Do you have some shorts and a sleeveless blouse? It's very hot down here, even in June."

As she walked to the bathroom, Lisa thought they would never stop asking questions. She and Daddy never talked this much in the morning. She promised him though that she would be nice to them, so she'll answer them. Whenever.

An hour later the three of them were on their way to downtown St. Petersburg. And then they drove all around a small lake right in the middle of the city.

"How do they water those flowers way up there?" Lisa asked, pointing to the daisies at the top of each street lamp. Gram and Grandy looked at each other. Josh, Lisa's father and their son, had told them how observant she was. But they didn't expect her to question the flowers being out of reach.

Grandy answered, "They're not real, Lisa."

"They have artificial flowers in Florida? How awful! Sometimes we have them in our malls because it doesn't get warm till May. But Daddy said it was flower season all year down here."

"I agree with you, but it would be almost impossible to keep them watered way up there," Gram said. "You are an observant one! Your Daddy told us to watch for that talent of yours."

"It's not a talent. You just have to look."

They pulled up to a curb near the lake, got out of the car, and walked over to a bench. Grandy explained that what they were looking at was also artificial—an artificial lake dug out of the sandy ground to add beauty to the center of the town. All around the lake were benches, several filled with old people and some children. Grandchildren probably. As they settled down, Lisa looked at her grandparents and then at the other gray-haired people.

"Daddy said there would be lots of grandmothers and grandfathers down here. How come?"

Laughing, Gram explained how life was so much easier in Florida than up north. No snow, no real cold winters. They didn't need heavy coats or warm hats or woolen gloves, and the electric bills for heating the trailer were quite low.

"And easy living," Grandy said. "Now how about a little lunch? You like hamburgers?"

"Sure. And a soda."

They walked around the lake and went into a huge drug store with a counter a mile long. Or it looked that way to Lisa. As they

11

scrambled up to three stools, a waitress was right there to give them menus. After ordering, Lisa looked around at the other customers and what they were eating. Then she heard an old man telling the waitress what he wanted, in a slow, soft voice. She was leaning over toward him with her pad and pencil and not saying a word, just listening. He finally got it all out. Then she asked him if he wanted milk or cream for his coffee. He smiled a little and said milk. She brought up a little jug of milk, placing it carefully by his right hand. Giving his order into a mike, she brought him his cup of coffee.

"Be careful," she said as she put it in front of him. "It's very hot."

He muttered, "Thank you."

After eating her last potato chip that came with her hamburger, Lisa and her grandparents continued their walk through the drug store to the toy department. Lisa was quiet as she looked at all the beach balls, small surfboards, and plastic floats.

"Choose what you would like to have for the beach, Lisa," said Grandy. Lisa chose a yellow ball. Then she asked if she could have one of the floats, too.

"No, a ball or a float for now," Gram said.

"I have money with me." said Lisa.

"Not now, Lisa. Choose which you would like." Lisa chose the blue float. "We'll get the ball another time," continued Gram. "Save your money for when you're down here a while and know more what you want. We have a pail and shovel waiting for you at home. One of our neighbors bought it for you. Catherine, next door."

"Is there lots of sand at the beach?"

"Lots." laughed Grandy. "We'll dig our way to China and maybe build a sand castle."

"To China?"

"That's only an expression. Would you like to build a sand castle? A big one?"

"Sure."

As they got into the car to go home, Lisa asked her grandparents about that waitress in the drug store.

"Did she know that man?"

"I don't think so," Gram said.

"She was so nice to him. At home the waitresses are always in a hurry. I don't think they would take that much time with anyone."

"That's one of the reasons Florida is so good for us senior citizens. Did you notice how each sidewalk ends in a smooth downhill to the road? That's for wheelchairs and walkers to go up and down easily."

"Show me at the next corner."

As Grandy slowed the car and pulled over to the curb at the corner, Lisa remarked, "What a great idea! Look, here comes somebody pushing a wheelchair right now. And it's going down to the road without any trouble."

Grandy smiled at Gram, pulled the car back into traffic, and started home.

"I'm going to come here when I get old," announced Lisa.

Chapter Four

As they walked into the trailer, Gram gently asked Lisa if she would mind not going to the beach today but go tomorrow. She and Grandy would like to have a little nap, rest a little.

"What about the sand castle? And my new float?"

"Do you have a book to read? I believe your Dad said that you loved to read and would bring some books down with you. Tomorrow will be another beautiful day, and we'll go to the beach early in the day. We'll have a picnic! And collect shells. Have you ever collected shells, Lisa?" asked Gram.

Grandy nodded to Gram and escaped to the bedroom.

"Okay," she said, pouting a little. "I'll read." as she got a book out of her backpack.

She remembered what her Dad had told her about Grandy needing to rest now and then. So she let Grandy go, but she wasn't happy about it.

"Where can I read? Here? Can I sit on the porch?"

"If you like, but it's very hot out there," said Gram. "You can plop on your bed if you want a nap. You've had a full two days."

"I don't need a nap!" She felt herself getting angry. She'd read. Out on the porch. Can I have a soda?"

"You had a big one at lunch. How about some lemonade?" asked Gram.

"No, a soda. I don't like lemonade."

"All right, Lisa, but then no more today, okay?" said Gram as she too disappeared into the bedroom. "See you later."

Lisa dug out a book from her bookbag, checked the title, chose another one and put it on the table near the door. Then she headed for the refrigerator. Pleased to find lots of cans of soda, she took one and headed for the porch. She settled down in a large canvas chair and drank most of the soda, thinking how awful to buy all those things and then not let her go to the beach.

She tried reading. It was a horse story, which was her favorite subject for books. She soon closed it though and wondered how long she was going to stay here. Only two days and she was bored. Finishing her drink, she tried the book again. Finally she went back inside and threw herself on the sofa. Her bed! Where did all the linen go? The sheets, pillows? It was a sofa again, but she didn't care. "I'll only stay a month." she thought. And fell asleep.

When she woke up, her grandparents were sitting in the kitchen, reading the paper. They weren't bad people, she thought, but they shouldn't have promised to take her swimming if they weren't going to do it. She watched them a while. Daddy looked just like Grandy. That's what he'll look like when he gets old. Her mother would never get old. She missed her mother. She never told anyone what her mother did and that she wondered if her mother really had loved her. Daddy told her that her death had nothing to do with her. But she knew it did. Well, she decided that if her mother left because of her, she would just not care anymore. About anybody. She did love her father though, and she knew he loved her. She missed him.

"I miss Daddy," she said to the two people in the kitchen. They both looked up.

"Of course you do," said Gram. "We can call him again tonight if you would like."

"Okay." She got up, took her book, and started out the door. "I'll be on the porch."

"Don't sit in the sun, Lisa," warned Grandy. "It's still a strong sun even at this hour, and we don't want you getting sunburned."

Settling into the big chair, she started reading. She didn't like that her grandfather was so worried all the time. The sun felt good after the air-conditioned trailer. In fact, it felt so good, she closed her book and moved over to what they called a glider. It was wide and long, had a back like a sofa, and moved back and forth with a little help from her. Here the sun was fully on her whole body and it felt good. She was about to fall asleep when she could hear her grandfather calling her from the doorway. Half awake, she looked at him as he told her to get out of the sun. Twice.

"Lisa, please move out of the sun." She got up but not too happily. She definitely was not going to stay the two months, if she could manage the month!

"Want to walk around the park?" Grandy asked.

"What park?"

"The trailer park. Right here."

"I can see it from here. I'm going to read."

Her grandfather went back into the trailer. He looked at his wife, shook his head a little, and put on the television. "Too early for the news, but I don't feel like reading."

"You were right to get her out of the sun, Carl. That's the least we can do for Josh. We'll call tonight and mention the sun to him."

"She's a strong-willed girl, Alice."

"Josh was a strong boy, remember? He wanted to do what he wanted to do, but he turned out just fine. She'll be okay."

Later, after the news, Gram opened the door and asked Lisa if she changed her mind about walking around the park. No, Lisa wanted to keep reading.

During supper, Gram asked Lisa how the book was. Lisa shrugged her shoulders.

"We have a very good library down here. You can take ten books out for a month. Why don't we go there tomorrow?" asked her grandmother.

"Why?"

"Your grandmother was trying to be helpful, Lisa. I think a trip to the library is a good idea."

"And miss another day at the beach?"

"You're right. Tomorrow is a beach day, our sand castle day. Okay, Alice?"

Alice gave him a quick wink and added, "Absolutely. Tomorrow is definitely a beach day."

When it was 10 o'clock and Lisa seemed to be asleep, Gram motioned to Grandy to join her on the porch. They quietly slipped out, and Lisa never stirred. Once settled on the glider, Gram waited a few minutes before speaking.

"Carl, we have our hands full. And we have a lot to learn. For one, we have to be more patient. We've been alone for so long, making up our own minds what we want to do, it's hard for us to really consider others."

"Our friends don't feel that way."

"Oh, they're going through the same thing. I remember when Veronica had her two grandsons down for a week, just a week, and she nearly went crazy. Whatever she suggested, they wanted something different. She let herself get angry and so they got angry. Of course, she was by herself. We have each other, and Lisa is the one that is alone."

"Yeah, I remember when the boys left; Veronica came over here and cried for two days. Well, what are we going to do? First of all, Lisa is not that difficult. She pretty much goes along with our ideas. I don't think we have a problem, Alice."

"But it could turn into one. We're the adults; we know better. She's a child and has been through a terrible time with her mother's suicide, and watching her father go into a slump for a couple of months. Maybe we should have stayed longer after the funeral."

"Or had her come down here with us."

"No, she had to be with him. Remember how she never left his side those four days."

"Well, Alice, what do you suggest to make it easier for us and of course for her?"

"Be more patient. And you could try having a grandfather to granddaughter talk once in a while."

"And you? I always thought women could talk easier with each other."

"No, not true. Like the sun bit. You were right to tell her to get out of the sun, but you could see how annoyed she was. It would have been better if you had gone right out to the porch and had a quiet talk with her. You were right, but you were a little abrupt."

"Well, I was annoyed that she didn't do what I asked the first time."

"Carl, you're the adult. She's too old to take her in your arms—unless she asks to be there—but do it mentally. You were always so good at that with our children. You would have quiet talks that I never even knew about till the problems were solved. The kids used to love those talks."

"I did, too."

"Try them on Lisa. Even if you don't know her very well, try not to treat her like a stranger. She needs your love, your warmth, your understanding."

"I know, I know. You're right as usual. I'll try. Let's make a deal. Whenever you feel I'm being too tough, give me a look or a kick, okay?"

"Okay. Now let's treat ourselves to a walk around the park."

As they left the porch and turned left down the street, Lisa crawled back into her bed. She had heard most of their conversation through the screened windows. What they said was awful! Was she that mean? Weren't they mean also? Not knowing what to do, she let the tears roll down her cheeks. Getting a tissue, she again went under the covers and prayed to be better—to do what they wanted like her father had asked.

Chapter Five

"What kind of sandwich do you want, Lisa?" asked Gram.

"What do you have?" Lisa answered. She was trying to cooperate, easy to get along with. Dad had warned her that his parents might not want to move as fast as she did—that she should go "easy on them." What she heard last night made her sad and a bit angry. But she would try.

"Egg salad, peanut butter, ham and cheese," suggested Gram. "Swiss cheese," Gram added, anticipating Lisa's next question.

"Okay, ham and cheese, with just a little mustard. Do you have any olives?"

"Sure do. How about helping with the drinks?" asked Gram.

"What do you want?"

"I'm having lemonade," said Gram as she took down a large thermos jug. "Ask Grandy what he wants."

"Lemonade," he called from the bathroom.

"Guess I'll try lemonade today," said Lisa.

"I think you'll like it. Nice and cold. And I'll bring extra sugar in case you want it sweeter."

As the lunch was being packed in the picnic basket, Lisa got into her bathing suit, her blue one. She grabbed her beach jacket, slipped on her sandals, and stood at the door ready to fly out.

"Should I get into the car?" she asked.

"Not yet. Too hot without the air-conditioning. Let me start the car and get it cooled off," offered Grandy.

Driving down to Ft. DeSota Park took a long time. Gram and Grandy talked about how beautiful the scenery was along the way. Lisa only wanted to get in the water.

Lisa couldn't believe how few people were on the beach. Two groups of ladies down aways, and a man swimming in the Gulf. That's what Grandy called it, the Gulf. Not the ocean, not a lake like they had at home.

"But it's so big, it could be the ocean," said Lisa. "It goes on forever."

"I'll show you a map when we get home, and you can see just how big it is. Stretches all the way down Florida and over to Mexico. But come on, let's go in!"

They piled all the food and towels and pail and shovel and her float near a wooden table and started for the water. It was warm, a lot warmer than the water at home. Lisa walked in with Grandy right at her side. She ducked under the water and came up giggling.

"It's salty!" she screamed.

"Your Dad says you can swim. Did he teach you or did you take lessons?" asked Gram.

"No lessons but we swim all the time at the 'Y'. Everybody can swim. Oh, look how easy it is to float," she yelled as she lay on her back. "I don't even have to move my feet. This is great." Staying on her back, she started to kick.

"Now don't kick yourself out too far, Lisa," Grandy warned. "Keep checking to see that you can touch the bottom."

"I'm a good swimmer, Grandy," she explained as she turned over on her stomach and started to swim away from them.

"Lisa! Don't swim out there. Please stay with us. Gram and I can swim, but we don't want to have to pull you out."

"Let me swim around you," she said, gurgling as she put her head in the water and kicked crazy-like between them and behind Gram. This went on for awhile with Gram and Grandy twisting and turning to keep her in sight. Then she swam between their legs, nearly knocking Gram off her feet. But everybody was laughing.

After more splashing and ducking and swimming, they decided it was time for lunch. They decided, not Lisa. She could have stayed in the water all day, but they all got out, sat down, and ate. Lisa was more hungry than she thought.

"Better put your jacket on, Lisa, and your hat. And more of that sun lotion." Gram suggested. She, too, put on her hat and towel over her shoulders. And more sun lotion on her legs. Grandy was already tan and thought he could take a little more sun. They all lay down on the straw mats, covering themselves with towels. Lisa wanted to throw off the towel over her legs, but Grandy insisted. "Maybe next week when you've had more sun. What we don't need is for you to get burned. Your Dad is worried about that."

"He worries too much," Lisa complained as she obeyed her grandfather and kept her legs covered. The sun made her drowsy and she soon fell asleep. But not for long.

Waking up hot and sticky with perspiration, she asked, "Can I go in again?"

"Keep your feet on the bottom," warned Grandy as he also stood up and got closer to the water's edge.

"This is fun," Lisa said laughing, splashing Grandy. "Can we come again tomorrow?"

"I don't think two days in a row is a good idea. We'll come back Friday. We thought we'd go to the Salvador Dali Museum tomorrow. Have you ever heard about him, Lisa?"

"No, who's he?"

"An artist. Bit of a wild one, but he's very famous. And we have a museum with just his paintings."

"What do you mean 'wild'?"

"Oh, he paints melting watches and tree branches that don't join a tree."

"Melting watches?"

"Want to see them?"

"Not really," murmured Lisa.

"Now don't judge him before you see his work."

Gram joined Grandy and Lisa. "Let's have lunch tomorrow on the pier where they have some rides. Then we can take a walk through the museum. If you don't like it, we don't have to stay. Grandy and I have been there lots of times, so we won't mind."

"Okay," agreed Lisa. "What kind of rides?"

"Don't know. I just heard about them. We'll check them out."

So they planned the next day as they built a sand castle. There was so much sand that they built a real big one, with tunnels, and bridges, and all kinds of towers. Every few minutes, Lisa would dash into the water to cool off. Then dash right back to the castle.

The time came to go home, so said her grandparents. Lisa didn't think so at all. She wanted to stay forever. They packed up everything

21

and got back into the car. Lisa was still wet, so she didn't mind the car being so hot. In fact, she asked if they could turn off the air-conditioning. They lowered it but didn't turn it off. They wanted it on, and they won. Why do older people always get their way, wondered Lisa.

Chapter Six

Lisa woke up and not hearing any noises than her own, she decided to stay in bed and do some serious thinking. This was now her ninth day in Florida, more than a week without Daddy, without Mitzi, without her friends. She liked having that long talk with Grandy a few days ago about not getting sunburned and not swimming out too far. He was gentle and made sense. But still…

She would stay three more weeks. She had promised that, and she would keep that promise. She also hoped to keep the promise to be cooperative and nice all the time. And be willing to try anything new. She was trying, really trying. But there were some difficulties. She knew she was wanting her way lots of times. But so were her grandparents. And they always got their way. They were nice but they did make all the decisions. Not like Daddy who let her make a lot of decisions.

She admitted to herself that she was sort of stubborn about going to the Dali Museum. Who wants to visit an art museum on a summer vacation? None of her friends would have wanted to go. But she went with the promise of a few rides after. The rides were awful—for little children, not her age. Gram felt badly. The museum turned out to be okay. The pictures were funny.

And the days they spent at home turned out to be okay, too. She now had two gardens next to the patio, a flower garden and a vegetable garden. She was growing begonias and gladiolas, which she had to water every day. And she had some beans and some tomatoes that hadn't ripened yet. But they would, and they would have them for lunch. She also did find some good books at the library. They even had more books here than at home. She guessed older people liked to read more.

She still thought she wanted to go home. Of course, that day in the boat that took them fishing way out in the Gulf was a blast. She caught four fish, and they had them for supper. Grandy tried to teach her how to clean the fish, but she didn't want to learn, so he did it. But she caught them!

She finally got out of bed, or rather out of her sofa, and squinched down in the big soft chair next to the window. It was already light enough to see down the three streets before her. So many trailers. Why? Why didn't they want houses? None of the trailers had much land around them. Little gardens and a half roof over some cement they called the patio. Pretty—but why not want a bigger garden, a bigger patio, a bigger house? Grandy said they didn't want to take care of a lot of house and a lot of land. She just didn't understand older people.

As she looked over the many trailers, the light in the sky became brighter. Several people were coming out. Some sat in the chairs on the patios; some got into their cars that were parked right next to their patios and drove away; some started walking down the street; some picked up newspapers on the front steps and went back into the trailers.

"Good morning, Lisa," whispered Gram.

"Hello. Why are you whispering?"

"Grandy is still sleeping. Guess we wore him out going to the beach again yesterday."

"But he wanted to."

Smiling at her only grandchild, Gram gently said, "Yes, he did, but sometimes he does too much. That's why we're going to stay home today and take it easy."

"Again?" Catching herself, she said, "Sorry. I can water my garden. And I can read one of my new books."

"Good girl. You can help me with the laundry. And we can play some cards."

"I don't like cards. Daddy plays bridge, or he did play bridge. Now he mostly plays what he calls 'poka' or something. But I don't like to play."

As Grandy entered the room, he burst out, "Why, there's no one here to tell "up and at 'em'. You're up already."

"You keep saying that. What does it mean—up and at 'em?"

"Learned it in the Navy. Every morning the loudspeakers would yell, 'UP AND AT 'EM" and "HIT THE DECK, YOU SWABS." Anticipating her next question, he said, "Swabs are the sailors on board the ship. Expressions to get everyone out of bed!"

Grandy sat down at the breakfast table and asked, "Well, what's on for today?"

"Nothing," Lisa groaned.

"Nothing? You're kidding. We can't have a day doing nothing."

"That's what I say. I can't read all day."

"Now who said you had to read all day?" Grandy asked.

"Gram."

Laughing, Gram said, "I didn't say that, Lisa. I have to do the laundry, and I thought we could just take it easy."

"I have an idea," Grandy said.

As Gram poured orange juice for her two customers and one for herself, she asked, "And what would that be?"

"How about going to the pier tonight and watch the old timers dance?"

"I don't think Lisa would be interested in that," said Gram.

"Yes I would. Anything just to do something. I love my new books, and I love my gardens, but it's fun going out."

"Carl, why don't we just lounge around today? Won't hurt you either to sit around, read, watch some television, maybe visit some neighbors."

"Oh, please, Gram, let's go to the pier," Lisa pleaded. "What did you say they did down there, Grandy?"

"Well, down here we have a lot of old, I mean older people. And a lot of them love to dance. So they got together a few years ago and hired a band and rented the large room at the end of the pier where they usually play bingo or have some entertainment. So now they have ballroom dancing every other Saturday night. And you should see how they dance! And how they dress! The ladies wear long, flowing gowns and the gents a tuxedo or a dark suit and white shirt. No casual clothes for this party. Your grandmother and I go down every now and then to just sit outside and watch them through the windows."

"Why don't you dance?" asked Lisa.

"Don't have a long gown," Gram said with a merry laugh.

"And we don't dance that well," added Grandy.

"But you could learn."

Laughing, he said, "Never did dance like that. Oh, we danced. The two-step. Even the waltz. But not the way they waltz. Wait until you see them. They cover the whole floor in three bars of music."

"Might be fun, Lisa. Want to try it?" asked Gram.

"Sure, but I'd like to see you two dance."

"When you see these people dance, you'll be glad that we sit in the dark outside."

Grandy scolded Gram with a twinkle in his eye, "Now, Alice, we're not that bad. So let's have a quiet day here and then head for the pier tonight."

"Settled," Gram said happily.

Chapter Seven

The next three weeks did go by quickly. Lots of days down at the beach; another wonderful day fishing out in the Gulf. And they did try a new beach on St. Petersburg Beach. When she wrote a postcard to one of her friends, she hoped she made her laugh by saying, "the town of St. Petersburg Beach has a beach that they call St. Petersburg Beach. We go swimming there a lot and picnic with the seagulls."

But Lisa liked Ft. DeSota better. There were more palm trees, and that's where they ate their picnics—under the palms to get out of the hot sun. They also explored the old fort at the end of the island. And one day they flew a kite! Not many people were around, and there was a good breeze. Grandy got it started by running along the water's edge with Gram yelling, "Take it easy, Carl. Let the wind take it." And sure enough the wind came along and lifted the kite way up to the sky. Then Grandy handed over the string to Lisa, warning her to hold on to it tightly. Otherwise, she would lose it. Lisa ran with it even though it was way up there; then she turned and played with it, pulling it in different directions and watching it bob up and down and sideways.

They had had a wonderful time at the pier, watching the "old timers" dance. The ladies in their beautiful dresses seemed to float around the room. The men, looking so handsome in their dark suits, white shirts, and ties, smiled as they led their partners around to the melodies of such pretty music. Lisa hoped they could go there again.

As she was thinking about everything she had done so far and looking forward to today's trip to the baseball game, she kind of decided that maybe she would stay a bit more than a month. Maybe.

Grandy was getting out of the shower and she could hear him singing, "Take me out to the ballgame, take me out to the crowd..."

Lisa chimed in, "Buy me some peanuts and Crackerjack; I don't care if I ever get back…"

Gram joined in with, "For it's root, root, root for the home team. If they don't win, it's a shame."

"For it's one, two, three strikes you're out at the old ballgame," the three of them sang together, finishing up the song.

"Tell me about the Old Timers, Grandy," said Lisa as they sat down to breakfast.

"Well, just like the dancers we saw couple of weeks ago, these men are what we call old. There are some in their eighties, one in his early nineties, but most of them are between 65 and 75. That's pretty old to be running around a ballpark! And in this sun."

"Is it a real game?"

"Oh, yes. There are two teams, nine men on a team. And they take it very seriously. You should see how they bat that ball and how some of them run. Some of them are very good at hitting the ball way out in the field, but they don't run well. They walk, then run a little, then walk again to the next base."

"Maybe that's why they make sure they hit the ball way out there."

"There she goes again, coming up with another solution." Gram said, laughing. "But you're right. The ones that don't run well don't want to get kicked off the team. So they hit that ball as hard as they can and in the direction of the outfielders who don't run very well either."

"Most of them," said Grandy, "played ball when they were younger, not professionally but either in college or where they worked. I used to play with the fellows I worked with. In Central Park. I think we had the field every other Tuesday from May to October, right through the hot summer."

"In Central Park in New York City?"

"Yes, sir. I mean, m'am. Right in the heart of the city. And what a park it is."

"It's a beautiful park, Lisa," said Gram. "Some day you'll visit your Aunt Sally, and she'll take you there. Maybe even to a Shakespearean play in an open-air theatre in the middle of the park. For free! And you can have a picnic there before the show."

"I don't remember Aunt Sally too much. She came to Mom's funeral, but I was too mixed up to remember her."

28

"She's a lovely woman. Our oldest child. She comes down here at least once a year to visit us."

"A high school principal, that Sally is," added Grandy. "Went right up to the top. She only has a few years left before retirement, right?"

Gram quietly answered him. "Eight more years. Don't know what she'll do then. Travel, I suppose. You'll meet her some day. Maybe next summer when your Dad sends you on another adventure."

"Like this one," commented Lisa. "This is turning out to be an adventure with something different every day. Well—almost every day.

"Now we've got some errands to do before the game," said Grandy. "Have to go to the post office and then do some food shopping. And I think you have some books to return to the library, Lisa. And Alice, you have some laundry to do. We'll have a light lunch here and then eat hot dogs at the park. It starts at 4, but we want to be there by 3:30. They always have some fun things before the game."

"Well, let's go shopping," said Lisa as she wiped her mouth and excused herself from the table. "We got lots of food to get. And more soda!"

Chapter Eight

Thinking it would bring her closer to her Dad, Lisa held the phone very close to her ear as her father continued talking, "I don't think so, Lisa. Gram and Grandy would rather you didn't. And I think you have to go with what they want this time."

"But I've seen lots of kids go up. And they come down okay. Parasailing is safe, it really is, Daddy. Gram and Grandy worry too much."

"That's what you're always telling me, Lisa. That's our job—to worry. Well, not to really worry but to be concerned. They believe it's just a little too dangerous. We all know you can swim, and you're probably a much better swimmer now. Still, if the wind should take that parachute far out and you lost the rope, you would be way over your head."

"Daddy," Lisa screamed into the phone, "there's no wind today! Well, there's a little wind. Oh, please. They'll let me if you say so."

"No, Lisa. Now this phone call is getting too expensive. Please let them decide. With me helping them. You are still enjoying yourself down there, right?"

"Yes. I really like them. It's just that..."

"You don't always do what you want to do. Lisa, you've done so many great things with them. These four weeks have been a great adventure, right? And you said you wanted to stay another four, right? I'd have to put you back into camp if you came home now, and you wouldn't like that. Arts and crafts all afternoon."

"No, Daddy. I want to stay another month. We really do have a good time. And I even love now to stay home every other day. I read a lot. About things I didn't know before. They have a wonderful library. And those gardens of mine are doing great. It's fun to eat tomatoes that come out of the ground. And I have a few friends down the street, even though they're old."

"I heard about the retired science teacher who does all kinds of experiments with soil and chemicals. Just think what you can tell Mr. Moody in September. An 'A' for you in science."

"Daddy, how's Mitzi? I miss her."

"She's fine. Seems to like all her new friends."

"Will she remember me?"

"Of course! Remember, she sleeps in your room, sometimes on your bed, every night."

"You let her up on my bed?"

"No, but if I go out for the evening, I find your bed all mussed up. She misses you."

Lisa quietly asked, "Where do you go when you go out?"

"Oh, to the movies or out to dinner."

"Who do you go with?"

"Lots of people. And Barbara now and then."

"I don't like her."

"Now, don't say that, Lisa. You hardly know her. She's a lovely woman. I've told her all about you and what you're doing down there. She's looking forward to seeing you again."

"Well, I don't want to see her."

"Don't be like that, please. Let's not end this conversation with outgrown habits."

"What do you mean?"

"I've had such good reports about you, and some of them from you. You don't always demand your own way. I've heard how willing you are to cooperate with others. Being with Gram and Grandy has been good for you. Since Mom died, I haven't been a very good father. I'm afraid I've spoiled you."

"Oh, Daddy, don't say that. I love you and I don't want you to be mad at me," said Lisa, crying a little.

"Okay, let's forget it now. This phone call has gone on long enough. Gram and Grandy won't be able to afford any food next week."

"Oh, they have plenty of money," Lisa said, starting to laugh. "Grandy says they're the richest people in the world. And Gram always tells him not to say that too loud. Want to talk to them again?"

"For just a minute. I'll talk to you next week. Bye, Lisa. I love you."

"Goodbye, Daddy. I love you, too. Scratch Mitzi's ear for me." She then handed the phone to Gram.

"Hi! From what we heard, you two had a good talk. I'm glad we don't have to send her into the blue skies with that balloon. She's such a good child, Josh. We have good times, even when we stay at home. Tomorrow we're going on that Ft. Myers trip for a few days. We'll call you when we get back. Goodbye, dear."

"Bye, Mom. Thanks a million for everything you're both doing for her."

With the phone hung up, Grandy suggested they all go for a walk around the park and then come back for some ice cream. As they left the trailer, Gram said quietly, "Lisa, tell us more about your mother. Your Dad loved her so much. And yet we don't know too much about her. They spent a few days here and then up north we were together once in a while. And of course we talked on the phone."

"Well, you know she committed suicide," Lisa answered with anger in her voice.

"Yes, but that's not what we want to hear about. We want to hear about her. We know that she was a good mother and that you loved her as she loved you. What are some of the things you did together? You never mention her, but we know how well you two got along. What are some of the things you did together? Did she teach you how to cook? To sew? Or knit? Did she go swimming at the 'Y' with you?"

As they walked around the park, Lisa told them a few stories. Not everything, of course. But what she told them, they seemed to enjoy hearing.

Chapter Nine

On the way to the motel in Ft. Myers, they drove past Sarasota, which Gram explained was a small elegant town, again right on the sea. Grandy said he liked the town, but his favorite part was one of its islands, Anna Marie Island.

"Why?" Lisa asked.

"Because of its beautiful white sand, the way its sea rolls softly up, and its seagulls. Lots and lots of seagulls."

"We have seagulls at our beaches."

"Not like these. Seems they're whiter, fly more dramatically, swooping down to watch you picnic."

"So they can take some of your food!"

"They are actually very patient, just surround you and wait for you to toss them something. We'll have to go there some day."

"How about now?" asked Lisa.

"No time now—maybe on the way home."

Watching the town go by, Lisa asked, "How much longer?"

"Well, that's better than 'Are we there yet?'" commented Grandy.

Gram added, "We'll be there in less than an hour. How about a game about famous people?"

"I don't know any famous people, unless you count the movies."

"And what about your history lessons?"

"Like George Washington?"

"Of course. These famous people can either be alive or dead. We go through the alphabet. Grandy, you go first. Then Lisa. Then me."

"Okay, A – I'll choose John Adams."

"Who is he? Never heard of him."

33

"One of our founding fathers who signed the Declaration of Independence. And one of the most important signers. A smart man although a bit outspoken."

"What does that mean?" asked Lisa.

"Anyone who has more to say than people want to listen to."

"Was he as good as George Washington?"

"Oh, yes. He worked with Benjamin Franklin and, of course, Thomas Jefferson. They all wanted to make this country free from England. Independent. The United States of America. It was John Adams who got up and spoke about it the most."

"Now it's your turn, Lisa," said Gram. "Sometimes Grandy is like John Adams! The letter B, Lisa."

"B —— Anne Bancroft. She played Helen Keller's teacher in the movies."

"Very good. That was a wonderful movie. But that was a long time ago. Do you have the video?"

"Yep. Play it all the time. Now it's your turn, Gram. The letter C. Know someone that starts with a C? Can it be the first name or just the last?"

"Either one," answered Grandy. "Come on, Gram, the letter C."

"Charlie Chaplin."

"Who's he?"

"Another movie star but way before your time. A very funny actor. You should see one of his movies," suggested Grandy. "We'll rent it when we get back home."

"I don't know if she's old enough to enjoy him," said Gram.

"Sure she is. We'll try for the one where he eats his shoe because he's so hungry."

"Eats his shoe! That doesn't sound very funny."

"You'll see. Now it's my turn. The letter D. Dwight Eisenhower."

"Another old movie star?"

"Another president. John Adams was our second president. Don't know what number Eisenhower was, do you Gram?"

"No, I don't, but he was also a general, during World War II and helped win the war for us. And the people liked him so much, they voted him in as president."

"Like George Washington! He was a general first."

"Say, I'm getting hungry. Here's a good place to stop. Okay, Gram?"

"Why don't we wait until we get to Ft. Myers. Then we can go right to the motel and get into our bathing suits."

"But then we can't go swimming if it's right after eating." said Lisa.

"See, Gram, she's on my side."

"There are no sides. But she's right about eating and then going right into the water."

"Not an 'old wives tale'?" asked Grandy, laughing.

"I'm hungry now, too. But we passed it," said Lisa as she watched it go by.

"We'll catch this next one. Here, how about this?" asked Grandy as he pulled the car into the parking lot of a restaurant.

"Nobody answered you, Grandy."

"Thank you, Lisa," said Gram. "I'm so glad you're alert, especially to your grandfather's outspoken way, like John Adams."

"This is a nice place, Alice. I believed we stopped here before."

"You two don't really argue, do you?" asked Lisa.

"There was no cause for an argument there," Grandy said. "Gram just likes to make a fuss once in a while."

"No, we don't argue. We pretty much agree on everything." said Gram.

"Daddy and Mom argued all the time."

"I didn't know that, Lisa," Gram said.

"All the time. It was awful, I mean to hear them arguing."

"Well, let's go in, shall we?" asked Grandy. "I'm still hungry."

Chapter Ten

Lisa walked into the motel room, looked around, and wondered out loud, "Why is it so dark in here?"

"Well, let's open the curtains," Grandy said, "and you can put on that corner lamp, Lisa."

As he pulled the string and the curtains opened, Lisa sighed, "That's better. We don't need the lamp on. Where's the pool? I only see lots of cars out there."

"Probably in the back. But you want to go in the Gulf, don't you?"

"I'd like to try the pool. I've never been in an outside pool."

"Alice," said Grandy, "do you mind if I take a few winks?"

"No, you lie down. Get your suit on, Lisa, and we'll go look at the pool."

"Aren't you going swimming?" asked Lisa.

"Well, I'll put on my suit, but I won't promise I'll go in. Probably would wake me up though."

After putting on her suit, grabbing a towel and her float, Lisa made for the door.

"Lisa, just a minute. I'll be right with you," called Gram as she disappeared into the bathroom with her bathing suit. Lisa sat on the floor and plopped over onto her float.

"I'm always waiting!" she said out loud.

"And that's what children do," murmured Grandy from the bed next to the wall.

"It's not fair."

"Oh, yes it is. When children are old enough to take themselves on trips, then they won't have to wait."

"We don't go on trips at home, and I'm always waiting for Daddy."

"But you don't have to take care of anything, like locking up or checking the stove or the dog. You just get what's yours and you're free to go."

"Grandy, are you mad at me?"

"No, but I didn't like the way you spoke to Gram. We talked about this before. And you have been much better, you know. You were much grumpier when you first came down. We know it hasn't been easy for you. Well, let me tell you it hasn't always been easy for us. Gram tries so hard to please you. No, don't cry, Lisa. It's not that serious. I just want you to be kinder to Gram."

"I try, I really do. I just get all mixed up when things aren't done right."

"You mean when things don't go your way."

Gram came out of the bathroom already to go. "Ready, Lisa? Thought you were sleeping, Carl?"

"I am," he said as he rolled over.

"You know, I really feel like taking a dip into that pool. Let's have a look at it." Gram said as she looked down at Lisa still on the floor. "You okay, Lisa?"

"Yes. Come on. Let's go." And out the door they went.

As they walked to the pool, Lisa quietly said, "I don't think Grandy likes me."

"What a silly thing to say. Grandy loves you. Why do you say that?"

"He yelled at me for the way I spoke to you."

"Oh, well, he does get a little touchy about things like that." After a few minutes, she added, "We know or we think we know just what you've been going through these last two years. No child should have to go through that. Your mother's suicide had nothing to do with you or with your Dad. She was sick, and I guess she just couldn't take any more. It was not right to do what she did, leaving you and your Dad to figure out why. Suicide is really not a very good answer to one's problem. It's almost a selfish thing to do. I'm told that when people get so tired and angry, being sick all the time, that they can't think of other people, only of themselves."

She looked down at Lisa who had become very quiet. "You okay?"

"I don't like Mommy being called selfish. She was very good to me. And to Daddy. She always thought about me and what I wanted. All the time. Some people say she spoiled me."

"All mothers spoil their children. I spoiled mine. Well, we've talked enough today. Let's get into that pool. Look, we have it to ourselves."

"I miss my mother, no matter what people say. I wish I could have helped her with her sickness. Why couldn't the doctors help her? She had a lot of doctors."

"I don't know, Lisa, I just don't know. I do know that you have come a long way these few weeks. Your Dad was right sending you down to us; you two were almost too close this past year. Becoming involved with other people, especially your family, was a good idea. In the beginning you never wanted to listen to Grandy. And now you two have wonderful conversations. He wasn't scolding you before. He was just trying to help. Let him try, okay? Now, last one in is a rotten egg!"

"That's what Daddy always says." And they both jumped in. No rotten eggs!

Chapter Eleven

"It won't take long, Lisa. About 25 minutes as I remember," said Grandy as he got into the car.

"But there are shells right here!"

"Not like on Sanibel Island."

"Grandy told you about the pail they give you for collecting shells, didn't he?" asked Gram.

"Yeah. You can only collect a few. That's not fair. If there are shells on the beach and you pick them up, you should be allowed to take them home. Rules, rules, rules. Why so many rules?" complained Lisa.

"I told you why. There were some people who came down here and collected barrels of them and would take them home to sell. Greedy people. That's why we have rules and laws. They protect us from greedy people." explained Grandy.

"Why punish us because there are bad people? I just want to bring some shells home for my friends. I don't want to sell them."

"Most rules are good for most people." Gram added. "Like the ones we have in our trailer park. Remember the one about not putting clothes on your patio to dry?"

"I understand that now. But I sure thought it was silly not to be able to put your wet bathing suit over a chair, Then I saw that man hang his shirts and underwear all over his patio!"

"Well, Mr. Crosby just moved here and didn't know that rule. But didn't it look awful? Imagine all the patios full of laundry!"

"Yeah. You wouldn't be able to see down the street. And the washing machines and clotheslines are really not that far way."

"And what about the rules telling you not to drive over 15 miles an hour in the park? You don't drive, but some of the young people who visit down here were whipping around at 40 or 50. Near killed a couple of people. Most of us who live here don't walk very fast to get out of the way of some wise guy," argued Grandy.

"Yeah. Some rules are still silly."

Almost over the bridge, they spotted a beach ahead with beautiful palm trees and picnic tables and just a few cars parked nearby.

"Here we are! A beach waiting for us. A swim first? Then some shelling?" asked Gram.

Grandy pulled up next to the other cars. The three of them unpacked their straw mats, umbrella, shovels, float, and a picnic lunch. Grandy did most of the carrying.

As they got near the beach, a man in a funny sailor suit handed each one a small cardboard pail. Grandy gave Lisa a friendly grin that she returned.

"I can have your pails, right? Three pails will be enough," commented Lisa.

"How about a swim first? I'm warm," said Gram.

The Gulf was the same warm temperature at Ft. Meyers, but just to get wet was cooling. They splashed around a little, then took their pails and started down the beach. In three minutes, Lisa's pail was full.

"How come my pail is full, and you have hardly any in yours?" asked Lisa.

"Because we're more choosy. Come look here," said Grandy as he showed her the shells he had collected. He only had five shells but they were beautiful and perfect, not a crack or chip on any of them: a round small one with a shiny brown curve; a flat one that looked like a fan; a tiny corkscrew shell; a long curved one with a smooth opening; and a large one with a point at one end and an wide curling opening.

"Listen to the ocean," as he put the large one against Lisa's ear. She giggled.

"You can really hear it! And it's perfect and pretty."

"Now let's look at yours," her grandfather suggested. "See all those broken edges. Don't bother with them. Look for the perfect ones. We have all day."

They shelled almost all afternoon with a little lunch and little swims in between. And Lisa had the prettiest shells! She even became more fussy than Gram or Grandy. She found some unusual ones by going in the water over her ankles—shells that were buried in the sand. The water cooled her feet from the hot sand. Grandy and Gram had flip-flops on, so it didn't matter how long the sun heated the sand they walked on.

Lisa asked finally, "Can we rest for awhile? I'm getting tired. Can I float on my float?"

"Haven't you had enough sun?" asked Gram.

"No," she said as she smiled. "I'll be careful. Don't worry, okay?"

"Look," suggested Grandy, "you lie down on the float with your hat over your face, and I'll cover your legs with your towel."

"But it'll get wet."

"So what? It'll dry, and we have extras if you want to dry yourself," Grandy said.

"Come on. I'll even wet it on purpose to cool your legs."

So Lisa lay on her blue raft with her wet towel over her legs and her hat over her face, with Grandy standing two feet from her.

"This is the first time I ever did this," Lisa said. "I've done a lot of 'firsts' with you and Gram. First time in a motel. First time in an outdoor pool. First time picking up so many beautiful shells."

"And first time watching old timers dance," added Gram.

"And play baseball," said Grandy.

"And first time in a plane," Lisa reminded them.

"First time catching fish way out at sea. And off a bridge," Grandy continued.

"And first time swimming in salt water!" said Lisa. She took a deep breath and a moment of silence. "A lot of firsts."

Chapter Twelve

"Ready, Lisa?" Gram asked.

"A few more minutes, Gram," Lisa yelled from the bathroom.

Grandy stretched his long arms and reached down to his toes as he stood by the patio door and mused, "Hard to believe almost eight weeks have gone by. Going to miss that kid. First two weeks I couldn't wait till she went home. Now I don't want her to go."

"She'll come back for a vacation. And Carl, it might be nice to get back into our old routine," whispered Gram.

"I don't know," said Grandy. "Just you and me. What'll we talk about?"

"We'll find something. Oh, here you are," she said, as Lisa bounced out in her new bathing suit and beach robe.

"Wait till Dad sees my new clothes. And wait till I go to the pool! Is everything out in the car already? Anything I can do?"

"All done. Don't you look fetching!" remarked Grandy. "That's another word from the ancient past."

"Fetching? Strange word, but I guess you paid me a compliment."

"Sure did. Alice, let's go. I got the thermos."

"And I have the soda. Off to Ft. DeSota," said Lisa as she got into the car.

Driving down the now familiar road to Ft. DeSota Beach, Gram asked Lisa why she chose this beach for her last day in Florida. "I thought surely you would pick St. Petersburg Beach."

"Well, I wanted to choose Anna Marie Island. That beach was awesome. And nobody there but us. The seagulls and the sea were super!"

"More alliteration. What a gal!" gasped Grandy.

"But I knew we could never make it in one day. And Ft. DeSota has more palm trees, and anyway I'll be at St. Pete Beach tonight for the sunset. This way I can say goodbye to both beaches."

"We're so glad you got to love our sunsets," Gram said.

"Remember how I didn't like them," said Lisa laughing. "I thought they were so boring, but when you explained about the clouds and the colors, I just got to like them. I'll think of you two whenever I see a sunset. We don't really have them at home. The sun just goes down. No clouds. No colors."

"They're there. You just have to look more closely." Grandy said as Gram turned her head to look at Lisa with a big smile. "But you're right," continued Grandy. "They're not as colorful as down here. We're closer to the Equator."

"We thought we'd never get to see another one while you were here," Gram said, laughing.

"Such a fuss you made!" added Grandy. Imitating Lisa, he yelled, "We saw one last night!" adding moans and groans.

"That's enough, Carl. Lisa got to like a lot of things—after a while. A new place always takes some time to get used to, like the Dali Museum."

"Best of all," said Grandy, "was getting to enjoy staying home every other day. That was the toughest, but you finally liked it almost as much as going out."

"Almost. That was because you found the best library books for me. And the videos we took out. Like the real old ones that were so funny. And the gardens I planted! I loved staying home. Oh, Gram and Grandy, I'm going to miss you so much. Like I missed Daddy in the beginning. And my friends."

"Will you write to us?"

"Of course."

"And we'll send postcards of all the places we went to. But you'll be busy when you get home, Lisa. Just getting to know your Daddy again. And Barbara. I do hope you two become friends," Grandy said.

"I'll try. I really will. And I'll let you know."

"And," reminded Gram, "you'll have lots of work at school. It would be wonderful if you did join the French Club."

"Only if my friends join. The schedule said it would be twice a week. That's a lot. I have swimming twice a week, remember? That leaves only one day free to go biking or roller skating or just hanging out," explained Lisa.

"You've been here so long, did you forget that your Dad doesn't get home from work until 6 o'clock. We agree with him that you shouldn't be alone in the house, especially when it starts getting dark in October. You'll only be ten come October, and that's a bit young to be alone, whether you agree or not," chimed in Grandy.

"There you go worrying again. Dad worries too much, too. So I'll be used to it. By the time October arrives with my birthday and the change in the clocks, I'll find a place to stay. Maybe at Mary's again, if she joins the French Club. I know she still wants to swim. But please don't worry. I can take care of myself. And I have Mitzi. She'll bark and scare anyone away."

"Yes, she probably would. But the world is a little crazier now, Lisa. We just have to be more alert. I promise you that your Grandy and I will not worry. We'll just be thinking about you—all the time."

"And maybe by October, Barbara will be around more often," said Lisa as she gave Grandy a tap on his shoulder. "I sure hope I like her and that she likes me."

"Well, we can vouch for you. If she doesn't like you next week, she'll be crazy about you by October and from then on. Maybe we should write to her, Alice."

"Now you just mind your own business, Carl. Lisa can take care of everything."

"Maybe it wouldn't hurt, Gram, if you let her know how wonderful I am," said Lisa with a big laugh. Then, seriously, she added, "Do you think Daddy will marry her?"

"We have no idea. He seems quite fond of her. He told us how good she would be for you. It might be nice if they got married—for everybody's sake. She won't be a stay-at-home mom, but she gets off at 4 o'clock from school, right? That was a good idea to become a school secretary. The hours and holidays are much better. Just perfect for you. And for your Daddy to have a real home-cooked dinner. No more pizzas or McDonald's. Except on weekends, of course. I hope she likes to cook."

"Alice, we don't even know if they're going to get married. They'll do the right thing. We better stay out of it," chirped Grandy. Gram looked at Lisa and winked. Grandy continued, "Our son is a smart boy. He'll take the best care of this little one."

As he slowed down the car, he shouted, "Here's the beach, Lisa. Ready to jump right in?"

"Could I have a soda first?"

Gram frowned and gave Grandy a worried look.

"I'll split it with you," suggested Grandy.

"Fair enough!"

"You say that more than I do now. When your Daddy hears that, he'll have a good laugh."

"And "Up and at 'em'" and "Hit the deck, you swabs.'"

"Last one in is a rotten egg!" added Gram as the car came to a stop.

"Oh, I love you both so much. What will I do without you?"

"And us without you?" asked Grandy. "It's been a great summer. And now get ready for a great swim."

"And after a swim, a great picnic! Olives, pickles, potato chips, Swiss cheese and ham on potato bread, and watermelon!" Gram said.

"A soda first, right, Grandy?"

"Half a soda."

Gram smiled as she handed him the can of soda.

The End

Book Two
Lisa on Long Island

Chapter One

Lisa got off the plane at Kennedy Airport, New York's largest airport, and looked for her grandmother. The flight attendant and she walked around the terminal looking carefully at all the people, but no one was there to greet Lisa. She got a little scared, and the attendant told her not to worry, telling her he would not leave her.

"She'll be here soon," he said. "Did she drive? Or take the jitney? Sometimes the traffic out here can be miserable."

"She knows I'm coming. We wrote her the time the plane got in. And we called her last night. Where is she?" asked Lisa.

"Not to worry. Is this her? The woman with the large black hat?"

"Maybe. Yeah, that's her."

"Hello, Lisa, sorry I'm late. How are you, darling?" the attractive woman said as she approached them.

She didn't bend down to kiss or hug Lisa, but she had a friendly smile and happily signed the necessary papers. She ignored the attendant, but Lisa gave him a big smile and a thank-you whisper as she said goodbye.

Lisa and her newly-found grandmother walked to the baggage claim section to pick up her suitcase. As they left the terminal, her grandmother, Isobel, explained that she had come on the Jitney bus and that's how they would return.

"We have about 20 minutes for the return Jitney," said Isobel, looking at her watch.

"What's a Jitney?" asked Lisa.

"A small bus, a van, that travels to and from Southampton. Well, it runs the length of Long Island. A bit expensive but much better than the train."

"Does it go all the way to Southampton? That's a long ride. We studied some maps of Long Island. My grandfather in Florida showed me how to use maps."

"And how are your father's parents?"

"Great. I had a wonderful summer with them last year. They showed me all kinds of things. Took me fishing, and a place where they have beautiful shells, and to the pier where we watched old people dance. And we went to a baseball game where all the players were over 65. Lots of places."

"My, you were with a lot of old people," commented Isobel.

"It was lots of fun."

"Well, my dear, I don't believe you're going to see a lot of places and do a lot of things with me. We're very quiet here. And I have a dress shop that I must go to every day. Your father knows this but still thought you could have a good time. Guess that's why he sent you only for a month."

"I know you're near the ocean. I'd like to go swimming there. The Atlantic Ocean, right?"

"Yes, but I can only go there on Sundays when the shop is closed."

"Oh, okay. The water down in Florida was called the Gulf. It was like a lake but it was salty. So you could float on your back and not sink. The ocean is salty, right? I would like to see what the waves are like. We don't have waves where I live either. So it would be fun. Could I go alone during the week?"

"I don't think so, Lisa. There is a lifeguard at the Southampton Beach, but ten years old is a bit young to be on the beach alone. Did you bring some books to read?"

"Yes, but only three. Do you have a library?"

"Of course. But it's in town. Too far to walk from the cottage."

"I'm a good walker. What about a bike? I'd love to go biking. Do you have one?"

"No, my dear, I do not have a bike. But I have seen a young girl down the street riding her bike. Maybe she'll loan you hers."

"What shall I call you? I called my grandparents in Florida Gram and Grandy. Do you have a favorite name for yourself? I know you have three other grandchildren who live in Carmel. That's in California, right? What do they call you?"

"Isobel," she answered almost curtly.

50

"Oh, good! I wanted to call Gram and Grandy by their names, Alice and Carl, but they didn't like the idea. I think it's cool to call you by your name. Isobel. Pretty name."

"Thank you," which came out rather stiffly.

"Is this the Jitney?" asked Lisa looking at the small, dark blue van pulling up to the curb.

"Yes. Go right in. I'll give your suitcase to the driver."

"Can I sit in the front?" Lisa called from inside the van.

"Anywhere, dear."

After they settled into the two front seats and started down the road to another building to pick up more people, Lisa wondered if she was going to have a good time with Isobel. She certainly liked calling her by her name. That was so grown up. And she was sort of nice. A bit serious. Very beautiful, but not warm and hugable like her other grandmother. She wasn't at all like she remembered her at her mother's funeral. Tears continuously running down her check without a sound. But then it was her daughter who died.

Four more people came onto the van and soon the inside lights went out as they took off onto a big highway. Lisa felt comfortable and closed her eyes. Soon she was sound asleep.

Chapter Two

Lisa woke up in a strange bed, in a small room. She vaguely remembered leaving the van and climbing into a taxi. And then climbing into bed. Isobel offered her some hot chocolate, but she fell asleep before she could answer. Now she would love to have something like that. She was hungry. At home she would have gone to the kitchen and made herself some toast and poured her orange juice. But she didn't even know where the kitchen was. She heard a shower in the next room going full blast and figured out that Isobel was up and getting ready to start the day. She got out of bed, opened the door, and looked into the room next to her. It was the kitchen! She was standing there a few minutes when her grandmother came out of the bathroom, dressed in a beautiful bathrobe, pink and white with lots of ruffles.

"Good morning, Lisa," Isobel said without a smile.

"Good morning, Isobel."

"Sleep okay?"

"Yes, thank you."

"Want some orange juice?"

"Yes, thank you."

"I'm going to have some bacon and eggs. Would you like some?"

"I don't know. Maybe some bacon with some toast."

"All right. Wash up or take a shower if you'd like," pointing to the bathroom. "Then come in here." Isobel nodded towards a small room off the kitchen that had a table, two chairs, a large window next to the table. And outside the window was a beautiful garden filled with all kinds of flowers. Lisa quickly decided to just wash up and then go out to see the garden. She never saw one so beautiful! But after the shower which she decided she needed, Isobel asked her to sit down and eat

52

her toast and bacon and, of course, drink her orange juice. Lisa thought that everyone in the world must have orange juice for breakfast. Isobel was nothing like Gram and Grandy, but they all had the same breakfast.

As they ate Isobel explained that she was on her way to the shop, and Lisa could read her book. She would come home for lunch, and they could decide what to do with her in the afternoon.

Isobel got dressed and left. Lisa got dressed and read. It was another horse book and although she was enjoying it, she was curious about the garden. She quietly opened the only door to the cottage, as Isobel called it. Gram and Grandy had a trailer; Isobel had a cottage. Nobody had a house. When she looked out, she saw a lawn, some trees, a road and a few houses across the road. No garden. Then she realized the garden must be in the back. She cautiously walked outside, leaving the door slightly opened. She didn't want to be locked out. Walking around the cottage, she came to the garden. It was even more beautiful than it was through the window.

There were roses of all colors, and lilacs, and daises, and sunflowers. They had all these where Lisa lived but somehow they seemed more beautiful here. Maybe because they were all close together with just a small path that went in and out around them. With a bench and a birdbath and a bird feeder. She would read out here.

As she went back inside to get her book, she saw a girl riding her bike down the road. She waved, but the girl did not wave back. She probably didn't see her. The girl looked nice and about her age. Maybe she could rent a bike, and they could go biking together. The girl disappeared over the hill, and Lisa went into the cottage.

She got her book and this time she tested the doorknob to see if she could close it and not be locked out. It worked. So around to the back she went and was glad that the bench was in the shade. The sun wasn't as strong as in Florida, but still it was July and too hot to read in. Then she realized that the house, the cottage, wasn't air-conditioned. Yet it wasn't hot indoors. The windows were all opened, and she guessed that was enough. The air was much cooler than at home or in Florida.

She sat down and got to reading. Several hours passed by. She was about to start a new chapter when she heard a car stop right in front. It must be Isobel, she thought. And sure enough, Isobel came walking around the side and into the garden.

"So you found a place to read. You're a smart girl," said Isobel.

"I checked the door first to make sure I wouldn't get locked out."

"That was also smart," commented Isobel.

"What am I going to do this afternoon?"

"Let's have lunch and discuss it."

They went in for lunch and as they ate, or drank, a bowl of cold peach soup, Isobel suggested that Lisa come back into town with her and either go to the library or just walk around town.

"Be sure to get yourself back to the shop by 5:30. And we'll go out for dinner."

"OK. That's sounds great. Can I wear shorts?"

"Yes. This is a beach resort town. The only time we get dressed up is for dinner in a fancy restaurant or going to the theatre. A lot of people dress for the movies, also. Some wear pants with a good-looking top."

"I'd love to go to the movies. And I'd like to go to the theatre if it's a play I can understand."

Picking up Lisa's empty bowl, Isobel asked, "Is that enough for you to eat? You can have a sandwich. I have hard-boiled eggs or cheese."

"No, I'm fine. I thought the soup was going to be awful when you told me what it was, but I enjoyed it."

"I'll be ready in a minute. What about you?"

"In a minute," said Lisa as she went into the bathroom to brush her teeth.

"We'll have to decide on a bathroom schedule. Don't be too long."

They closed up the house and got into the car, which wasn't hot at all. The sun here wasn't like Florida's sun. Something to do with the equator.

The ride into town was somewhat interesting. Some big houses and some small ones like Isobel's. Isobel explained that the small ones, like hers, were once where wealthy people kept their carriages. No, she didn't know where they kept the horses. When the automobile came into fashion, the 'carriage house' was turned into a living space for one or two people. Isobel liked the new name of "cottage" better.

"It doesn't reek of elitism."

"What does that mean?"

"It doesn't smell of the grand snobs."

"And what is a grand snob?"

"Someone who thinks he is better than anyone else. We have a lot of them here."

"That's funny. Can I meet someone who is a grand snob?"

"Come into my shop anytime. Not all my customers are snobs, but some of them believe I'm their servant or slave."

"And how do you treat them?" asked Lisa.

"Honey, I have to sell clothes!"

"Oh,…. so you don't tell them what you think."

"You are one smart girl."

They reached the main street and drove around to the back of the long building that held all the shops in that block. There were lots of parking places back there, and Isobel parked in front of the sign "ISOBEL'S".

"Well, I won't forget the name of your store."

"Shop."

"Right, shop."

"Come in for a minute."

She unlocked the door, turned off the alarm system, turned on the lights. It was a bigger store – shop – than Lisa had imagined. There were lots of dresses. And jackets and pants and shorts and even some hats. A pretty place.

"This is nice, Isobel," said Lisa.

"Thank you. Now let me show you where the library is."

She walked out the front door and pointed to her right. "Almost three blocks down there. Tell them who you are. They'll give you a temporary card for the month. I've already told them you were coming. Remember to come back here by 5:30. And stay on the main street. Don't walk down any side streets."

And out Lisa stepped into the charming town of Southampton. There were lots of people walking up and down the sidewalks, some looking in shop windows, some talking in small groups, others coming out of the various stores that lined both sides of the street. Lisa walked until she found a white wooden building that simply said LIBRARY over the front doors. She walked in and found several people already at the front desk, checking out books, so she joined the line. She got her temporary card and then meandered up and down the aisles, looking for a book. Her watch told her she had almost five hours to herself. What could she do for five hours? She decided to get the books she would want later so she wouldn't have to carry them around town. Leaving the library, she told the librarian that she would be back later. It also closed at 5:30 so she had two reasons to watch the time. At 5:00 she would stop whatever she was doing and go back to the library and then to the shop.

Where should she go? Well, she decided to give the town a good examination. Suddenly she missed Gram and Grandy. They never left her alone. Of course, she was a year older now but still....She saw lots of stores in the five-block walk one way and five blocks the other way. And she still had more then three hours!

As she reached the end of the sidewalk across the street from ISO-BEL'S, she saw a huge white house with lots of blue shutters all the way up to the fourth floor. What could this be? Too big for just a family she thought as she crossed a road to get a closer look. There on the lawn was a neat sign SOUTHAMPTON GUEST HOUSE. Oh, she decided, a place for tourists. At home they had a guesthouse that was also large and neat looking and filled with antiques. She decided to go in and have a look.

"May I help you?" said a voice from the other side of the room that Lisa entered.

"Hello. May I look at your guesthouse? I saw the sign. I'm staying with my grandmother in a cottage a few miles away. She brought me into town. She owns a shop across the street. May I see your guesthouse?"

"Oh, sure. What shop does your grandmother own?" The lady, whose voice she had heard, came into view. She was dressed in a long skirt and a short-sleeve white blouse. It was of thin material with lots of embroidery on the sleeves and neckline. Lisa thought she looked like a Russian peasant she had seen in her geography book. That thought would have pleased Abigail, owner of the guest house. She was a left-over from the true hippy era but to Abigail the times of the laughing revolutionary who could storm the courts with screams and curses with impunity were to be here forever. America as far as she was concerned was more wonderful because the little people could scare the big ones. And keep them in line without the use of too much violence.

"ISOBEL'S. That's a beautiful blouse. And I like your skirt."

"Oh, yes, I heard you were coming to town. Welcome! Your grandmother let everyone know, as usual. Thought about a room here for you on the fourth floor where the rent is cheap and the temperature in the nineties."

"She was going to put me in this house? Why? I have a room to myself in her cottage."

"You mean carriage house, don't you?"

"Well, yes, but she says only stuck-up people call them that," said Lisa.

"Really? Nobody more stuck up than your grandmother."

"Oh? She doesn't seem stuck-up to me," Lisa said quietly.

"I'm sorry, honey, I shouldn't have said that. She's your grandmother, and I must remember that. Anyway she never came back after hearing the price of that room."

"I like it where I am. What's your name?" asked Lisa.

"Abigail. You can call me Abby if you want. Or Gail. Or anything you wish. And what do people call you?"

"Lisa. I have no nicknames. Just Lisa."

"That's a pretty name. Never knew anyone named Lisa. So, welcome to the Southampton Guest House. Can I show you around? See some of the rooms?"

"Yes, I would like that. This room looks old-fashioned," said Lisa.

"Right. All the rooms are old-fashioned. All Americana. Some in the 1776 style, some mid 1800's, some early 1900's and some as old-fashioned as 1980."

Lisa decided she was going to like Abigail. She also decided she would call her Abby. Less formal and less syllables. And if she didn't like Isobel, that was her business. So far she liked her grandmother, but she only knew her for two days. Isobel had never written to her like her Florida grandparents had or sent her presents. She didn't care. What she liked the most was that she was her mother's mother. Somehow that was important.

"Could we start with the 1776 rooms? I just finished learning about the American Revolution and I got to like some of the people. I'd like to see how they lived," Lisa said.

"Of course. Let's go. Up to the third floor."

On the way up the stairs, Lisa asked, "Where are all the guests? I don't see anybody."

"Most of them come on the weekends. People who work in the city come out on Friday and leave either Sunday or early Monday. We do have a family here now for a week's vacation. They're out at the beach right now."

"It's a little hot up here, but I see you have all the windows opened. You don't have air-conditioning?"

"No, not for this big house. But, except for the attic rooms, it cools down in the evenings. Some people tell me they're glad to be out of air-conditioning."

"So each floor is cheaper according to the heat?"

"Lisa, you are observant and curious. A great combination. Yes, the prices change but the second floor is the most expensive, even more than the first floor, because there is more breeze up there."

Moving to the next room and seeing the fresh flowers in two of its vases, Lisa remarked, "The flowers are real. Do they come from your garden?"

"Yes, look out this window. This is the back garden where we eat breakfast."

"So many flowers! My grandmother has a beautiful garden, too. Even more beautiful than we have at home. My mother used to grow lots of flowers but not like this. And, of course, now we don't have any."

"Why not?" asked Abby.

"No one to take care of them. Dad's too busy at work and Barbara, that's his new wife, well, this is her first summer with us. She says she'll do better next spring."

"Lisa, is your father Isobel's son?"

"No, my mother was her daughter. Sounds confusing but it isn't."

"Now that you say that, I remember reading in the paper that Isobel's daughter passed on. About two or so years ago."

"Almost three years. She committed suicide," Lisa said softly. She had decided that she was going to be friends with Abby and so didn't mind telling her the truth.

"She what! Isobel's daughter committed suicide? Oh, I'm sorry, Lisa, I didn't mean to blurt it out like that. But I had no idea. Isobel was so quiet about it and even became more cool and unfriendly. I'm sorry, again. But this is such a shock. I feel like I haven't been fair to her. What a tragedy for her. And for you. Forgive me, Lisa for going on like this."

"It's okay. I'm used to it now. And I decided if we were going to be friends, you should know all about me."

"Of course. And we are going to be friends!" said Abby with a great big smile.

"Come on, let's move into the early 1800's."

They walked down to the second floor and into a room filled with clothes all over the place. The door was open but they didn't go all the way in. The guests who were now at the beach lived in this room.

"How many children do they have? I see oodles of little clothes. Any of them my age?" asked Lisa.

"Three. Ages four, six, and nine. The nine year old might be fun to play with. He's a boy and a little wild. But I bet he'd be good with you. They'll be back for dinner. Can you stay around till then?"

"I have to be at the library at 5:15 and then at the shop by 5:30."

"Dinner's at 6:00 so you might not meet him today. Maybe tomorrow. Will you be going to the beach at all?"

"I don't know. Isobel has to work every day and said we'd go on Sunday."

"But that's three more days. What will you do by yourself?"

"Read. And walk around town," Lisa answered.

"Do you have a bike?"

"No."

"Well, I have a bike you can use. I keep several here for the weekend guests. You can have it until then."

"That would be great! I'll come in with Isobel tomorrow morning and come over for it. Okay?"

"Okay. You're a mature little girl, aren't you? Make all kinds of decisions. Guess you had to these last few years. Yes, Lisa, come anytime in the morning and have breakfast with me. We'll both go for a ride."

"Abby, I knew I would like you. And I would like you to like my grandmother more. She's had a terrible time with Momma leaving us the way she did. I don't know her yet myself but I think she'll be all right."

"Of course. I'm going to rethink all the things in the past and give them a new slant."

They said goodbye after looking over the guest rooms on the first floor, and Lisa walked to the library where she picked up her books. Then she walked to Isobel's shop.

Chapter Three

On the way home after a good dinner at a local, but not fancy, seafood restaurant, Isobel told Lisa that she had decided that Lisa shouldn't be going over to see Abigail in the morning.

"Why?"

"I'm glad you met her and that she was nice to show you the house and invite you to breakfast, but Abigail is not the type of person I would like you to be friendly with. She's a little far out. I know you don't know what I mean, but you'll have to take my word for it." said Isobel.

"But she was so nice. She wasn't "wild" or crazy. She was friendly. Oh, Isobel, please let me go over there. We were going bike riding after breakfast, and she said I could keep the bike until the weekend."

"I believe I can rent you a bike from a shop downtown. I'll find out tomorrow. But please understand my decision is for your own good. Abigail is not a monster but she leads a different life from the rest of us."

"What do you mean?"

"Never mind. Just let me decide."

"I think that's mean. You tell me what I can't do and you don't give me a reason. That's not fair," exploded Lisa.

"Young lady, you don't talk to me like that. Now that's enough."

They reached the house, got out of the car and into the house without another word between them. Isobel went to the message machine by her telephone and settled down to take notes. Lisa went to her room. She got undressed for bed and took her book into the kitchen.

"Can I have a coke?" she called into the living room.

"Yes."

After a few minutes, she called out, "What am I supposed to do tomorrow?"

"I'm on the phone."

Lisa drank her coke and let the tears roll down her cheeks.

"This is going to be a terrible month," she muttered.

She opened her book and tried to read but the tears came again. What could she do? She would have loved to pack her bag and go right home. Or down to Florida where her grandparents understood how to treat children. Her mother wasn't like this. How could HER mother be so different? She calmed herself down with thinking about her mother. They had been very close, shared everything that Lisa liked and disliked. But her mother hadn't shared her problems with her. She should have done more to help her mother. But she didn't know. She was only seven years old and thought everything was just fine. She wondered what made life seem so mixed up. She heard her grandmother coming into the kitchen so she quickly dried her tears on a napkin and started reading.

"Lisa, I've had a very busy day at the shop. And I just got some more work to do over the phone. I'm going to bed in a little while. Now you took five or six books out of the library today and with your three, that gives you a big selection for tomorrow morning. I'll come home again for lunch. Then you can either go to the library again or stay home and read. There's also the television. The next day, which is July fourth, we've been invited to a barbecue in East Hampton. That should be a lot of fun for you. There'll be several children there."

"Okay. I'm sorry I got mad, Isobel. But I know Abby is going to try to like you."

"Oh, is she? That's nice of her. I never did anything to her," snapped Isobel.

"I'm sorry. Let's forget the whole thing. I'll read tomorrow. I'm going into my room now. Good night, Isobel."

"Good night, Lisa. I'm sorry, too, we said those things to each other. See you at breakfast."

Lisa went into her room. She put on the lamp over her bed, crawled under the covers with her book, and started to read. The phone rang, and she heard her grandmother answer it and talk a little bit before calling her.

"It's your father, Lisa,"

Lisa hopped out of bed and flew to the phone.

"Daddy!" she yelled. "Oh, how I miss you. What time is it there? I'm already in bed."

She listened to her father for a few minutes, then took over the conversation.

"Oh, everything's fine. I have a nice room, and there's such a pretty breakfast room off the kitchen. They call this a carriage house sometimes, but Isobel and I call it a cottage. And she has such a pretty garden in the back. Lots more flowers than we have. All kinds."

After a few minutes of listening to her father, Lisa started up again. "I've been all over the town of Southampton and to the library and we had dinner last night in Hampton Bays. Remember that on the map? And on the Fourth of July we're going to East Hampton to some friends for a barbecue. And there'll be lots of children there."

She listened some more. Then she bubbled again. "We're going to rent a bike for me, maybe. Okay. Yes, I'll be careful. No more worrying, okay? Here's Isobel. Yeah, I call her Isobel. Isn't that cool? I'll go back to bed. Talk to you soon."

She handed the phone to Isobel and went right into her bedroom. When she heard Isobel put the phone down, she put her book down on her chest and listened.

After knocking on the door, Isobel called out, "Lisa, may I come in?"

"Yes."

"You are a very good little girl. So diplomatic. I really appreciate that. I wouldn't want your father to worry about you. And he would if he knew we had a squabble. You're very kind."

"That's okay. I don't want him to worry either. That's been our biggest problem since Mom died. Worrying about me," said Lisa sitting up in her bed.

"I know you're my daughter's child, but it's hard to realize that the daughter I lost was your mother. It must have been just as hard on you as it was on me."

"Maybe worse."

"Because you're a child?"

"Because you have another child. I only had one mother."

"Oh, Lisa!" Isobel cried. And then she really started crying. She sat on Lisa's bed, put her arms around her, and they both cried. Long and hard. And then they started to laugh a little. As they both wiped their eyes and blew their noses, Isobel sobbed, "I needed that. How I needed that. I was so afraid to meet you. I thought you would remind me of Joanna and I couldn't stand that."

"Do I look like her? To you?"

"Not really, but some of your mannerisms are like hers. She was a lovely woman. A lovely child and a lovely woman."

"Tell me about her, when she was a child," Lisa whispered.

"I will, I will. But not now. It's late, and I really must get some sleep. I'll tell you what. Tomorrow evening we'll eat here and have a long and good talk about your mother. Get some sleep yourself. I'll see you at breakfast. Good night, Lisa."

"Good night, Isobel."

Chapter Four

After breakfast the next morning and after Isobel left for work, Lisa took herself out to the garden with one of her new books, a mystery about a cat. She had read some other cat mysteries before and wondered why no one wrote mystery books about dogs. She had heard about some of them, but one seemed too adult for her and one too sad. Maybe she would write a book about Mitzi. She missed Mitzi. Her Dad told her she was doing just fine and "not to worry." She laughed because that was what she was always telling her Dad – not to worry. Barbara told her once that whenever anyone told her not to worry, that's when she started to worry.

She heard a noise from the road and got up to investigate. It was the same girl riding her bike past the house. And this time she was singing. Lisa started to call out but the girl was too far up the road by that time. She would love to talk with her. Maybe if Isobel could rent a bike, she'd ride up to see if she could find the girl's house.

Lisa returned to her book and somehow couldn't get interested in it. It wasn't the book she decided. It was this awful feeling of being alone. She had never felt this way before. She had been alone many times at home with Dad at work and Barbara at the computer, but she didn't feel lonely. She knew where they were. She knew her house so well. And she had Mitzi. But here in a house and neighborhood she hardly knew and nobody around, she felt strange. Lonely was all she could call it. A new feeling and she didn't like it. She forced herself to read. She went inside to get a coke and check the time. Isobel would be home in three hours. Three hours!

She finished the chapter. Then she finished the book. Checking the time again, she had only one hour to wait. She went in to watch television.

When Isobel drove up, she met her at the door, never so glad to see someone. They had a quick lunch of egg salad sandwiches and milk. Then her grandmother was off to work again. But she told Lisa she would be home early—by 4:30—and they'd have a roast chicken she would pick up at the grocery store. And they would have their long talk about Joanna. Lisa wanted that but 4:30 was almost four hours away.

When Isobel left, Lisa almost cried. In fact, she did. She lay on her bed and felt so sorry for herself. Nothing, absolutely nothing to do! Television with its dumb soap operas was boring and her books began to be boring. The only thing she could do was think. So she thought.

She thought about all the fun times she had in Florida with Gram and Grandy. As she reviewed them in her mind, she got an idea. She would write to them. Right then and there. But she didn't bring any stationery. She looked around the cottage and found nothing but brown grocery bags and discarded envelopes in the wastebasket. So that was what she wrote on, the envelopes. Neatly crossing off Isobel's name and address, she told her paternal grandparents how lonely she was. How she missed them. Then she complained some more but at last tore it up. No sense making them unhappy. She took another envelope and told them first how she remembered all the wonderful times she had had with them last summer. Then she told them about Abigail and her huge guest house. And about maybe renting a bike. And the girl up the road whom she might get to know. And about the July fourth picnic tomorrow. That alone filled three envelopes.

She then said goodbye and told them how much she loved them. And maybe she could visit them again. She would be eleven next summer and would be much less of a pest. She laughed and then she cried a little. This time she went to bed and slept for an hour.

When she woke up, she went in for a shower. There was only an hour left of waiting. She would try another book, out in the garden, with another coke. That's one thing that Isobel didn't do—limit her cokes.

After a delicious supper, Lisa and Isobel did have a wonderful talk about Joanna.

Lisa wasn't able to give any more information about Joanna's suicide. She told what she knew, but Isobel already knew that. Together they tried to figure out what made Joanna so unhappy. They both knew you don't commit suicide if you're happy. But they couldn't come up with an answer. They cried a little and tried comforting each other a lot.

Later in the evening there were lot of laughs when they told stories of some of the good times each had had with Joanna. Isobel told about her childhood which Lisa loved hearing. Her schoolwork, her acting in school plays, her closeness to her father who was an actor on Broadway, even though his parts were always small ones. Isobel let her know how angry she was about that! But she told Lisa how successful he was on television, with ads and again, small parts in several sitcoms. He had made enough money for them all to live comfortably.

When Joanna's story grew thin, Isobel told stories about her son, Derek, who now lived in Carmel, California. And some of these stories were very funny. Derek and Joanna got into silly scrapes together and had a close relationship. Lisa said she wished she had a brother.

They had a piece of pie with ice cream and then happily each went to bed. Lisa was feeling good—about her mother, even about her grandmother, and about being where she was. And tomorrow was July 4th!

Chapter Five

On the drive to East Hampton, Isobel continued her stories about Joanna and Derek when they were children. Lisa was enthralled to learn so much about her mother. She felt she was meeting a new person whom she already knew very well. Mixed up but wonderful.

Just before getting to the barbecue, Isobel gave Lisa some names to remember: Johnny, age 11; Mike, age 9; Claire, age 10; and Debby, age 9. Their fathers all worked in the big city, and the women and children stayed out here for the summer. The men would come out every weekend on Friday and go back on Sunday night. Or Monday morning if they had a high enough executive position. Most of the children went to the beach every day. Most of the mothers played bridge or took their turn at watching and feeding the children.

"Do they bike to the beach?" asked Lisa.

"I don't know. By the way, we can rent you a bike for a week. So I thought we'd go there on Monday during lunch and get you one."

"That would be great, Isobel. Maybe if we make friends today, I can bike down with the kids. To show me the way."

"I don't know how you'd get to East Hampton. We have a beach only a few blocks from the cottage, but I don't like the idea of you biking there alone. Not very populated and no lifeguards, so you couldn't go swimming. Try to make some arrangements today. Otherwise I want you to bike just near the cottage. Maybe get to know that girl you told me about who bikes up and down the road. Now your father has told you, I hope, about not talking to strangers."

"Of course."

She was going to say more but Isobel was pulling up to the house. There were lots of people there. More than she could count. She saw some kids running around and that's exactly what she wanted to do.

"Can I go?" she asked Isobel.

"Not until I introduce you to the host and hostess. Come with me till I find them."

As Lisa passed some kids, she smiled at them and waved her hand a little. They smiled back but that was all. Isabel started weaving in and around little crowds of people, greeting each as she passed. Lisa just followed her. Finally, Isobel started waving her arm above the crowds and quickened her walking. Lisa had to run to keep up.

"I want you to meet my granddaughter, Lisa," said Isobel to a beautiful gray-haired lady.

"Hello, Lisa," said the lady.

"Mrs. Compton, Lisa," said Isobel.

"Hello."

"Glad you could come, Isobel. Good for you to get away from your work once in a while. Have you met my new neighbor? Come meet her," said Mrs. Compton.

She and Isobel went off to the right, and Lisa decided she didn't want to follow any longer. So she stood still and stared at all the people. And she looked for the kids. Then she gasped! There at the edge of the crowd was Abigail, chatting happily away with several guests. Lisa almost yelled out her name. Instead she managed to break through the crowd and got right up to her friend.

"Abby!"

"Well, my goodness, if it isn't my young friend, Lisa. And where were you yesterday morning? I near starved to death waiting for you."

"I'm sorry. I wanted to come but....couldn't. Things came up. I'm sorry, Abby."

"Everyone, I want you to meet Lisa. Lisa, everybody."

They all said hello and talked to her about things in general. "Are you staying in East Hampton? Who do you live with? Your family out here? Who did you come to the barbecue with? Do you want something to eat? The food just started to come out." And so on. She couldn't answer all the questions at once so she just smiled at everyone. Her grandmother's friend, the hostess, wasn't this friendly. In fact, she wasn't friendly at all. She wasn't surprised that Abby's friends were so nice.

"Let me introduce you to my friend, Howard," said Abby.

She led Lisa over to a good-looking man with just a tinge of gray in his hair and with a wonderful tan like her grandfather in Florida.

"Well, hello, Lisa. I've heard a lot about you. Gail told me how you got to see all the old-fashioned bedrooms and how much you knew about American history. We both waited for you yesterday. I was going to take over the chef's job and cook you some pancakes."

"He is the chef!" laughed Abby.

"I'm sorry," said Lisa with a disturbed look on her face.

"That's okay," said Abby. "Kids can't always make decisions at home, right?"

"Right," Lisa said quietly. She didn't want to tell on her grandmother, but Abby did deserve an explanation. Some day she would tell her.

"How about a coke, Lisa?" asked Howard. "I'm going to have a glass of beer but I bet you'd love a coke. Gail, a beer?"

"Sure," as they walked over to the table with beverages. Abby and Lisa waited off to the side as Howard went up to order the drinks.

"He's nice, Abby. Is he your boyfriend?"

"Yep. All mine. Or at least he says so." Abby laughed as she looked down at Lisa and said she thought that might be the reason she didn't show up for breakfast.

"Why?"

"Well, you're a little young to explain, but Howard and I aren't married and some people think we should be."

"Is that their business?"

"No….and here is the culprit with our drinks," whispered Abby.

"He called you Gail. Is that more romantic than Abby?"

"Ask him." As she took her beer, and Howard gave Lisa her coke, she told Howard that Lisa wanted to know if the name Gail was more romantic than Abby.

"Absolutely," he said with a merry laugh.

As they wandered back to the edge of the crowd again, Abby asked Lisa if she thought she could come another morning.

"Not yet. But soon. I'm renting a bike on Monday. Then I can ride over on my own."

"Please walk your bike across Main Street. Even if no cars are coming. Okay?"

"How will I know if you'll be there?" asked Lisa.

"We hang a flag on the roof when the queen is home." said Howard, laughing. "She's always there. I am, too, but usually working somewhere on the property. The Handy Man I am."

"Don't listen to him. But I am there most of the time. Come whenever you can. Now, Lisa, I see a group of kids looking for another kid. Right over there. Finish your coke and go have a good time. I'll see you real soon, I hope."

"Okay." Slurping up her coke, she said, "I'll be over soon. Thanks, Abby, and Howard."

Chapter Six

Lisa enjoyed playing with Johnny and the rest of the kids, but it was soon known that Southampton was too far away from East Hampton to make arrangements for biking together. Or for even seeing each other. Mike gave her his phone number in case Isobel was ever going to be near where he lived. Lisa took it down in her memory and liked Mike for doing that, but she felt it was not to be.

On Monday after a quick lunch Isobel drove Lisa to the bicycle shop off Main Street, and she chose a red bike for the four days of rental. Isobel drove home very slowly as Lisa followed her, mostly on back roads. There she was left with instructions not to bike across the highway which is what Main Street is called outside of town. She promised.

"See you at 6:00. Don't lose that key," said Isobel as she drove off.

Lisa opened the cottage door and looked for a piece of string so she could tie the key around her neck. Finding none, she took the rubber band off her photo album, looped the key on and put it on her wrist. Grabbing a can of coke, she locked the door and smiled at her red bike. It was beautiful. She wished she could show Abby but she was not one to disobey her grandmother's rule. She got on the bike and slowly rode out of the lane and up the road. There was no girl in sight so she just kept riding around the various roads that collected at corners. And drinking her coke.

"Hi!" a voice called out from the front garden of a large and beautiful house. It was the girl!

"Hi, yourself," yelled Lisa and she turned her bike around and pedaled up the lane to the girl's house. "I've been looking for you."

"For me? Do I know you?"

"Not yet. But I've seen you this last week riding up and down the road in front of the cottage where I'm staying. My name is Lisa."

"My name is Francesca."

"That's a pretty name."

"Think so? Lisa, eh? Don't know anyone else with that name."

"I do. Too many. But I don't know any Fran....how do you say it?"

"Francesca. It's Italian. I'm Italian."

"I'm American."

"Well, so am I, silly. Just wanted you to know where the name came from."

Lisa laughed a little. "I don't know where Lisa came from. Sorry."

"Are you visiting someone here? What house are you staying in?"

"My grandmother's and it's the tiny cottage at the end of this road. Just two blocks from Main Street."

"Oh, I know her. She owns ISOBEL'S." She laughed. "Your grandmother!? You don't look anything like her."

"No, I look like my father. Isobel was my mother's mother."

"Okay. She has a nice shop. My mother buys a lot there. Something almost every day. Is that Isobel's bike?"

"No. She rented it for me."

"It looks rented. The front wheel looks crooked. Let me get my bike, and we'll ride down to the ocean. Only a few blocks."

"Great." As they took off down the road to the left and passed her new friend's house, Lisa said, "That sure is a nice house. Big. Do you have lots of brothers and sisters?"

"Not a one. I'm the only child."

"Me, too," screamed Lisa.

"Awful, isn't it? For me anyway. My parents are always out. Well, my Dad works in the city and my mother is always going somewhere."

"Is that why I see you ride up and down the road a lot, and there's never anyone with you?" asked Lisa.

"No kids around here my age. Lots in New York, but there's no one here. So I bike a lot. Now I can bike with you. Look ahead, there's the ocean. We can't go swimming. No lifeguard. And the ocean's rough. Let's park our bikes and take our shoes off and wade."

"Great."

As they biked, conversation came easy for both of them. "What have you been doing this week—before you got the bike?" asked Francesca.

"Nothing. Reading some books. Not much fun. I was hoping to meet you. I waved to you when you biked past, but you never saw me. It was awful not having anyone to talk with. Boring."

"I spend a lot of time on the computer. But that can get lonely, too. It's better to have someone to bike with."

"I did meet someone who I liked. A lady named Abby. She owns the Southampton Guest House."

"You mean Abigail! Did you get to know her?"

"Sure. We had a good time together. She showed me all the rooms in her house. All decorated in what she called Early American. From George Washington's time right up to Theodore Roosevelt's. Have you ever seen them?"

"No. I'm not allowed to go there. Abigail is off limits."

"Why?"

"I don't know. Just that I'm not allowed to go there. I hear she lives like a gypsy."

"I don't know how gypsies live, but the house was pretty. And she wore pretty clothes. But Isobel won't let me go there again, either."

"Isobel? You call your grandmother Isobel?"

"Yep. Don't you like that?"

"I don't know. It sounds funny. I can just hear my mother allowing that." Stopping her bike without notice, she said, "Here. We leave our bikes here by this crummy old fence. And walk down to the water."

As they walked, they talked about names and grandmothers, and parents and houses. Francesca told her about her school in New York and her apartment on Fifth Avenue. Big and also lonely. She did have an Italian cook to talk with, even though she was fat and fussy. She also had school friends come over once in a while, the ones that were smart in school, and they'd do their homework together. Lisa told her about her father's new marriage. She didn't talk about her mother. Just that she died. She told her new friend about her school and her after-school activities: swimming and the French Club and biking and roller skating or ice skating. They were soon splashing water at each other, and it was cold, not like Florida. Then they sat in the sand and watched the seagulls. Lisa told her about the seagulls on Anna Marie

Island. Francesca told her about Central Park and the swans in the lake.

"I have an aunt in New York. And I'll probably visit her some summer. Next summer I'm going to Carmel, California, to visit my uncle and aunt," said Lisa.

"You get around a lot. With relatives all over. I don't visit anyone but I do get to go to Europe once in a while. And I like that."

"Europe?"

"France, mainly. Lots of good roads to bike on. I have more friends over there than here. In Southampton I mean. How long will you stay out here?"

"Till the end of July. Just three more weeks," answered Lisa.

"I can show you my scrapbook. I collect silly things but I love them. Want to come back and see all my stuff?"

"Sure. I don't keep a scrapbook. I have a friend who does. But I never know what to put in it. Let's go in again. The water's cold but it feels good in this sun."

"Lisa, what do you do when you get lonely? Besides read."

"Not much. I've never been lonely before this week. Right up to the Fourth of July barbecue. And it was awful."

" Which? The barbecue or being lonely?" asked Francesca.

"You're funny. I like you being funny," added Lisa as she saw her new friend frown.

"My mother says I shouldn't be so funny. She thinks it's rude. It's just that sometimes people say and do such stupid things that I have to say something funny. Silly, eh?"

"No, not really. Do I say or do things that are stupid?"

"No. You seem smart. Good in school? I mean do you get high marks?"

"Sometimes. You?"

"No. I have trouble with math. Even with a tutor. And science is not so good."

"Me, too. I love English and Social Studies."

"Me, too." They both laughed. "I bet we can become good friends. Let's go back, and I'll show you my scrapbook."

"Okay, race you to the bikes." screamed Lisa.

To Lisa's amazement and horror, the scrapbook was filled with things like a wing of a butterfly, the tail of a mouse, a photo of a dirty old woman sitting at the bus stop, a magazine picture of naked boys and girls at a beach. She said nothing. Francesca kept smiling and tenderly turning the pages.

Lisa said it was time for her to go home. After setting the time to meet the next day, she got on her bike, waved, and breathed a sigh of relief. Francesca was strange.

And mean, too.

Chapter Seven

Lisa and Francesca met and biked for the next three days, all around the ocean side of Southampton. Lisa saw such beautiful houses and cozy cottages. She told her new friend what Isobel had said about cottages and carriage houses. Francesca laughed and told Lisa she thought her mother was a snob, too. They both laughed. Life sure was strange and funny and fun. But it was good to have a friend to bike with and talk with.

"I have to return my bike tomorrow at noon but I can get it again on Monday. Do you think we can walk together over the weekend?"

"Not really. Mother usually has plans for me on Saturday and Sunday. Dad is here then and we go out to Montauk or East Hampton to visit friends. Have you been out there?"

"Went to a barbecue on the Fourth of July in East Hampton. What was the name of the other place?"

"Montauk. You have to go there. You have to see all the fishing boats. Not for pleasure, for business. They bring in loads of shrimp and lobster."

"We had fishing boats down in Florida. I went on one and caught four fish. We had them for lunch."

"My Dad goes fishing once in a while, but I've never gone. Mother says she'd rather have me eat my fish at a restaurant. They have great restaurants in Montauk. Get your grandmother to take you out there."

"Maybe on Sunday. That's her only day off."

"Try to go to The Dock. It's a noisy place and crowded, but they have lobster and shrimp combinations and they also have smaller portions for children. Mother likes that better than Dad leaning over and finishing what I can't eat. You see, she's a snob."

76

"The Dock. I'll remember that. I'll see you on Monday. In the afternoon, right after lunch. Same place, okay?"

"Okay. See if you can get Isobel's permission to cross the highway. I'm allowed to. Tell her we'll walk the bikes across and be very careful."

"That's what Abby told me, to walk the bike across. At the light. Do you think if we do that, we can visit Abby?" asked Lisa.

"I don't know about that. But, of course, once we cross, it's hard to say which direction we'll go biking. Maybe right up to the Guest House. Sometimes it's better to not say too much."

"What do you mean?"

"Just get permission to cross the highway. That's all. It's too easy for them to say no if you tell them too much."

"Wow." Lisa took a deep breath. "Of course Isobel told me that she didn't want me visiting Abby, nothing about crossing the highway. Or was it both?"

"Well, then you'll have to work on getting those restrictions lifted."

"You didn't. About visiting Abby." Lisa said.

"Let's take one more ride to the old lighthouse before I go home."

"Good idea."

As they rode toward the lighthouse, Lisa asked, "Do you really think it's haunted?"

"Sure I do. I told you how my Dad saw an old man coming out and going in a rowboat on a stormy night and then coming back with three men, walking out of the fog and going right inside."

"And he wasn't making it up just to scare you, just a fun story?"

"No, he meant it," Francesca said with a twinkle in her eye.

"You're fooling me then."

"No, I'm not. Why can't you believe in a haunted lighthouse? It's more than a hundred years old. Why couldn't the ghost of an old man be living there? And three ghosts visiting him?"

"Cause I don't believe in ghosts. It's not haunted. It's just some old man living there. What's wrong with that?"

"I told you the police told my father that they checked it over and it was empty."

Joining in the scary fun, Lisa whispered, "Maybe he sneaks in and out cause he doesn't want to pay rent. He only goes there to sleep. I was thinking maybe he takes his boat to some other part of the shore where he really lives and only comes here once in a while to get away from his family."

Laughing, Francesca added more to the story. "Maybe he has a crabby wife and screaming kids. And comes here to his second home that nobody knows about. But then wouldn't the police find some kind of a bed or a toothbrush?"

"No. He comes for a few hours and just sits on the floor. Then goes home when the kids are all asleep and his wife, I don't know, is also asleep."

"Or drunk! That's it. He is not a ghost but a man who wants to be alone once in a while—away from his drunken wife," giggled Francesca.

"That's awful, a drunken wife. Did you ever know anyone who gets drunk?"

"Sure, my mother."

"Your mother?" asked Lisa in a shocked voice.

"Yep. Doesn't—didn't your mother ever get drunk?"

"No. She didn't drink at all. My father drinks beer but not my mother. We did have a neighbor who they said drank too much. But I didn't know her."

"Didn't know a neighbor?" asked Francesca.

"No. She never came out of the house. We'd see her once in a while hiding behind the porch curtains."

"If she never came out, how did she shop for food or for liquor?"

"A man, they say it was her son, came every week with a box of stuff. Food I guess. I saw him once in a while but never spoke to him. But she moved last year. One of the kids said she died, that he saw them carry out a stretcher with a sheet over everything. But that kid, Joey, liked to make up things. So I don't know."

"Lisa, it's almost five o'clock. I have to go. Race you back to my house."

"See you Monday," Lisa yelled as she pedaled on.

Chapter Eight

Saturday was a long day for Lisa. It was a busy day for Isobel—she couldn't even come home for lunch. Lisa read a lot, wrote to her father and Barbara on decent writing paper Isobel gave her. Had several cokes and only cookies for lunch. And again, she thought a lot.

She was pleased to have a friend during the week to go biking with and to talk with but she felt a little strange around Francesca. She was funny, but sometimes, a lot of times, she was funny in a mean way. She was mean about her mother. And about Isobel. And about some of her friends in New York. Lisa laughed most of the time about the people Francesca described but she didn't like unkind things said about her grandmother. And nobody should say mean things about her mother. Besides being mean, she was always finding fault about something. "They never fix these roads." "Too many fields with high grass that they supposed to cut." "Not enough water pressure from the faucets." And the complaints always included people who were stupid or lazy or fat. Lisa would try to change the subject, but Francesca picked up the complaints somewhere else. When they biked on a long stretch, it was a relief to get away from all that.

Lisa thought maybe she shouldn't see Francesca so much. But how could she do that without being mean herself. And she did like having someone to talk with. That's why this day wasn't going to be a lonely day. She was going to be alone all day, but it was almost a relief to only have herself for company.

She read another book. Wrote a letter to her grandparents. And thought some more. And of course had more cokes. She began feeling a bit bloated.

She decided to write a letter to Abby. Talk to her through her writing. Abby would understand and not tell anyone else. Maybe Howard. That would be okay. She brought the writing paper out to the garden, sat on the bench among the lovely flowers and wrote and wrote. It would take two stamps to mail this one. Oh, how she wished she could visit her friend in person. And tell her how she felt about Francesca and things in general. She felt sure Abby could set her straight.

Tonight she would talk with Isobel and ask again if she could visit Abby. And tell her why. She had two more weeks in Southampton and she had to do something.

Tomorrow being Sunday, Isobel would take her out to Montauk. And to another restaurant. After, of course, a wonderful swim in the Atlantic Ocean.

In the meantime, she still had most of Saturday left. She decided to take a shower and put on her new shorts and shirt from Isobel's shop. She wouldn't get them dirty but she wanted to feel special and not so lonely. So far she wasn't really lonely but she didn't want it to sneak up on her as it did a few times last week.

She was on her sixth book and began feeling good about herself, her books, and her decision to have a talk with Isobel. And her decision to not see so much of Francesca. Isobel would help. But there it was again! She started feeing lonely. It was an awful feeling. Awful!

The phone rang, and she ran into the cottage. It was her Dad who knew Isobel would be at the shop and that maybe Lisa would be home. What a wonderful Dad he was. He talked as if he had all the time in the world and slowly Lisa unburdened herself and told him about Francesca, about Abby, about Isobel. He told her that he had faith in Lisa and thought some of her decisions were good ones. And added that perhaps she wouldn't be bothering Isobel but could actually help her by sharing all her problems. Isobel was also alone a lot and maybe she was lonely. He warned Lisa not to suggest that, but let it come out naturally. "Just tell her about your feelings." He agreed very much about Francesca being too critical and maybe too snobbish as Lisa blurted it all out. She thought maybe all of Southampton was snobbish. But Abby wasn't.

Her father told her she was very fortunate to be learning such wonderful lessons so early in life. "Not many people experience these kinds of honest feelings and then have the occasions to learn from them when they're young. Of course, be sure your words and actions are not mean, not snobbish, not critical—the very behaviors you object to." Her Dad was so smart. How lucky she was to have him. He was gentle, kind, down-to-earth and seldom critical. He was the one teaching her, not the others as he said.

They talked for almost an hour. But her father said it was worth every nickel. He wished her well with her talk with Isobel and said that he would call her during the week to check it all out.

She then had a thought she thought she would never have! She asked if she could talk to Barbara. It surprised her as well as Barbara. The two of them had a good conversation about her friends who were in the neighborhood and of course about Mitzi. And about some plans Barbara was making about August when Lisa came home. After some ten minutes, they hung up and both people were glowing happily. Lisa was so glad her grandfather had had those great talks with her about accepting Barbara into the family. Suddenly Lisa wanted to go back to the garden and continue her book. And suddenly she realized she wasn't a bit lonely. She was happy to be alone with her book, her coke, and her thoughts about life in general.

She was still alone and she wasn't lonely. How could that be? After a morning of feeling so horribly lonely! What changed? Her Dad's call helped and so did talking with Barbara. Was it her suggestion that she talk with Barbara? Was that it? If so, where did that come from? Oh, she couldn't figure it all out but this she knew: Life was good and full of good people. And definitely being alone is no cause for loneliness. Did this mean she was growing up?" Then by all means, "Keep growing!" she told herself.

She checked the time and she had two hours to go to be by herself. This was Isobel's busy day at the shop. Everybody wanted to shop on Saturday. So she'll come home tired and hot and wanting some peace. Maybe she, Lisa, could cook the dinner. What a great idea. Where do these ideas come from?

She went through the food closets and the refrigerator. Neither her mother nor Barbara had taught her anything about cooking so she carefully took the two cook books down from the top shelf. For the next hour she poured over the recipes and not one could she understand. But it did give her some ideas of her own. She could cook spaghetti and heat up some tomato sauce, both of which Isobel kept in her closet. There were some onions and tomatoes for the sauce or for a salad. She remembered always having a salad with spaghetti. She'd use them for a salad and even add some garlic power—or should that go into the sauce? She was having fun.

She found in one cookbook how to cook spaghetti. She opened the tomato sauce, added some garlic power, salt, and some pepper. And put them all into a saucepan to heat. For the salad she cut the tomatoes very carefully and the same with the onions. Then she put the salt, the pepper, and the garlic power on the table. The table! Oh, she had to fuss with the table. Her mother used to say half the meal was in the presentation.

She found a tablecloth in the linen closet and chose four hand towels for napkins and bibs (so as not to splatter the blouse or dress.) Then not finding a vase, she took a large glass, filled it with water, and placed it in the middle of the table. She went out to the garden to pick the prettiest flowers, hoping that Isobel wouldn't mind.

The sauce was hot, the salad was sitting in the fridge and the water boiling for the "pasta". She got that name for spaghetti from the cookbook.

It was a few minutes after six and she heard Isobel's car come into the driveway. She held her breath.

Opening the door and greeting Isobel with a big smile was just what Isobel needed. She perked up immediately and when she entered the cottage and saw the table dressed for a party and heard the water boiling, she laughed and teared up at the same time.

"What a lovely surprise, Lisa," she murmured.

"Well, I knew you'd be tired with all your customers going through all your clothes. And you wouldn't feel like cooking. And we have to eat! So there you are. I hope I did everything right."

"I know you did. What a thoughtful thing to do. Let me wash up and I'll be right out. Do you want to put the spaghetti in the water or do you want me to do it?"

"I'll do it. Eight minutes boiling time, right?" asked Lisa.

"Right. Do we have any rolls or bread sticks in the house? No, I don't think so," looking all around the closets. "I'll have to get some. But why don't we toast some rye bread and cut it up in quarters?"

"Okay. You get washed and I'll finish up."

"Be right there," said Isobel as she disappeared into the bathroom.

Lisa took out the salad bowl and placed it near the bowls for the pasta and the sauce. The pasta went into the pot and she started watching the clock, counting off eight minutes. She poured the sauce into its bowl and put the rye bread into the toaster. Maybe she should have done that first and the sauce after. Oh, she just wanted everything to come out right. Isobel hadn't noticed the flowers. Is that bad?

When Isobel came back to the table, she picked up the glass of flowers and smiled.

"How wonderful to have fresh flowers on the table. That's another thing I must do in the future. Thank you, Lisa, for making everything so beautiful and smell so good. I see the cookbook over there and I'm proud of you. You're very mature for ten years old. Your mother, my daughter, would be very proud of you."

"Thank you, Isobel. I wanted to make you happy, and I have. That makes me happy. Oh, the spaghetti! It's done. How do I get rid of the water?"

"Here, let me help now. You take off your apron and I'll use this colander and voila! We have a spaghetti dinner!"

They had a great time as they ate. Both talked at once about silly things. Both laughed together and both did a lot of smiling.

"Now how was your day, Lisa? Seemed long for you, of course. But fussing for this dinner took a lot of time." said Isobel.

"I learned something today. In the morning I was a little upset, facing seven hours without you or Francesca or anyone. But as I thought about her and you and Abby and how I was feeling, I made a decision to forget all that and to read my books and to have another coke and some cookies. When I forgot everything that was bothering me, I began to feel better. Honestly, I began to feel not so lonely. And my dad called and we talked and talked and talked."

"Good for him. Tell me more about not feeling so lonely. This sounds interesting."

"Well, I hinted to you this week about how Francesca is always complaining about things and people, and how it was bothering me. I don't know why she does it, but I decided I just wouldn't listen to it. I would bike ahead or try to start a new conversation. I decided that maybe next week I won't spend so much time with her. Maybe just a few hours. And now I can. I know I can be alone and not feel lonely.

"Wow. You are something. In a way I did the same thing years ago after your grandfather passed away. I wasn't going to let loneliness run my life. But I was an adult, fifty something. You're a child and you did the same thing. Amazing."

"I had to. I just had to. My only friend was getting on my nerves. I don't know where the ideas came from about all this, but they came and I really had a fun afternoon."

"Good girl. Now let's clean up or rather I'll clean up. You did enough."

"No, I'll clean up. You worked hard all day."

"We'll both clean up. Put that apron back on," Isobel said as she put one on herself.

They finished the dishes and put everything away. The flowers went on the table again but this time without a tablecloth. Isobel opened her mail and Lisa got into her pajamas and robe. Later in the evening they both enjoyed some ice cream. They discussed tomorrow's trip to Montauk, swimming in the Atlantic, and what restaurant they would try. Maybe they'd go to The Dock to see if it was too fancy in dress and money.

"I'm going to bed, Isobel, and thank you for enjoying my dinner. I had such a good time," said Lisa.

"Good night, Lisa, and thank you—for everything. Our next two weeks is going to be a blast. I love you, Lisa."

"And I love you," said Lisa as she left the room.

Chapter Nine

After church on Sunday, Isobel and Lisa set off for the town of Montauk which seemed to be the end of the world. A peninsula almost surrounded by water, it was indeed a terrific place to swim. But Lisa had to be careful with the rough waves and somewhat of an undertow. She remembered what her grandfather had taught her, to keep checking to make sure she could touch the bottom. That way she wouldn't drift out way over her head. She could swim and swim well, but oceans were tricky waters. That's what lots of people told her and she believed them.

Isobel went out a little further and was glad when Lisa didn't follow her. There was enough activity with the high and powerful waves to keep Lisa busy and happy.

After their swim, they dried their skin, hair, and bathing suits in the warm sun.

And laughed a lot while doing so. Putting on their cotton muumuus Isobel had ordered from Hawaii, they drove to the end of Montauk for a late lunch or early dinner. After checking the prices of The Dock which Francesca had recommended, Isobel took Lisa to a restaurant just beyond, to a more casual place called The End of the Pier, which it was. They ordered some lobster and a few shrimp on the side and sat back to enjoy the wide span of ocean before them while they waited. They both decided they liked this place even better than last week's because of the view.

"I hope the food is as good," remarked Isobel.

"Everyone seems to be enjoying their meal," said Lisa and just as she said this, a seagull came swooping down to the table next to theirs. It passed over one of the plates and took with it a large shrimp. Stole a piece of food right under the noses of the people sitting there. Lisa couldn't believe it. Everybody laughed and then carefully guarded the rest of the dinners.

"I don't believe what I saw. They have no manners, those seagulls. Or at least that one. In Florida, seagulls come down and circle you. They watch you carefully as you take out your food and then almost beg for something to eat. And, of course, we always threw them a piece of bread. We would throw it way up high and five or six of them would fly after it, sometimes fighting over it. But they never came near and took food from our blanket!"

"I never saw that before either. But then I don't come out here too often for a meal. They must be so used to people that they're just not afraid. Oh, look, Lisa, there's a sign PLEASE DO NOT FEED THE SEAGULLS. That's what happened. People fed them and fed them probably from their hands as they were eating until some of the gulls just went a step further. Look, here comes another one, swooping right into that lady's plate. Over there."

Lisa looked and saw again how a seagull gets its food on a pier in Montauk. This time it took a large piece of fish the lady had cut off. For herself, not for the seagull. The lady and her companion screamed, almost in delight but also with a bit of irritation.

At that moment their waiter appeared and put down their dinners. Lisa immediately covered hers with her arms. The waiter laughed.

"That's what people get for feeding them," he said. "These seagulls are very smart and know they don't have to work so hard getting their food from the ocean. I believe some of them even prefer cooked fish. A compliment to the chef, don't you think?"

"I might stand by the railing later and give up a piece of my fish, after I've eaten what I want," said Lisa.

"Watch your fingers!" warned the waiter. "Do you need anything else?"

"The iced teas," said Isobel.

"Of course, I'm sorry. I'll bring them right out."

"Now enjoy your meal, Lisa, but keep on eye on those gulls," said Isobel.

It was a delicious meal, especially the lobster. Isobel taught her how to eat each section and how to dip into that wonderful butter. Lisa wondered how she could get some when she's home.

Just as she was finishing her last shrimp, there came a seagull swooping down but instead of trying to take it from her, it landed on the table and merely looked at her,.

"He's begging for it. Should I give it to him?" giggled Lisa.

"It's only encouraging them to steal their food. Go to the railing."

"I'll give him half." As Lisa moved to the railing, she bit the shrimp in half and held out the piece for the gull. Before she could say anything, the shrimp was gone and so was the seagull.

"He didn't even say 'thank you'!" wailed Lisa. "Where are your manners?"

Isobel laughed and said, "He doesn't speak English. He probably thanked you, but then you don't understand gull language."

They finished their drinks and got ready to leave when they heard a woman laughing so loudly that everyone turned around to see what had happened. It was nothing but a party of newcomers to the restaurant, all giggling at the lady who was now screaming with laughter and being so silly. She could hardly walk straight, leaning on the arm of one of the men. A pretty woman, dressed in beautiful sport clothes, and spilling the drink she was carrying. Then she fell and laughed even harder. Isobel made a few quiet remarks, asking Lisa not to look at the lady. She quietly explained that she was one of her customers, one of her best customers, and that she was seen often in restaurants carrying on like this.

"She's a lovely lady, but with a few drinks in her, she becomes disgusting. Her husband is very kind to her and tries to save the day. She has a young daughter who always looks familiar to me. Oh, there she is in the back of the crowd."

"That's Francesca!"

"The girl on the bicycle? Of course. Now I remember seeing her on our road, riding up and down. Your new friend. The poor child. She must be so embarrassed."

Still looking with wide eyes, Lisa whispered, "She told me she's used to it. I don't mean like this in restaurants. But she told me her mother drinks a lot. Maybe that's why she's so funny and mean sometimes with her remarks about people. Should I let her see me?"

"You might not have a choice. But don't mind. Let her know that you still like her and act like you didn't even see her mother," suggested Isobel.

"Golly, how can I do that?"

"Be natural. Say hello, then tell her that you'll see her tomorrow. Come on, let's go."

As Lisa and Isobel left the restaurant, Lisa waved to Francesca and mouthed, "I'll see you tomorrow. 1:00." Francesca waved back and nodded "yes." She showed no embarrassment.

"She's used to it all right," said Isobel. "Poor kid."

"Maybe that's why she says those awful things about her mother."

"Yes. What else can she do? I'm sorry her father doesn't try to protect her more."

"What can he do?" asked Lisa as they got into their car.

"I don't know. And obviously, he doesn't know."

On the drive home, Lisa was mostly silent, thinking about her friend and about life in general. Why was life so mixed up? Why were there so many terrible things happening to everyone. Why were people sometimes unfriendly to others? Then she had an idea. She and Isobel were getting along so well now, she might ask her about Abigail.

"Isobel, do you think I can ever meet Abby again?" Lisa asked, coming right to the point.

"I knew you'd ask that some day. I've been thinking about it. I don't know. The things I've heard about her boyfriend and the crazy parties they give with their weekend guests. I just don't know."

"She never said anything crazy to me or did anything crazy. She was just friendly and fun. She knows I'm only ten so she won't say or do anything wrong."

"I'm sure....I tell you what. Why don't we both go over some time and you can show me some of the house. Would she mind?" asked Isobel.

"That's a wonderful idea, Isobel. When?"

"We could ask her to have lunch with us. Maybe take her to lunch although I don't know why."

"Isobel, I haven't spent any of the money Daddy gave me. Why don't I take both you and Abby to lunch?"

"You are the most generous child I have ever known."

"It would be easier that way, don't you think? Then Abby wouldn't feel she'd have to take you sometime. I go home soon. We have lunch and I say goodbye the following week and maybe you have a new friend."

"You are something. My little girl's little girl. I'm glad you're my granddaughter and that I finally got to meet you. But, let's give your idea some more thought. Okay?"

"Okay. When you decide we can do it, can I call her or go over to ask her?" asked Lisa.

"We'll see."

Chapter Ten

Isobel prepared a light supper to eat while watching the 7:00 news. It was her belief that Lisa should know what was going on in the country and in the world. The program they watched did not have sensational news or gossip so she felt safe having Lisa watching it. Over the two weeks Lisa almost learned to enjoy it. Almost. She asked a lot of questions. "Where is Palestine?", "Who is Hussein?" "Why are all those children so hungry?"

After the news, they settled into the living room each with a dish of ice cream. Strawberry this time.

"Can you tell me about my grandfather? I only know his name and that he was an actor and that he died in an accident."

"Well, John was quite a man. A lot like you. Maybe that's why you're so bright and eager and responsible. All the qualities he had. He also had a terrific sense of humor, something you'll develop as you grow older. And he was kind. Which you are already."

"What did he act in television? I never saw him but I remember Mom telling me I was too young to watch. Police stories or something."

"Yeah, he got into a lot of those and some shows we call sit-coms. But his main love was acting in plays in the theatre. He was fortunate to be in eight Broadway plays, small parts, and three off-Broadway shows. The television work paid the most though and the contracts lasted almost a year."

"My mother loved him. She used to tell me how he would race with her in the ocean. And how he and Derek would help her build great big sand castles.

"He loved his kids."

"She told me she felt so sad to leave you and him when she got married and had to move out west. Did you ever visit her?" Lisa asked as she took her last spoonful of ice cream.

"No, he was either in a play or a sit-com. Theatre is not a business you can work your own schedules too easily. We always felt terrible about not visiting—both Joanna and you. Especially when you were born, but that time he needed me for rehearsals in an important Broadway play. Joanna did come east several times and one time brought you. You were only two years and quite adorable."

"When was the accident?"

"Right after that visit in fact. She came right back, without you of course. And she stayed with me for a few weeks. Your father's sister-in-law, Mary Joan, from Charleston, went to your house to care for you. I believe she stayed the whole time Joanna was with me. Nice of her. She had lost her infant son a couple of years before so she was free to do that. Except her husband was complaining about being so lonesome."

"There's a lot of sadness around, isn't there?"

"Yes. But there's a lot of happiness, too. This is my seventh year alone – seven long years – sad years but for the shop which kept and keeps me quite busy. And now you're here and giving me my best summer."

"Did my grandfather know this cottage?"

"No, we came out here only for a few weekends each summer. We both loved it. So when he died, I just had to come back. And it just seemed right to settle in here.

"I'm glad you did! It's a wonderful place to live. And visit!"

"My shop started to really grow around four years ago, and I was almost as busy in the winter as in the summer."

"Then you came out for Mom's funeral. Almost three years ago."

"Yes."

"It's a nice shop, Isobel. The nicest shop I've ever seen. You have such pretty clothes."

"Thank you. Now enough looking back. Would you like to watch a video? I have BAMBI and THE SOUND OF MUSIC. Both very old but maybe new to you. Which one?"

Isobel held up both videos to show Lisa the pictures.

"I think BAMBI. I like deer. We have some at home if you go out to the park."

"Be prepared to cry a little. I did when I was a child. I might even now." said Isobel with a laugh. They watched BAMBI and they both cried. And of course laughed a lot. Lisa fell in love with Thumper, the rabbit, and with Flowers, the skunk. But it was Bambi, the beautiful deer, who gave her beautiful dreams that night.

Chapter Eleven

This week Lisa chose a green bike. At 1:00 after a hard-boiled egg for lunch, she met Francesca at the corner of her house. Francesca was the same. She never talked about her mother in the restaurant. But she was still saying mean and funny things about the old lighthouse, about the dirt roads; about the field of high grass that nobody else cared about. Lisa kept quiet. She was trying so hard to be nice to her friend.

"Did you ever see a video called BAMBI?" asked Lisa. "We saw it last night."

"Isn't that a little babyish for you? I had that when I was little."

"It's beautiful. When Bambi's mother dies in the forest fire, I cried. So did Isobel. But it had funny parts, too. I had never seen it. I liked it."

"Sometimes you are so strange, Lisa. A little on the goody side. Guess that's from where you live."

"Don't say that. That's not nice."

"See what I mean? What do you mean, 'not so nice?' That's a stupid thing to say."

"Oh, come on, let's go. Let's go to the beach today. And take a long walk. Can we leave out bikes for a long time?"

"We don't have thieves out here, Lisa. You must have thieves where you live."

"Francesca, I'm going to go home if you don't stop picking on me. How come you enjoy making fun of everybody?"

"Silly girl. There's no one else here. You're the only one I'm picking on."

"You do other times. You pick on your mother all the time. And on your neighbors. And some of your school friends."

93

"That's none of your business. Maybe you better go home," said Francesca and tears started to well up in her eyes.

Seeing this, Lisa said quietly, "Come on, Francesca, let's go to the beach."

They biked to the sandy edge, took their shoes off, and parked their bikes next to the sign that said in big letters NO LIFEGUARDS ON DUTY. They walked down to the water without saying a word.

"Which way?" asked Francesca.

"I don't care."

"Then we go to the right."

After walking a while, Lisa spoke up.

"Let's try to find shells. Did I tell you about the shells I found on Sanibel Island?"

"No."

"I know what I can do. I'll send you some when I get home. You're only able to pick up a pail full. But I had the pails of my grandparents. So I'll send you a couple."

"You're so cheerful. Sometimes it's annoying. To always be so happy."

"Would you rather I was crabby?"

"Yes."

"That's silly." She waited a few moments. "Francesca, I'm sorry about what happened yesterday at the restaurant."

"Wasn't your fault. Let's forget about it. Come on, we'll look for some stupid shells."

They walked in silence. There were no shells to pick up. So they just walked. Neither of them did much talking.

Chapter Twelve

With Isobel's permission, Lisa dialed Abby's number and nervously waited through six rings. Then Abby came on with a full and pleasant voice.

"Southampton Guest House. May I help you?"

"Abby! It's me, Lisa."

"Well, how are you? Long time since that barbecue."

"I know. Can you have lunch with us?"

"Whose us?" asked Abby.'

"Isobel and me. I'm treating."

"Two surprises. Isobel wants to have lunch with me. And you, you ten-year old squirt, are paying? Where will you get all that money? I eat a lot."

"Daddy gave me money when I came out here, and I haven't spent a cent. Isobel has paid for my new clothes and my bikes and at the restaurants. So I have lots of money and I can't think of anything I'd rather do than have lunch with you."

"You are something."

"Can you do it? Can you get away from your job for maybe two hours?"

"Two hours? Where could that restaurant be?"

"I don't know yet. But it takes time to get anywhere and by the time you order and we all talk, it could be almost two hours. Even Isobel is arranging that much time from the shop."

"You are a magician. How did you ever get your grandmother to want to have lunch with me?"

"She just did. I suggested it. No, I think she suggested it. Anyway, is Thursday a good day?"

"A perfect day. I always need a fun time before all my guests arrive on Friday."

"Oh, great, Abby. Isobel suggested we pick you up at 11:30 or 12:00. Which would be better?"

"11:30 in fact. Say, this is a welcomed surprise. 11:30 on Thursday."

"Okay. See you. Goodbye."

"Goodbye, Lisa."

"She's coming," yelled Lisa into the kitchen where Isobel was preparing dinner.

"Good. Thursday, 11:30. It's going on the calendar. Now come on and set the table and tell me about your day."

"Well, it was okay. I felt sorry for Francesca. She got all upset over nothing and almost started to cry. I didn't know what to say. But we took a long walk up the beach, and I think she felt better by the time we got back on our bikes."

"The poor kid. The restaurant and her mother weren't even mentioned?"

"Oh, I did. When I saw her crying, I said something. And all she said was that it wasn't my fault. That was all she said. And all I said. We just walked and watched the waves and sat on the warm sand. She did say I was a goody goody. I don't think I am and I told her so."

"Good for you. You are good but no goody goody. And you have spunk."

"What's that?"

"Courage. Willing to take a stand for what you believe. Not too many people have that. Some think they have it, but what they have is really self-will. You don't have any of that. So it's courage."

"I had some of that self-will last year. When I first went down to my grandparents, I wasn't always nice. I wanted things I couldn't have. I don't know why. But my grandfather started to have little private talks with me and got me over it. In a way. He was very smart. Like my father. I was much better by the time I got home. Even Daddy noticed the difference."

"I bet he was happy. I hardly remember him, except he took my daughter away. She was crazy about him. Well, are you meeting Francesca tomorrow? For more biking?"

"Yep. It will probably be better tomorrow."

As they finished eating, Isobel said, "Now, how about SOUND OF MUSIC?"

"Great. Tell me about Derek's children. Lawrence, or do you call him Larry?"

"Lawrence. His mother insists on full names. Doesn't like nicknames. That's why I'm glad I chose Derek. Can't make a nickname out of that. But Lawrence is surely Larry in the schoolyard. And Suzanne will become Suzy. And Helena maybe Helen. His wife is trying awfully hard to keep the proper names."

"My name is hard to be made into a nickname."

"Yes. Derek's wife's name is Rochelle and someone once told me that as a child she was called Rocky. Which didn't make her very happy," Isobel said, laughing.

"I have a friend who name is Robin, and the boys sometimes tease her by calling her Redbreast. Don't you think that's mean?"

"Kind of, more silly. I hope she laughs it off. If she doesn't, they'll keep calling her that."

"Well, she didn't at first. In fact, she cried. But our teacher told her the same thing you said. So she tried it. They almost don't do it now."

"Good for her. Good for the teacher."

"Suzanne is my age. Is she like me?"

"I don't know. Haven't been out there. Derek only brought his family here for your grandfather's funeral. And they were little then. So I don't know. I write them now and then, and they answer with short notes. They even write little thank-you notes when I send them presents. Which is unusual for today. So I'm pleased they have manners."

"What made him go out there? There are lots of banks right here in Southampton."

"Did you count them? Kidding. Derek fell in love with an artist, and she felt that Carmel had a lot to offer artists. No more than we have right here, but they do have a lot of art exhibitions. Derek liked it, so they stayed. The children go to a very good school out in the Valley. They seem to be doing quite well. So everyone's happy."

"Three thousand miles is a long way. It would be nice if you could visit them more often."

"I'm not too much on traveling. And neither of my children got the traveling bug. So we write and we telephone. Your Dad's parents don't come up very often to visit you, do they?"

"No, but I think that's because they're older. Much older than you are. How come?"

"I married quite young. Seventeen."

"Seventeen! I can marry in seven years?"

"Not unless it's a guy you're crazy about. I met your grandfather, and that was it for me. I didn't want to meet anyone else. He was twelve years older than me, but we both felt that it didn't matter. And we had a terrific marriage."

"That's why it was so hard for you when he died. Both your children were far away, and then he left."

"Left? That's an interesting way to put it. But that's why these past years have not been easy. Without the shop, I don't know what I would have done."

"Seventeen, wow! Did your mother like that?"

"She didn't care. I think she was glad to get me out of the house. I had five brothers and two sisters."

"Wow! Eight children! That's a lot."

"It's getting late. Let's get that movie on. By the way, there's a wonderful song in it about falling in love when you're sixteen. Ice cream now or later?"

"Later, please. I ate a lot and I'm full."

"Right. Want to get comfortable? In your pajamas?"

"Okay. Let's both get comfortable. See you out here in five minutes," yelled Lisa

"Right. First one out gets extra ice cream."

They both got back to the living room at the same time. So when they got to the middle of the movie and wanted a break, they both had extra ice cream.

Chapter Thirteen

Thursday came and went with excitement, joy, and promise. The three ladies chattered until it was difficult to distinguish which one was talking. Isobel was enthusiastic in her calm way, not cool and distant which Lisa was afraid of; Abby was low-keyed and lady-like and careful, yet bubbling underneath; Lisa was Lisa. And the two women gave her much attention. They went over all the activities she experienced the past three weeks and gave lots of friendly advice and compliments.

Francesca was seriously discussed. All of them came to the conclusion that there was nothing any of them could do and there was nothing Francesca could do. They decided the awful situation was probably what made Francesca critical and funny in a mean way. They also decided that it's almost impossible for a child to turn a parent around. All Francesca could do was grow up and eventually, out of the situation. And try to be patient, waiting for a right moment to maybe be of help. And if it never came, just grow up and out. Sad.

They discussed Joanna's suicide, Isobel starting the discussion after Abby apologized for not knowing about it and giving her condolences. Isobel apologized for holding it all in and not accepting small moments of people reaching out. Lisa didn't have anything to apologize for, but to change the subject, she did say she was sorry she was going home in a week.

Abby asked Isobel if Lisa could bike over some morning and have that breakfast with her. Isobel smiled and said yes, but she had to be careful about crossing the highway. Then Abby had a suggestion for Lisa.

"How about bringing Francesca over some afternoon? Not the day we have our breakfast."

"Great. Okay?" she asked Isobel.

"That's Abby's decision. It might be better to check with Francesca's mother."

"She won't care," remarked Lisa.

"But she did tell you that she wasn't allowed to go to the Guest House. I wouldn't get involved with a family decision, Lisa."

"My Guest House is so popular! But your grandmother's right. You can ask Francesca and let her find out if her mother will allow it. At least it will make her feel good about being asked."

"Okay."

On Friday she asked Francesca who in turn got very quiet and said nothing.

"But you will ask, won't you?" Lisa said. Francesca nodded.

The following Monday, Lisa's last week, she got a blue bike and met Francesca at 1:00 for their afternoon of biking and talking. Lisa was glad she hadn't cancelled it. She did explain that she wouldn't be able to meet the next day as she was going to have breakfast with Abby and then they were going to take a bike ride.

"I'll meet you Wednesday. Okay? Did you ask your mother about going over to Abby's with me?" Francesca shrugged her shoulders.

"Can I come to your garden instead of biking tomorrow? I'll bring some cookies."

"I'll ask Isobel but I'm sure it'll be okay."

"There you go again, being so good. Isobel would never know I was there. I'll even brush away the cookie crumbs."

"Francesca, it's her garden. Don't you think she should know who will visit?"

"Okay, ask her. Let's go to the beach now. Race you there."

And they raced. And they walked. And they talked.

The next day, Lisa had the most wonderful breakfast at the Guest House. Abby made pancakes with blueberries and maple syrup. They took almost two hours to eat, talking about Lisa's lunch and laughing about life in general. Abby told Lisa how happy she was that Isobel was now friendly and may even become a friend. All because of Lisa.

They had a fun bike ride through the countryside of Southampton, on the other side of the highway. They rested in a field of wild daisies. Lisa said it reminded her of home.

"May I write to you, Abby?"

"Of course. And I shall answer. Not long letters but happy ones to my new friend of the west."

"Mid-west."

"Okay, mid-west. Wherever that is. Been out to the west coast, California. But nowhere in between. Maybe on my next trip to the coast, I'll stop over and say hello."

"Would you, Abby? We have plenty of room in our house. And I know Daddy would like you. And Barbara, too. And you'd like them. Oh, please come."

"We'll see."

"That's what Isobel always says, "We'll see.""

"Well, it's better than saying, "No.""

"Yes. So we'll write and we'll see."

"Lisa, what do you want to do when you finish college?"

"How did you know I was going to college?"

"Every child should go. I didn't and I'm sorry. I don't know half the things I'd like to know. So what do you want to do with your life?"

"Don't know. I'm happy right where I am. I'd like to stay ten forever. We had a teacher last year who gave as our composition title, "Why I Like Being Nine Years Old." I couldn't stop writing. A boy in my class left his paper blank. When the teacher asked him why he wasn't writing, he told her that he didn't like being nine. So she told him to write why he didn't like being nine. He filled the paper."

"What did he write?"

"Don't know."

"Well, I was thinking about how you love to read and wondering if you'd like to write books for other children to read."

"I could. You know what I'd write about? You and Isobel and Southampton."

"There you go. Now, let's go back home. I have some work to do."

"Maybe I'll see you again with Francesca. I'll call you, okay?"

They biked back to the Guest House, said goodbye as Abby escorted Lisa across the busy noon-time highway.

On Wednesday Lisa met Francesca at the usual time and as they rode along the ocean road, she told her that Isobel said it was all right for her to come to the garden. Anytime. Even for lunch. Lisa and Francesca decided they would meet the next day in the garden about 10 in the morning, and Lisa would make ham and cheese sandwiches.

101

And then they'd go biking after lunch.

So Thursday Francesca showed up at 10 sharp with a bag full of cookies and a book, in case Lisa wanted to read. She admired the garden and all its flowers. Said a few things about it needing to be weeded. Lisa reminded her about her finding fault with everything.

"Well, I just thought how about us weeding it?"

"Oh, that's an idea. I never thought about that. Okay, let's do it right now. Before lunch."

They took off their shorts and shirts and weeded in their bathing suits. They decided to be very careful not pull anything up that could be a flower—just the big ugly weeds. They filled three grocery bags with them! The garden certainly did look better. Lisa hoped that Isobel would be pleased. Maybe she should have asked. No, she thought, she will love it, like the dinner she made. Surprises are fun.

Francesca and Lisa both washed up with the hose, put their shorts and shirts back on and went into the cottage to make lunch. Took the sandwiches and milk out to the garden and laughed a lot. Ate the cookies with more laughter. Then Francesca asked some serious questions.

"Is my mother very wrong to drink so much? She does seem to enjoy it. And she doesn't do it all the time. Most of the time only when we go out with Daddy. During the week she only does it just before she goes to bed. Nobody can see it, and me neither. I go to bed way before she does. Most of the time."

"I don't know, Francesca. I don't know if it's very wrong. I think it's a little embarrassing for you and your father. But I don't think it's terribly wrong. She doesn't hurt you or anybody."

"No, she doesn't. She doesn't even say mean things. I do that. And I don't know why I do it, Lisa."

"You're better than you were. When I first met you, you really hurt my feelings. But now, not so much. You're better."

"I think it's because of you. You said a lot of hard things to me about it, and I think it helped. You're a good kid, Lisa. You're not goody good like I said. I just get all upset cause I can't be like that. You know, kind, nice."

"Yes, you can," said Lisa.

"I've tried and it always comes out wrong."

"Just keep trying. That's what I did last summer in Florida. It'll happen. I like you, Francesca, and I would like to keep you as a friend.

Will you write to me? I'll send you those shells and then you'll have my address. But I need your address first. And your last name. Let me get some paper."

Lisa took down Francesca's address, put it in her book, and knew she had another friend.

Chapter Fourteen

Lisa's last weekend was a mixture of good and bad. Thursday's possible arrangement of Lisa and Francesca going over to visit Abby was broken the last minute by Francesca's mother. No reason given. What that meant Francesca didn't know, but she was used to her mother's sudden and unfair decisions, and she learned to live with them. To fight and try to demand what she wanted always proved disastrous, like some punishment being carried over to New York. She decided it just wasn't worth it. So Lisa went alone. She enjoyed another delicious breakfast and while they were cleaning up, Abby quietly said, "I have some happy news for you."

"What's that?"

"Howard and I decided to get married. Make everything legal, you know."

"Wow! Abby, that's awesome!"

"Yeah, we think so, too," said Abby with a big grin.

"When? When? Oh, I won't be here, will I? When did you decide?"

"The week after that July fourth barbecue. Howard said he was tired of being the "handy man" and would prefer to be my husband. When you asked him if the name Gail was more romantic, he thought about it, and that did it."

"I had something to do with it then!" cried Lisa.

"Guess you did, squirt. We finally decided to share the same last name, just two days ago. How about that?"

"When? Where?" asked Lisa.

"Can't take any time off during the summer so we thought we'd go to City Hall some day during October. Then go on a cruise or something to celebrate."

"What's City Hall?"

"A government building in New York where they perform civil marriage. Takes ten minutes. You fill out the forms, pay the fee, and the judge marries you. We don't want any fuss. We just want to be married. But I sure would love having you there."

"Oh, Abby, me too. Maybe Isobel can go."

"No, honey, no fuss. Just the two of us. And I'd rather you didn't tell Isobel just yet. I'll write you and tell you the date and then you can tell her. Who knows? Maybe I'll be telling her myself over some lunch next month. We may become good friends by then."

"Will you have some pictures taken? Will you buy a new dress? A bouquet of flowers?"

"Yes, yes, and yes. And I'll send you some pictures. Oh, Lisa, you're getting me all excited now. I was happy, real happy, we decided to do this. But now I'm excited. And now it's time for you to go home. There's a lot to be doing around here. I'll be in touch." said Abby as she walked Lisa to the door.

Lisa was so happy with the big news, but she sure would miss her new friend.

On Friday Lisa and Francesca spent the day at the beach. They took two long walks, one each way along the shore. And then they carefully walked into the ocean but only up to their waists. Francesca tried to get Lisa to go in further, but Lisa proved stubborn and wouldn't budge. Francesca was afraid to go out alone. But they still had fun. They splashed a lot, lay on the warm sand, and talked: long discussions about families, growing up, school, each other, and life as they knew it. They walked some more, rode their bikes home, and finally said goodbye. But not sadly because they both knew their friendship would last through letters and phone calls.

That night after dinner Isobel and Lisa also had some long discussions. They talked about Abby and her life style. Lisa had a difficult time not telling her grandmother the good news. They talked about Francesca and her chances for happiness despite having an alcoholic mother. They talked about Joanna whom they both missed. And they discussed how they would keep in touch with letters, phone calls, and maybe a visit now and then.

Saturday was no longer a lonely day for Lisa. She had conquered that devil. She read out in the garden with cookies and milk during the morning and with soda and potato chips in the afternoon. There were two more books that had to be returned to the library so Lisa read rather quickly. The title of the one she really thought she would like she committed to memory. She would get it out of her library at home. She also started packing, leaving out clothes for dinner that night and for church the next day. Just thinking about going home made her both sad and happy. Sad to leave Southampton and her new friends; happy to be seeing Daddy and Mitzi. And Barbara.

As promised Isobel came home early. She helped Lisa finish her packing, took a shower, and dressed for dinner in a special restaurant in Hampton Bays. Going there was mainly to avoid meeting Francesca's family who always dined in Montauk. The restaurant Isobel chose for their last dinner was, of course, a seafood restaurant. It had a room with lots of huge fish tanks against all the walls. They held the beauties of the sea, which the waiter claimed were not used for cooking, just for looking. Lisa loved it. After ordering her dinner, she joined the other children walking around the room, also watching and talking to her new friends of the sea—the lobsters, shrimp, clams, scallops, flounder, mackerel.

They had a happy time at dinner, laughing about some of the antics that go on in dress shops: women trying to squeeze into dress-es much too small for them; customers trying to exchange clothes they had already worn; young ladies, without their mothers looking on, trying on mature and sexy outfits. Isobel enjoyed them all and never insulted any of them. She was a good businesswoman and never lost a customer.

After dinner Lisa joined other children, checking up on the activities in the tanks.

That evening was a quiet time. A little talk, checking on the final packing, making sure they both had correct addresses of each other and their new friends. To help the evening, Isobel taught Lisa a new card game, double solitaire. It caused a lot of laughing and screaming as each tried to beat the other to the growing pile in the middle of the table.

Isobel told Lisa that she wanted to see Abby again and that she would try to say hello to Francesca now and then. Both of these ges-tures made Lisa happy.

There was too much excitement the next morning to allow any gloom. They ate a good breakfast, got to church, went home for the suitcase and a cold drink. They caught the jitney in plenty of time, Isobel naturally going with Lisa to the airport. She was early for the plane, but Isobel stayed with her until boarding time. Then they waved to each other with big smiles across their faces.

Isobel cried softly part of the ride home, feeling she had connected again with her daughter. Lisa cried softly in the early part of the plane ride as she ate her lunch, feeling she had her mother again so close to her.

The End

Book Three
Lisa in California

Chapter One

"We're almost there, Lisa," said the stewardess as she passed her seat, checking that all passengers were buckled in correctly.

"Then San Francisco really is close to Carmel!"

"By air. Four or five hours to drive. Did you get a chance to see San Francisco?"

"No. But my uncle and aunt told me we would probably be taking a trip there some weekend."

"Good. You'll love it. Lots of things to do and see. Ever been to New York City?"

"Not yet. That comes in two more years. When I'm 13. How did you know I was going to go there?"

"I didn't, but I was going to explain how San Francisco is like a small New York. It has a Chinatown where you can get the most delicious meals. There's a business section like New York's Wall Street and several streets of fabulous shops like New York's Fifth Avenue stores. They have Macy's, Lord & Taylor's, Saks, along with a few of their own fine department stores. Do you like to shop? For clothes?"

"Not really. My grandmother in Southampton owns her own shop with very beautiful clothes, and I enjoyed shopping there," said Lisa with a big smile. "Everything was free."

"I have to sit down now. We're coming in. I'll come back when we land."

Lisa looked out the window again, studying the airport for comparison. It was much smaller than San Francisco's or Kennedy's or even Tampa's. Only a few airplanes on the ground, two hangers, and a building that could be for offices.

The plane stopped, and the stewardess was next to her as soon as the other passengers had left. Lisa unbuckled, picked up her backpack, smiled nervously as she stood up. She wasn't really nervous, but still, meeting an uncle and aunt and three cousins she had never seen and staying with them for more than a month, was a little scary. They sounded nice on the phone, and her Southampton grandmother assured her that her son and his family were good people, although her grandmother really only knew her son. Still, suppose they didn't like her. Suppose the three children were stuck-up or mean or wild and noisy. Well, she decided, she could always go home. Her Dad was not that eager for her to travel so far away, but Barbara thought it would be a great experience and she should definitely go. So she went. And here she was.

Getting off the plane, she saw a man and a woman walking toward her, both wearing huge smiles.

"Lisa, you must be Lisa, my world traveling niece," said the tall man.

"Yes. That's me. Not really a world traveler, a country traveler. Hello, Uncle Derek, Aunt Rochelle."

"We left the three Indians at home."

"Indians? American or from India?" asked Lisa.

"No, no. They're just a bit wild. We call them our Indians."

Lisa smiled but didn't know what to say. She never thought of Indians as wild. Oh, well, there was always something to learn. Her uncle signed the papers, and the three of them took off for the one suitcase she had checked under the plane.

As they walked to the car, she felt good about the weather. It wasn't hot like Florida or misty like Southampton. Here it was in the middle of July and it was cool. Smelled fresh and clean and what her Dad would say, *invigorating.* Maybe too cold for swimming which would sadden her. She so wanted to swim in the Pacific Ocean. Perhaps this was just a colder day than usual.

Their car was a big one. A big SUV. Uncle Derek explained that with three children and two dogs, they needed lots of room. When Lisa heard they had two dogs, she was beside herself. What fun! She would miss her Mitzi, of course. No dog like Mitzi. But two dogs, wow!

As they rode through the streets of Carmel, Lisa saw lots of small shops like her grandmother's and most of them had baskets or window boxes filled with the most beautiful flowers. Lots of geraniums and begonias. And some she didn't recognize. They passed several people her uncle knew and everybody waved. With the town so full of friendly people and pretty shops, Lisa decided she could have a wonderful summer. Of course she still had to meet the three cousins! The Indians.

They pulled into a curving driveway and faced a large, wooden house with lots of corners coming out here and there. Like it was put together at different times. But it was very beautiful with all its porches, sections with window boxes overflowing with flowers, and several entrances with flowers coming from baskets and pots. It was almost like a story-book house. And it had three floors with lots of windows. From one window came a head of a laughing boy with bright red hair. From another window on a different floor and a different corner came a young girl, about Lisa's age, with brown hair braided down her back. And from one of the entrances, came a younger girl with dark red hair curled all around her head like a powder puff. The girls were smiling and waiting to meet Lisa. The boy disappeared. They looked friendly. Her Aunt Rochelle helped her out of the car by pulling back the heavy door and led her up the path to the terrace that surely was the main entrance. Lisa suddenly felt shy. And she had never felt shy before. Why was she nervous? What made her feel intimidated? The house? Just because it was large and impressive? She'd been in beautiful houses before. Francesca's was unusually large. But she was going to live here for a month.

Uncle Derek brought her suitcase up the steps and motioned them all into the house.

"Well, hi there, cousin," yelled the boy from another upstairs window.

"Hello, Lisa, welcome to Carmel," said the girl with the long braid, from her window.

"Hi, Lisa, we're glad you came to see us," said little powder puff girl, standing now at the entrance they were entering.

Well, Lisa thought, they certainly are nice to greet me so enthusiastically, and they look like normal and happy kids.

"My name's Suzanne," said the braided girl.

"My name's Helena," added the curly top.

"And guess who I am?" He waited a minute. "Come on, you know my name. Formally it is Lawrence, but when Mom's not around, you can call me Larry."

"Hello Suzanne, Helena, Lawrence."

113

Aunt Rochelle gave Lawrence a strange look, then told them that lunch was ready and waiting in the kitchen. The five of them went into the house with the terraces and entrances and flowered corners. The front door was shut, and a black poodle greeted them with a wagging tail.

"His name is Buttons, and he only obeys Lawrence. But he's a good dog," said Suzanne as she gave him a big hug.

"My dog's name is Mitzi, and I miss her already," said Lisa.

"Girl's, let's go," Aunt Rochelle called.

Chapter Two

Suzanne led Lisa up to the second floor to the guest room. It was a large room with two beds, a large desk, a small desk, a make-up table with a huge mirror and a low chair, an open closet with lots of empty space and lots of hangers. Lisa hoped she said the right things as she admired all the furniture and curtains and bedspreads. She didn't feel so shy with just Suzanne there. When she saw that she would have her own bathroom, she ooed and aahed so loudly that Suzanne laughed.

"After lunch I'll show you the rest of the house. Let's just put your suitcase here till later. Want to wash up?"

"Yes, please. I've been traveling for hours. Since 7 this morning." She walked slowly into a blue and white bathroom. "Everything is so beautiful. Are these towels all for me?" asked Lisa as she washed her hands and face.

"Yep. All yours. My room is right next door so when the door is open, just come in, whenever. Helena is on the other side of me, and my mother and dad have the large room at the end of the hall. Lawrence, or Larry as we call him when Mom isn't around, sleeps upstairs. He has the biggest room of all. But it's not fixed up. Just a big room with lots of tables for his animals."

"Animals? What kind of animals?"

"You name it, he has it," giggled Suzanne. "Gerbils, hamsters, snakes, frogs, lizards, and a large turtle."

"Is he going to be a doctor or a vet I mean?"

"I don't think so. He just likes small animals. Maybe he'll own a zoo some day. Come on, let's go down."

Aunt Rochelle was waiting for them, and so were the others, as one of the rules of the house was that nobody ate until everyone was there. Unlike the rest of the world.

"Everything all right in your room?" asked her aunt.

"It's beautiful!" exclaimed Lisa. "And my own bathroom is simply awesome. Wait till I tell Isobel."

"That's right! Isobel is your grandmother, too," yelled Lawrence.

"You see how bright our brother is? He doesn't miss a trick," said Suzanne.

"What's Isobel like?" asked Helena.

"Nice, real nice. We had a great month together."

"How is my mother doing, Lisa? She's well?" asked Uncle Derek.

"Oh, yes. She has a wonderful shop—all kinds of clothes, mostly for sports."

"And the shop is doing well?"

"Yes. She's a good business woman." Lisa chuckled. "She's nice to all her customers, even those that are stuck up."

"Oh, we know some stuck-up people, don't we Suzanne?"

"That's enough, girls," warned Aunt Rochelle.

Derek got up to get some more coffee. "Anybody need anything while I'm up? More coke, Lisa?"

"No, thank you."

"I'll have some more," Helena piped up.

"No, dear, you've had enough," said Aunt Rochelle.

"Well, what are the plans for this afternoon?" asked Uncle Derek.

"Don't you have to go back to the office, Derek?" asked his wife.

"I have a meeting at 3, but we can do a little sightseeing before that."

"Let's show her the Presidio in Monterey," suggested Suzanne.

"How about the dolphins?" asked Lawrence.

"The dolphins! Yes! You brought some shorts, didn't you, Lisa?" asked Helena.

"Yes. And I'd love to see the dolphins," agreed Lisa.

Suzanne grinned. "I'm always out numbered. Lawrence suggests something and dear Helena goes right along with him. What's he got on you, Helena?"

"Nothing. I just like dolphins."

"Never did before."

"Children, that's enough. Derek, do we have time to drive to the beach and still get you to the office on time?"

"Absolutely. The beach is a great way to start a tour of Carmel. We can also show her the tide pools."

"Yuk!" moaned Helena.

"Hey, Curlytop, some day you'll appreciate the creatures that live and die in those tide pools," said Lawrence.

"What's a tide pool?" asked Lisa, as she finished her sandwich.

"You find them among the rocks," her uncle explained. "When the tide comes in, it brings with it lots of tiny sea life—baby clams, miniature lobsters, even tiny sea horses—and when the tide goes out, it leaves a small pool behind, with some of these creatures. Quite fascinating."

"Yuk!"

"Helena, that'll be enough. I agree. I think Lisa would enjoy seeing the ocean as well as the dolphins and the tide pools. Why don't you change into your shorts and a long-sleeved shirt and sneakers. Did you bring sneakers? You'll need them to walk among the rocks." said Aunt Rochelle.

"Let's go, Lisa. We can unpack your stuff when we get back," Suzanne suggested.

They all cleared the table and stacked the dishes for Miranda, the cook. Suzanne and Lisa took off for upstairs. Uncle Derek and Aunt Rochelle went out to the car with Helena and Buttons. Lawrence telephoned a few friends to deliver a short message: "She's here. Not bad. Seems timid but it might be an act." He finally went outside and played with his dog till the girls came down. Then off they took for the beach, a mile or so from the house. Again they passed so many quaint-looking houses and shops, all sprinkled with flowers. Lisa said she'd never seen so many pretty houses and shops.

Lawrence laughed as he told Lisa that one of San Francisco's famous newspaper writers once wrote that Carmel was a town "built by the seven dwarfs." Lisa didn't get the connection and started to ask about it, but Aunt Rochelle was quick to change the subject.

"I'll tell you later," whispered Lawrence.

"Did you swim in the Atlantic Ocean? You won't be able to swim here. Much too cold," explained her aunt. "Helena likes it. But anybody over ten ignores it."

"There it is!" said Uncle Derek as he drove up to the parking spaces just a ways from the ocean.

"It's so blue," Lisa said. "And sparkly. Wish we were wearing our bathing suits."

"Oh, no, you don't," said Suzanne. "That water is really ice cold."

"You need a wet suit to go into this ocean," said Lawrence. "Got a wet suit?"

Lisa laughed. "I don't even know what it is."

Uncle Derek explained. "It's a rubber suit that is only a 16th of an inch or so from your skin. That space allows the water that comes in to become the temperature of your body. So it's like swimming in 98 degrees water. Clever idea."

As they walked to the beach, Lisa saw her first tide pool. "Is this a tide pool?"

"Yup. See all the clams and sea horses?" asked Lawrence.

They all gathered around with Lawrence pointing out various sea creatures. Derek and Rochelle then walked to the water's edge. Lisa caught up with them and asked if they had wet suits.

"No," said Derek. "I did years ago, but I'm too busy these days. Suzanne wants to take scuba lessons when she's 11, which is in two weeks. Lawrence rents a suit when he goes diving with his friends. We should get him his own suit, Rochelle."

"Not until he stops growing. Too expensive to buy a new one every year."

"I might be able to wear his old one, Mom," Suzanne suggested as she caught up with them.

"We'll see."

Lisa laughed to herself. No matter where you are, parents always say "We'll see" when they're not sure what else to say.

"Lisa, would you like to take lessons? You're 11, right? That's the age you can take lessons. It's a little dangerous. You have to be very careful to follow all the rules. You like the water? Enough to want to go down under and breathe through a tube in your mouth?" asked Suzanne.

"I love the water. And I'm a good swimmer. And I'm not afraid. Sure, I'd love to take lessons."

"We'll have to ask your father, Lisa. Scuba diving can be dangerous, but as long as you know that and respect the rules and your fellow divers, you can have a lot of fun. Searching the ocean floor can be exciting," Uncle Derek said.

"And beautiful. And the fish you meet! Your Uncle Walter and Aunt Mary Joan go to the Caribbean for their vacations and scuba dive. Don't have to wear wet suits down there. He told me the fish there come in all colors and shapes. Schools of them pass in front you:

yellow with blue stripes; pink with polka dots; blue with orange fins. I sure would like to see that. Dad, you said we would visit them some day. They live in Charleston, Lisa. Ever been there?"

"Next year."

"How do you know that now?"

"Every summer I visit another relative. At least I did these past three years. First I went to Florida to visit my father's parents. That's what started my travels. Dad wasn't married yet to Barbara, and we didn't know what to do with me for the summer months."

"How about camp?" asked Helena.

"Sticky question. I'm not crazy about arts and crafts, and that's what they teach most of the day. So Dad shipped me off to his parents."

"Don't like arts and crafts?" Helena burst out. "I love them."

"That's cause Mom teaches it," Suzanne added.

"You teach that stuff? With all the cutting and white paste and everything?"

"Yes, I do," answered her aunt. "I'm a professional artist most of the year. But in the summer there are so many children with nothing to do, I decided to give them some of my talent."

"Can you give talent?" asked Lisa.

"I share it with them. Is that better?"

"I'm sorry. I didn't mean that, the way it sounded. Isobel told me you were an artist. I should have remembered. She said you had a lot of exhibitions here in Carmel."

"I have had my share. Also in San Francisco."

"She's quite an artist," commented Derek. "She sells quite a bit."

"I'll show you some when we get back home," said Helena.

"If you like scenes of ocean in all times of the day, you'll love her work," said Suzanne.

"It's not easy to paint the ocean with all its colors and the way it moves. Mom is an expert at it."

"You see how I train my children. They are my forever fans. And collectors. There are several in your room, but even more in the children's rooms."

"Rochelle, I've got to get back now. You can drop me off and come back here if you wish."

"No, I think we've had enough for the day. Suzanne can help Lisa get settled in. And I have a few chores."

"Okay, everyone, back to the car. Lawrence, did you clean out your tanks yet? Maybe Lisa would like to see you do that."

"Yes, I would. Larry, …Lawrence. I would also like to meet your other dog. What's his name?"

"Her name is Cinderella," called Helena.

"That's a great name. Do you have a nickname or do you go through the whole name every time you call her?"

"In this household? It's Cinderella all the time," giggled Suzanne.

"You chose the name, Suzanne," corrected her mother.

"I know, Mom. I'm only kidding."

As they piled into the huge car, Lawrence whispered to Lisa, "Remind me to tell you about the seven dwarfs later."

Chapter Three

"That was Michael," whispered Suzanne.

"Where? Downstairs?" Lisa said, also whispering but she didn't know why.

"No. On the phone. They want to meet you. We can take a walk after dinner and meet them in the library."

"Why are we whispering?" asked Lisa.

"My mother doesn't care for Michael. Simple as that. Says he's too brazen whatever that means," said Suzanne as she plopped on Lisa's bed.

"Will she mind if we meet them later?"

"She won't know. We'll just take a walk. She allows that, of course. Bring a jacket. It gets cool in the evening. And the library is five streets away."

"Okay. What time is dinner?" asked Lisa.

"At six. Want to see my room?"

"How about coming up to see my room?" interrupted Lawrence as he appeared in the doorway.

"Sure. Either one."

"I'm about to feed my creatures. You'll enjoy that. Mealtime is exciting."

"Disgusting. Lisa, do you really want to see live animals eat other live animals?" asked Suzanne.

"I'd rather not.... Do you mind, Larry?"

"Suzanne, there you go again. Ruining my relationships! Even with my cousin. You're such a twerp. Go play with the boys and let Lisa do what she wants."

"Go, go, go creature lover. We're having girl talk," said Suzanne, pushing her brother out of the room and shutting the door. "Now where were we? Michael, right. He's so cute. And so is Timmy. You like boys, don't you?"

"Sure. Why not?"

"I mean more than girls. You like to be with them, right? They're so cute and so funny."

"I don't know too many boys. Most of my friends are girls. There are some nice boys in my class, but they seem very shy. So I hardly get to know them."

"Well, Michael and Timmy are not shy! Michael is fourteen. Timmy's only thirteen but he knows what Michael knows."

"About what?" asked Lisa.

"About us, girls. What we like and what we want to do. Lisa, have you ever kissed a boy?"

"Good heavens, no. I told you the boys in my class are shy. And they're only eleven like me. They don't even know we, I mean I, exist. They only pay attention to baseball and soccer. That's all they know."

"They'll find out soon. Michael started after me when he was twelve and I was only ten. He would walk me home and make me laugh all the way. But the next year he started writing to me, on my computer so my mother wouldn't know. He told me how pretty I was. How smart I was. How much he liked me."

"Did he ever kiss you?" asked Lisa shyly.

"Yes. Lots of times now. But we didn't kiss till last year. He's a good kisser. Of course, I haven't kissed anyone else so I really can't compare. But he's nice. Soft. Maybe all the boys are soft like that, but in some of the movies I see, some of them can be rough. I wouldn't like that. Michael makes my heart pound something awful. You can almost hear it. And see my blouse move. I'm embarrassed, but Michael laughs."

"Did you ever tell your mother?" asked Lisa.

"Are you kidding? No way. She's pretty hippy in lots of ways but not as far as boys go. She still thinks I'm Helena's age. Would you tell your mother?"

"I don't have a mother."

"Oh, I'm sorry, Lisa. I didn't mean that. Of course I know your mother died a few years ago. I forgot. It must be rough not having a mother."

"It was in the beginning. But I have Barbara now. She married my Dad last year. So she's sort of my mother. She tries. She's good to me, but I don't think I would talk to her about boys. Besides…. I don't know what I would tell her except who's the best soccer player or who is the smartest in the class. Or what I would ask her."

"You're sort of shy, Lisa. Or terribly polite. But I think shy. My mother teaches us to stand up for our rights, even Helena. So there's no room for being shy. Especially with boys, but my mother doesn't know about that. And I don't want to ever discuss boys with her."

"Why not?"

"She's too old. She wouldn't understand what girls our age think about."

"But she was once eleven."

"A million years ago!"

"She's not that old," screamed Lisa, laughing as she rolled off the bed.

"Almost."

"You're so funny, Suzanne. I have a friend, Jackie, who's funny like you. She makes me laugh right in the middle of class sometimes."

"Are you good in school? Smart? Like getting good grades?"

"Sometimes. I get good marks in English and Social Studies. Not so good in Science or Math."

"Me, too!" shouted Suzanne.

"We have a lot in common. Well, we are cousins."

"Boys are good in science and math. But they're awful in English. Michael almost flunked English this semester. He's in Middle School of course. It's harder up there. But he's a whiz in math."

"You're in sixth grade now, right?"

"Yes, and I can't wait till I get out. Boring. I go to Middle in September."

"Me, too. And we have a swimming pool in our Middle School. Do you?"

"No, but I don't care. Swimming is not my favorite sport."

"I love swimming more than anything. What sport do you like?" asked Lisa.

"Boys!"

"Oh, stop it. I mean what sport do you like playing?"

"Boys!"

"Suzanne, I can't tell when you're being funny or serious."

"We have four weeks together for you to learn. Let's go down and set the table for dinner. And have some iced tea on the porch."

123

Chapter Four

After a wonderful dinner, the family broke up into five sections: Uncle Derek went to a meeting at the Community Theatre, where tryouts for the next play were being held; Aunt Rochelle left to attend a meeting at the high school about their summer workshops; Lawrence biked over to a friend who shared his love for zoology; Helena was picked up by a friend's mother for a girl scout meeting; and Suzanne took Lisa by the elbow and pushed her out the door for their walk to the library. It was still light outside but cool enough to wear jackets and walk briskly.

In the early dusk, Carmel seemed like a storybook. Like Lawrence said. A light fog hugged "the little houses built by the dwarfs" and the sky was full of darkening clouds that outlined all kinds of shapes. Lisa was impressed with the beauty and the stillness. For a town this size, she thought, it's awfully quiet. No busses, no trucks, just a few cars, no loud radios, no kids screaming, no parents yelling. Where were they all?

"You're so quiet, Lisa," murmured Suzanne.

"Not me. The town is quiet. Where is everyone?"

"They're around. Lots of activities going on. One street over is the Community House, where all the lights are. It's opened every evening and has six large rooms and four smaller ones for all kinds of activities. Helene is there now for her girl scout meeting. I used to go but they got silly. I tried to join the boy scouts!" she laughed as she teased Lisa.

"You didn't!"

"Yes. I knew it was a joke and that they'd never let me in, but I wanted to see what they would say. They laughed."

"Is Michael in the boy scouts?" Lisa carefully asked.

"No. He was in the cub scouts but quit when he found it too baby-ish. No, he's into research and the library. That's where we meet most of the time."

"What does he research?"

"Don't know. He doesn't talk about it."

"Maybe nothing. Just to get to the library and meet you."

Suzanne laughed. "I hope so. The librarians are getting suspicious, but they're so nice that nobody has asked us to stop going there."

As they approached the library, Suzanne spoke more quietly and Lisa took the hint.

"I always start off in the mystery section. Where would you like to look?"

"I don't know. I'll just walk around and see what they have. I used to read a lot of horse stories. Think I've read them all. I'll see." said Lisa.

They entered the main room of the library and Lisa gave a loud "Wow". Everyone looked at her. What took her by surprise was the huge fireplace, crackling its wood with enthusiasm. It gave the whole room a warm and cozy feeling, and Lisa was drawn to it, right up to its screen.

"Why does this amaze you? Doesn't your library have a fire-place?" asked Suzanne.

"No. It doesn't. What a wonderful idea. Especially on a cool night like this."

"It never really gets warm enough in Carmel not to have a blazing fire in here. And in a lot of homes. We have three fireplaces, but when everyone goes in different directions, you know, for different activities, we don't light them. We light them more in the rainy season."

"When is that?"

"January, February. We'll have to light a few of them while you're here though. Maybe some Saturday or Sunday when families become the activities. We can roast marshmallows or pop corn. You have done that, haven't you?"

"Only on a camping trip. Over an outside fireplace. One we've made ourselves. I loved that. I sure would like to see one of your fire-places and pop some corn."

"I'll suggest it. Mom loves to do that, too." Seeing Lisa's quizzical look, she added, "I know Mom doesn't look or act the part of a hippy but under that strict face, she is a bit wild. Except when it comes to my going out on dates."

125

"You're only ten, well, eleven really in two weeks. That's kind of young to be dating, isn't it? At home, we go out in a gang of kids. Like six or seven of us, boys and girls, will attend a baseball game or go to the 4H Club exhibition."

"What's 4H Club mean?" asked Suzanne.

Just as Lisa was about to explain, Suzanne looked to the front door and a big smile covered her face. Michael and Timothy walked in. And that's all she saw, all she heard. Lisa quit and got ready to meet the boys. Suzanne stayed put and with her smile, invited the boys to come to the roaring fireplace.

"Michael, Timmy, I'd like you to meet my cousin, Lisa, from the mid-west somewhere," said Suzanne with perfect grace.

"Hi, Lisa," they both said together.

"Hi," Lisa shyly murmured.

"Been here long?" asked Michael.

"In Carmel or in the library?" inquired Lisa.

Grinning, he joked, "Here, in the library."

"No, we just got here."

"Let's sit down," suggested Michael as he motioned them over.

The four of them sat at a nearby table and quietly giggled over nothing. Lisa because of shyness; Suzanne because of feeling guilty; Michael because he liked being the center of attention; and Timmy because he didn't know what else to do. With Michael around, there was not much one could say. So he listened.

"Gonna look for a book?" asked Michael.

"I might," said Suzanne, "in a few minutes."

"I have to get a book on airplanes. Not on how to fly them. How to build them. The engines. A little research for science class," Michael proudly spoke.

"See, Lisa, a wiz in math and science. I have to get a book on plants. See the difference? Girls get the easy assignments."

"Suzanne, you're only in sixth grade. Relax. Though I don't think I did one on plants. Probably soil and trees. The big ones up the coast," quipped Michael.

"The sequoia trees?" asked Lisa.

"Yeah! What are you going to look for?" Looking around, he quietly added, "We have to mosey around here for about half an hour."

"I think I'll just walk up and down the aisles. I usually find something interesting."

"Don't get lost. And don't forget the upstairs. Up that circular staircase. Lots of books on poetry. Do you like poetry?" asked Suzanne.

"Not particularly."

"But you love English!"

"English also means stories and biographies. Found a wonderful book about Louis Pasteur one day, just by walking up and down the aisles. Probably would have never asked for such a book. It was great."

"Timmy, you got a science report to do?" asked Suzanne.

"Yes, electricity. Sort of. Dynamos," said Timmy quietly.

"A man of few words," kidded Michael.

Lisa got up and hesitantly pushed back her chair. "I'll be back soon," as she backed away and down the aisle nearest her.

"Nice kid," said Michael. "Doesn't look like a trouble maker. Too shy for that."

"I knew she was shy, but I didn't think she was timid."

"Afraid of boys, maybe?"

"No, I don't think so. She's okay." Turning to Michael only, she whispered, "How are you?"

"Good, good. And you?" He laughed on that last remark as he tipped his chair on its two back legs.

"Fine. I missed you." She glanced over at Timmy who then took the hint and disappeared down one of the aisles.

"Wanna go on a family picnic next Saturday?" asked Michael, still balancing himself on those wobbly chair legs.

"I don't think I can. With my cousin here, we might take a drive down to Big Sur. Show her the scenic highway." Suzanne said these last two words with great affectation. Then she giggled. "But we're going to have a picnic the following Saturday. And I'm sure you and Timmy are invited. Out at Point Lobos."

"Can't you get out of "Big Sur" and come over?"

"I doubt it."

"You haven't played sick for a while. Lisa will have the rest of your family to amuse her. Come on. It's just family and Timmy here. We're celebrating Mom's birthday."

"Let me think about it. Talking about birthdays, I'm going to be 11 in two weeks – oh, maybe that's why the picnic—anyway, I can start my scuba lessons. Have you been diving lately?"

"Last Monday. Couple of guys from class went and we went way down. Had to use our flashlights. Some nice tunnels and caves down there. You'll be able to go down there soon. You'll catch on real quick. Timmy got caught in some kelp, and we had to cut him out. He got scared so don't say anything. Kept signaling he was out of air but of course he wasn't."

"How do you signal for air?"

"Run your flat hand sideways across your throat. Like a death sign," Michael said with a scary look in his eyes. Then he laughed. "Poor Timmy thought he had had it."

"Here comes Lisa already," said Suzanne softly.

"See you found a book, Lisa," Michael said as he put his chair on all four legs.

"Yes, I picked it because it's skinny and small. "On the Eve" by Turgenev. Ever hear of it?"

"No." they both said together.

"Never heard of ...how do you say his name, "Tur...?" asked Michael.

"Turgenev. Russian author it says here. I'll read a few pages here before I check it out."

Lisa went over to the fireplace and sat in a large leather chair. She felt so comfortable. So safe. Michael seemed nice and so did Timmy. They're weren't rough like she thought they might be. Suzanne was polite, not funny like she was earlier. Here less than a day and she already felt at home. She liked Suzanne and the family. And it was too early to be homesick. This was going to be a good month, she thought.

She opened her book and even with some unknown vocabulary, got caught up in the story right away. It was about her. The girl was Lisa, struggling with all kinds of confusing thoughts. Not knowing which were right, which were wrong. The boy was wonderful. Strong, decent, honest, kind. Not like she thought Michael might be. Of course she didn't really know him. Suzanne would tell her more tonight about him. In the meantime, she had her new friend in the story.

A light tap on her shoulder scared her for a moment. It was Suzanne signaling that they were ready to go. "Want to check the book out?" she asked Lisa.

"Please, yes. I love it."

"Okay, give it to me. The boys already left. They'll meet us on the corner. Come on."

The book was checked out and the girls made for the door.

"I hate leaving the fire. Can we come back here tomorrow or whenever."

"Sure. Come on."

As they left the library, Suzanne was busy pinching her cheeks.

"What are you doing to your cheeks?" asked Lisa.

"Making them pink. Didn't you ever do that? There they are by the phone booth. Oh, they rode their bikes here. That's unusual. But don't worry. We can sit on the handle bars."

"What took you so long? Thought you were studying for a test. Come on," ordered Michael in a humorous way. Lisa didn't like it anyway, serious or funny. He seemed like the bossy kind. She knew a fellow back home like that. Tony. He was popular with the boys and some of the girls. But not with Lisa. Tony asked her to a basketball game one day, but she turned him down, politely she hoped. She just didn't like his wisecracks, his comments about girls, or the way he looked at her. He didn't like her refusing him and he gave her the silent treatment for weeks. It didn't bother Lisa.

Michael grabbed Suzanne onto his handlebars in such a way as to make her giggle and even laugh a little nervously. Then they took off, leaving Timmy to offer Lisa a seat on his handlebars. She accepted and was glad he was not like Michael.

Timmy headed his bike toward the ocean front. When Lisa realized this, she asked him where they were going. He muttered something about walking the beach with Michael and Suzanne. Lisa's watch told her it was after 9 and she asked to be taken home. She had had a long day and hadn't even fully unpacked yet. Timmy hesitated. "Michael will be expecting us down there."

"You can go down after you leave me off at Suzanne's house."

"Suzanne will worry about you, won't she?"

"Tell her I was too tired to stay out any longer. Tell her I'll see her tomorrow morning."

Timmy turned his bike around. "Okay, but Michael won't like this."

"Thanks, Timmy, I appreciate this."

"How do you like Carmel so far?" asked Timmy.

"From the little I've seen, it's great. Where do you live?"

"A couple of streets down from the Community Center. On the same street with Michael."

"Born here?"

"Yep. So was Michael. We grew up together. Always in the same class. And on the same soccer and basketball teams."

"Nice."

"Say, be sure you get to ride down Route #1 to Big Sur. In a car though, not on a bike. It's the best ride in the world. The Scenic Highway they call it. My Dad lives down there, in Big Sur."

"Oh, you don't live with your mother and dad?"

"No, they divorced couple of years ago. He moved down to a cabin in the woods. My mother remarried. A guy named Warren. Nice guy but he's not my dad."

"My dad got remarried last year. My mother died almost three years ago. And he was lonely with just me. You got any brothers and sisters?"

"No, the only kid. What about you?"

"I'm the only one. Like you. We have a lot in common. Well, there's the house. Looks like a few of them are in already. Thanks again, Timmy, for taking me home. I'll see you again, I hope."

"Goodbye, Lisa. See you." He waited until she got into the house, then biked off.

Chapter Five

Lisa looked out of her bedroom window which was above the terrace in the back. It was a beautiful morning and everybody was sitting in various chairs. Derek (she was asked to do away with the words 'uncle' and 'aunt') was pouring more coffee for himself; Rochelle was on the telephone; Lawrence had a baby raccoon on a leash and in his lap; Suzanne was staring out into space from the lounge chair; and Helena was reading. It was only 8:30 and everybody looked wide awake. Even Suzanne, although Lisa did not know what time she came in last night. Lisa had passed Rochelle quickly and said "good night" before Rochelle could get off the phone and question her about Suzanne.

And now Rochelle was on the phone again, and Suzanne didn't look very worried. Lisa got dressed in shorts and a blouse and wore her sneakers again. When she entered the terrace, everyone but Suzanne turned and said hello. Oh, she thought, Suzanne is upset with me for leaving her without telling her she was going home. She hoped that Timmy went back and explained that he took her home. Lisa sat in a nearby chair.

"Some juice before breakfast is served?" asked Derek.

"Yes, thank you," as she got up to go to the table.

"I would have brought you some. You are our guest," Derek said.

"For this day only," said Lawrence with a laugh. "From tomorrow on, you just follow the crowd. And get your own juice."

"Lawrence!" said Rochelle as she put down the phone. "Lisa, when Miranda brings the breakfast, you have a choice of scrambled eggs, bacon, sausage, and toast. Is that all right? And of course you can have a glass of milk. What time did you get in last evening, Lisa? I was on the phone when you whizzed by and said good night. But I didn't notice the time."

"Oh, somewhere around 9 or a little after. I'm not sure."

"Did Timmy bring you home?" asked Rochelle.

"Yes, he did. He's a very nice boy. He was telling me about Big Sur where his father lives. Said the road to get down there is very beautiful."

"We're going down there on Saturday. It's a drive that can't be equaled. Even more beautiful than the Amalfi Drive in Italy. We'll have lunch at Big Sur Lookout, which is built out on the precipice," said Derek.

"Again? Can't we go to the Jungle or the Hamburger Pit?" asked Lawrence.

"Not this time, Lawrence. Not on Lisa's first visit there," put in Rochelle. "The Lookout has good food beside a magnificent view."

"Panorama!" chirped Helena, looking up from her book.

"Yes, my dear. Panorama. Helena has developed a wonderful habit. Whenever she learns a new word, she uses it over and over for days on end. It's a good way, Helena, to make it a part of your vocabulary."

"Our breakfast is here," announced Derek. As Miranda spread out the food, Derek motioned to all to join him at the table. Suzanne needed a little push from her mother but she did get to the table, sitting between Derek and Lawrence. She hardly looked at Lisa and when she did, she was stone-faced. This made Lisa nervous and she covered it by remarking how beautiful the roses were in the garden below the patio.

"I've never seen such large roses."

"Everything in Carmel is larger than life," said Helena.

"Who told you that, squirt?" asked Lawrence.

"Her name is Helena," Rochelle corrected him.

"Yes, Lisa, our flowers out here do tend to be larger than usual. It's the heavy moisture and lots of sun. Now help yourself," said Derek as he passed the platter of eggs.

"How did you like our library?" asked Rochelle.

"Very much. It's beautiful with that large fireplace. Wish we had one at home. I'd be in the library all the time."

"Daddy, did you get the part you wanted?" asked Helena.

"Thank you, Helena. Yes, I did. My family and that includes you, Lisa, can see your breadwinner playing the father in Eugene O'Neil's

"Ah! Wilderness", a very interesting play and the only comedy he ever wrote."

"Derek, I'm glad. Did you have any competition? I'm sure Mr. Travers wanted that part. Did he get anything?" asked Rochelle.

"Yes, he plays Sid. And he'll be good. As he pursues my sister and tries to hide his drinking habits, he'll have the audience laughing out loud."

"Who got the young boy's role?" asked Helena.

"Some kid from Pacific Grove. The director was hoping your Michael, Suzanne, would try out."

"Derek, Michael is not hers. And I'm not sure he has the discipline to carry out a large part. He's too flip. Timmy would have done a nice job," commented Rochelle.

"Isn't he a bit shy, Rochelle?" asked Derek.

"Is he, Suzanne?"

"I don't know. Lisa would know that. Is he shy, Lisa?"

"I don't know about being shy. He's a nice boy, polite."

Rochelle noticed the strain between the two girls. She was smart enough to change the subject. "Derek, it's getting late. Shouldn't you be going?"

"In a minute. Oh, well, you're right. I'll tell you about the rest of the audition at dinner. I'm having lunch with Al today. I'll be in rehearsal every night but Saturday and Sunday for the next three weeks. Sorry I won't have much time with you, Lisa. But I bet you'll enjoy coming to a rehearsal now and then. I do want to hear more about Isobel. Excuse me now, everyone," he said as he rose from the table.

"We'll miss you, Daddy," teased Helena.

"Excuse me, please," said Suzanne. And she left the terrace quickly.

"Suzanne, wait for me. I'm finished, too. Okay, Rochelle?" asked Lisa.

"It's okay, Lisa. I'll see you later," Suzanne answered for her mother.

Lisa was half up but sat down again, not knowing what to do. Rochelle gave her a soft smile. "She'll be all right. She's a little miffed because I questioned why she came in after 10 last evening. I like my children to be popular and to be different, but I do not like disobedience. She was asked not to see Michael alone and certainly not after 9. She first said you were still out and that she was looking for you. But she retracted that this morning. Let it go. She'll be okay. Did you leave her without telling her?"

133

"Not really, Rochelle. I asked Timmy to tell her. I shouldn't have done that. I'm sorry. I'll go talk to her and explain how tired I was and just had to get to bed. It was a great but busy day yesterday. I'm sorry if I caused any trouble."

"No. Let it go. It's not easy being 11, almost 11. It used to be that 13 was the difficult age. Now it's down to 11. We had a good talk this morning. She'll be okay. Stay with us for a while and let her get herself together. Do you play tennis, Lisa? All the children and of course myself, play almost every day." Seeing Lisa shake her head no, she asked, "Would you like to come to the courts with us and give it a try?"

"Come on, Lisa, I'll let you win a game or two," teased Lawrence.

"Yeah, Lisa, come with us. I'm pretty good but you probably will beat me. Just because you're older and bigger," said Helena with a laugh.

"Yes, Lisa, do come with us. Suzanne is a good player and she'll teach you a lot. She's been looking forward to this," added Rochelle.

"Okay, I'll try. The only game I play like that is badminton."

"You're in for a shock then. A shuttlecock is a lot different from a ball," said Lawrence.

"See you all in about an hour, okay?" asked Rochelle.

"Okay," said Lawrence, Helena, and Lisa.

Chapter Six

That afternoon and Thursday proved Rochelle right—Suzanne was back to her good humor, enthusiastic, energetic. She was a terror on the tennis court. But gentle with Lisa.

Saturday morning was busy with preparations for their excursion to Big Sur. They didn't bring lunch but did carry out a large thermos of water out to the car. Planning to walk some of the trails after their lunch at the Big Sur Lookout (it seems parents always win), they would want a drink as they headed for the trail that ran down to the beach. They all wore long pants and long sleeve shirts to protect them from the undergrowth and any flying insects that might be in season.

Suzanne was slowing down and finally sat, complaining of a stomach ache. They all ignored her as they got ready to go and were surprised to see her still sitting with a strange look on her face. She quietly murmured, "I'm not feeling very well. I feel like going back to bed."

"And miss your favorite trip?" asked Derek.

Rochelle went over to her and felt her head. "She is a little warm. Suzanne, won't you enjoy the ride down? You'll feel better after a good lunch."

"She's mad because we're not going to eat at the hamburger place!" said Helena.

"Nonsense. Suzanne, can't you try to snap out of it?" Rochelle asked.

"I really want to go back to bed. Do you mind, Mom? I've done this trip so often. It's not like I'm going to miss something," whimpered Suzanne.

"Do you want us to stay home with you?" asked Rochelle.

"No, no, you have to show Lisa Big Sur. And we have our birthday picnic next Saturday and Disneyland the following. And she'll be going home after that," she said as she smiled weakly at Lisa.

Rochelle continued being the mother. "Are you sure you don't mind that we go ahead? This is the only opportunity. I won't drive that road without your father. After a good sleep, you can call Josie or Wilma and ask them over for lunch. Plenty of food in the fridge. Are you sure?"

"Yes, Mom. I really want to go back to bed. I'll be okay. And I will call Wilma later."

"All right, darling. I'll call you from the restaurant. Before we take our walks."

"Okay. Maybe I'll walk over to Wilma's later. I'll see how I feel."

"Let's go. I don't want to race down Route 1 to make our reservation. You take care, Suzanne. We'll call you later. Ready, everyone?" said Derek, half-way out the door.

"Goodbye, Suzanne, I'll bring you back a hamburger," giggled Helena.

"Take it easy, little sister. Feed my creatures if we're not back by 5," Lawrence said.

"Bye, Suzanne, sorry you're not feeling well," said Lisa sympathetically.

Rochelle said one more goodbye and followed the others down the path and into the car.

"We're off!" screamed Helena.

"She's never done that before. She's never sick or even sickish," Rochelle softly said as they pulled out into the street.

"Now a little history for Lisa. The highway we're going to drive on is Route 1 and also known as the Scenic Drive. Because that's what you get from here to Big Sur: scenery galore. It is built right at the edge of the mountain and curves in and out of every ridge. Wait till you see it. The driver cannot take in the scenery. Too dangerous. Got to keep your eyes on the road at all times and drive slowly. Here we go. It starts right here," explained Derek.

"Tell her about the lady who fell down," suggested Helena.

"Is that necessary?" asked Rochelle.

"Yes." shouted Lawrence.

Derek laughed. "It happened years before we moved here, but it seems that a man and woman were taking in the sights when they wanted to take a picture. Evidently the man got too close to the edge of the road so that when the woman opened the door and stepped out, she really stepped out. Over the cliff she went, right down to the bottom."

"Was she hurt?" asked Lisa.

"Hurt? She was smashed. How far is it to the ocean, Dad?" asked Lawrence.

"At least 100 feet."

"It's more than that!"

"Oh, that's awful! Did that really happen?" asked Lisa.

"Now that's enough. Let's enjoy the scenery. From up here." suggested Rochelle.

The further they drove, the more beautiful it became. The ocean was a deep blue and it went on for miles, to the south, the north, and out as far as you could see. The white caps were barely visible and the porpoises not at all. The curves of the road and the brown hills above the road on the left side added to the beauty.

"Oh, my, this is awesome. Absolutely awesome," Lisa said as she sucked in her breath.

"See what I miss by driving? But when we're alone, Rochelle and me, she takes the wheel and lets me enjoy what you're enjoying. Brave Rochelle," bragged Derek.

"I don't like doing it. But the man has to know what we're seeing."

"Tell Lisa about the lady who came out here to teach and what the doctor told her," said Lawrence.

"I'll tell it," chirped Helena. "This lady came here from New York. The first day here she took this drive and was so excited about the scenery on Route 1 and about how beautiful Carmel was that when she went to the doctor for her physical, she told him all about it and how she felt "such peace", and he quietly explained to her that anyone who came out here and didn't bring peace with him, he wouldn't keep that newly-found peace very long."

"Helena, that story had no commas, no dashes, no periods," said Derek.

"But the point was made. Many people come here for that indescribable aura of peace and security. Then they find that the peace the scenery gave them begins to fade with life's normal activities. The doctor was a wise man," Rochelle softly said.

"I don't get it," queried Lisa.

"You will. It took Helena a few weeks to understand it, after our telling her the story several times."

"I'll think about it. Helena, you can help me, okay?"

"Sure."

"Now we are crossing the famous Bixby Bridge. Look down and get a thrill. This was quite a feat of engineering. Built in 1932," explained Derek.

"It's even more beautiful than the Golden Gate Bridge in San Francisco," said Helena.

"Another famous bridge?" asked Lisa, laughing with Helena.

"You'll like that one and you'll like San Francisco," piped up Lawrence. "When do we go there?"

"In a couple of weeks. If we don't have another free Saturday, your Mom can take you on a weekday," said Derek.

"That's better. Less tourists. We can eat in Chinatown and visit Ghiradella Square where they have a great chocolate store," Lawrence added.

"And go to Fisherman's Wharf where they have great fish restaurants," said Helena.

"Do the seagulls come down and swipe the shrimp you were going to eat? That's what happened in Montauk Point," said Lisa.

"Where's Montauk Point?" asked Helena.

"Girls, leave all that till later and enjoy part of the scenery in silence," Rochelle suggested.

And so they did. For the next hour there was little talking and lot of oohs and aahs. Especially from Lisa who was thoroughly enjoying herself. Here only four days, she thought, and she didn't want to go home. What a wonderful summer she was having!

Chapter Seven

Big Sur itself was dotted with cabins and handsome homes that were nestled in lots of foliage and narrow curving roads. They arrived at the restaurant with a little time to spare so they took advantage of the binocular machines to look over the land and the sea that spread out beneath them.

"Some of these houses seem to be all alone, miles from each other," commented Lisa.

"Artists fill these homes," said Rochelle. "And they like to be off by themselves."

"Tell her about what happened to Roger," said Lawrence.

"Lawrence, you keep more stories alive in your memory, ready to pop out at anytime. Why don't you tell the story?" responded his mother.

"Okay. It was during the days of the hippies. Not that there aren't any hippies around now. My Mom is one. Right, Mom? This happened in the late sixties according to Roger. He went out for the afternoon and since nobody in those days ever locked their doors, he came home and found a hippy taking a bath in his bathroom. Not even the guest bathroom, but the one that had three glass walls looking over the ocean. Roger said the man was very nice and apologized but explained that he was so tired of being dirty, that he hoped the owner wouldn't mind. Roger was a bit of a hippy himself. Even today, right? He said he laughed and gave him a towel and I think a bowl of soup. Crazy, eh?"

"None of my children can punctuate. Hardly any periods and forget the commas. But you tell a good story," said Derek.

"Is it a story or is it true?" asked Lisa.

"Oh, it's true. Roger doesn't live there anymore but he had a beautiful, spacious home in the middle of nothing but trees. The walls that formed his living room, had five long but narrow windows overlooking the ocean and the remaining Route 1. He called them his everchanging paintings of sea and land. He still talks about them."

"What do you mean?" asked Lisa.

"The sky with its clouds and shadows was always changing, giving him different pictures."

Rochelle told Lisa that Roger was still a wonderful artist. He lived in San Francisco now in a retirement home but still got out to paint his ever-changing nature. Especially the Eucalyptus trees. Lisa said she had never heard of such a tree and asked what it was like.

"Haven't you heard them?" asked Helena.

"You can hear them right now if you get away from people noise," said Lawrence.

"Come over here, Lisa," said Derek as he walked to the far end of the deck. "You hear that groaning, that "talking", that noise that sounds like people screeching?"

"Yes. And I heard it the other night outside my window. I thought at first it was someone on the patio but didn't see anybody. So that's a Euco – what?"

"Eucalyptus tree."

"The waitress is signaling us, Derek. Everybody hungry?" asked Rochelle. "You all go to the table. I'm going to call Suzanne and see how she's doing."

The four of them sat around a large table near a window and looked over the menu.

"Take your time. We'll wait for Rochelle before ordering," said Derek. "Anything look good to you, Lisa? You said you enjoyed seafood. Their lobster is a little different than my mother's area but they're real good. Helena, another hamburger? Lawrence is a vegetarian, naturally, so he only has a short list to choose from."

"I've heard of vegetarians but never knew one. Don't you miss hamburgers and hot dogs? And seafood?" asked Lisa.

"Nope. I don't understand how you people, my dear family, can eat innocent and beautiful creatures. They are God's creatures just like we are," wailed Lawrence.

"Now, Lawrence, that's enough. Everyone's allowed to choose what he eats," said Derek. "Here comes your mother. From her expression, it doesn't look good."

"No answer. I let it ring until the tape came on. Left a message that we'd try later, just before starting home."

"Probably went to Wilma's. Probably feels a lot better. Don't worry, Mom," said Helena.

"I'm not worried, dear. Remind me, Derek, to call after our walks though."

"Yes, now let's order. Rochelle, you want the clams, right? Me, too. They really know how to fix them here. Delicious. Lisa, what will you have?"

"A little bit of everything. It all looks so good. I'll have the shrimp, thank you."

As Derek ordered, Lisa began to worry about Suzanne. Not that she was sick but that she lied to them all and maybe went to Michael's picnic. Hoping nobody could read her mind, she felt sure that was what Suzanne did. She had told Lisa how much she wanted to go. But she knew her parents wouldn't let her leave their party, especially with Lisa here for the big trip to Big Sur. That annoyed her, she had said, being treated like a child. Not being allowed to have her own friends, go to their parties, spend more time with them. Lisa thought what her father would have said. "You ARE a child, my dear." Even her Florida grandparents. And especially Isobel. Of course, maybe her friend, Abigail, might have agreed with Suzanne. Sort of.

Chapter Eight

The following week went by so quickly that Lisa could hardly believe it was Saturday again and time for the picnic at Pt. Lobos. It was Suzanne's birthday and so a lot of fuss was being made with food, drinks, and gifts.

Suzanne had waited almost the whole week before confiding in Lisa about her day with Michael at his mother's picnic. What had happened was so predictable. Rochelle met Michael's mother, Catherine, at the grocery store, and as they both bought picnic food for the next day, Catherine mentioned how great it was having Suzanne with them the previous Saturday. Rochelle never let on but rather took the whole story in, asking what food they had, etc. Her harmless hippy days had made her a cool character. Catherine was surprised that Suzanne didn't tell Rochelle about their having a couple of Michael's fish he had caught the day before, for the entrée. And that Michael even cooked it like a French chef. Rochelle just nodded and explained how full their week was, what with Lisa visiting them, that she had hardly had a word with Suzanne. But she would certainly catch up on the details the next day at their own picnic. Carmel was certainly a picnic town.

That evening Suzanne knocked on Lisa's door and quietly told her the whole story. She explained how her mother was going to punish her after Lisa went home, like not letting her go to the movies for a week or so. Or whatever. Lisa was dumbfounded. How could Rochelle allow such lying go unpunished? Her father would have kept her from basketball games, swimming meets, and the movies. Lying to your mother or father was simply not done! At least in the midwest. Especially lying to someone like Rochelle who was rather open and freewheeling with all her children.

Suzanne cried a little and apologized to Lisa but she explained how desperate she was to be with Michael. And she could see no other way other than to fake illness. To her absolute surprise, Rochelle told her daughter that she had done the same thing to her mother when she was fourteen when she thought she was madly in love with the minister's son. Her mother severely punished her by keeping her in the house for two or three weeks. Rochelle said she never forgave her mother for that. She had had to miss two birthday parties, a fishing trip and three overnights. She promised herself that if she ever had a daughter, she would never do that to her. So here she was with almost the same problem. Suzanne had cried, and Rochelle wiped away her tears, trying to explain how wrong it was to try to fool your mother. When Suzanne said that she knew Rochelle would never had let her go to Michael's picnic, Rochelle bit her lip and softly said that maybe she, too, was learning a lesson. That maybe she would have allowed Suzanne to go to the picnic, if she had thought it over carefully, even if it meant not being with Lisa for the day. But they both decided it was over, that Suzanne shouldn't have lied, that talking things out would have been better that day, that her infatuation with Michael was temporary, an eleven-year old's infatuation. And that was that. Rochelle would tell Derek and maybe even Lawrence and Helena. She decided that the picnic tomorrow with Michael and Timmy as their guests would be a lovely day with no mention of last week. Suzanne could tell Michael everything at another time, but definitely it was over. Not to be mentioned again by anyone. That way there would be no embarrassing remarks or moments. Like it never happened except for the lesson Suzanne learned. Lisa always liked Rochelle even if she was a little nervous around her. But her admiration for her hostess now soared. She envied Suzanne a little but then realized that her father would be almost as thoughtful.

"How do you think she'll punish you after I'm gone?" asked Lisa.

"No movies for a while but that's all. She's pretty fair and she certainly doesn't want to ruin our time with you. I shouldn't have done it. I knew it was wrong all the time but,…oh, well, it's over now, thank heavens. Don't think I'll ever do that again. She did ask me to apologize to you, Lisa. So I'm sorry."

"It's okay. You told me everything now, and I'm glad you did. So let's all forget it," Lisa softly said. "Now what are you going to wear for your birthday picnic tomorrow?"

"My new pink outfit. You haven't seen it yet. Let me go get it and show you. What are you wearing?"

"Probably what I wore last Saturday. But then it will be new to you, won't it?"

They both screamed laughing. When Suzanne left to get her new outfit, Lisa thought about how she didn't feel nervous or shy anymore, around anyone. She wondered when those awkward feelings left her. Was it the beauty of Big Sur or Route #1, the tennis lessons she was having every day, hearing about Derek's rehearsals and looking forward to attending one next week, Lawrence's connection to his animals, Helena's openness and goodness and innocence? Or was it Suzanne's ability to brave the storm she had created and come out on the other side? Unhurt. Smarter. Or Rochelle's ability to keep learning how to be a mother.

This last thought made her miss her own mother, not painfully but with serious feelings. She still loved her mother, would always love her and would never let her go. Mothers are wonderful creatures, if you can call a mother a creature, and some day she would be a mother. A mother that not only loved her children but was willing to learn with her children. As she thought about her motherhood, Suzanne burst into the room wearing her stunning pink outfit Pants and two tops, all three with a sprinkling of sparkles. Lisa felt so free. So loved. So cared for. "It's wonderful! Just beautiful!" she said.

Chapter Nine

"I'm so glad your father said you could take scuba lessons with me," exclaimed Suzanne as they got into the van.

"Me, too. Although I don't have any idea what we're going to do."

"It's simple. Lawrence said we spend a couple of hours in the pool, practicing with all the equipment. After we pass some tests, we go out to the ocean!"

As they rode to the Scuba Scuba Hole, Lisa saw a lot of the ocean. It was so beautiful. So blue! She could hardly wait to get into it.

Derek was giving the girls some basic points as they pulled into the parking lot. "Listen to everything the instructor says. And do whatever he tells you to do. He's the boss, remember. Scuba diving is not a game. It's a sport and a serious sport at that. I don't want to frighten you, but it's a sport that can be dangerous. If you do what you're told, you'll be okay. Let's go."

As they walked toward the office, Suzanne whispered to Lisa, "I think he's more nervous than we are."

"I'm not nervous. A little unsure of myself. Like I know nothing," said Lisa.

"Well, I know a lot about it from Dad and from Lawrence. So I'm not nervous at all."

"Does Lawrence's suit fit you okay?" asked Lisa.

"Yep. The instructor will check it out though."

After signing up, the two girls were asked to put on their bathing suits, take a shower, and meet by the poolside. When they got to the pool, they found four other people ready to take their first instructions, too. They were all adults, young adults, but not kids. This made Suzanne and Lisa giggle.

"I want to see each of you swim the length of the pool six times, with strong strokes and kicking. It's important that you swim well so that if you should get into any trouble out there, you'll be able to rescue yourself," said Pete, their instructor, with a large grin. "Don't worry. If you do what I tell you to do, you'll have nothing to worry about. But what I say goes, right? No matter what you think you should be doing, you do what I tell you to do."

They all dove into the deep end of the pool and started swimming. Lisa felt so good getting back into water again. After six lengths, she felt ready to conquer the world.

Peter called them all to the side of the pool and gave each one a mask He showed them how to keep the plastic clear by spitting on the glass, rinsing it in the water, and putting it on right away. Giggling again, both girls followed Pete's direction and successfully tested their masks above the water and beneath. Lisa was amazed how clear she could see under the water. No blurriness, no water leakage, no fog hid the pool's secrets. Encouraged to dive to the bottom, she wanted to stay on the bottom but her breath gave out and she had to surface. Pete then introduced the snorkel to them. Standing in the pool while they practiced breathing through the snorkel's attached tube, they all coughed, spit, choked for a few minutes. It wasn't too long though till they all got used to this method of breathing and swam to the bottom, holding their breath. When they needed to breathe again, they surfaced. Then they followed Pete's instruction to come to the surface without lifting their faces out of the water. Relying on the tube that Lisa held in her mouth and letting it stick out into the air, she was able to breathe through the tube. She choked a few times in the beginning but soon learned how to measure the length of the tube that was out of the water. Her lungs full again with air, she closed her end of the tube with her lips, keeping any water out of the tube, and dove down to the bottom again.

One of the adults was having a difficult time keeping water out of the tube when he went to the bottom. But Peter was very patient and kept him trying over and over again until he learned how to control what went in and out of the tube. Air or water, it was the decision of the diver. Lisa learned quickly because of her love of the water and practicing quick dives and quick intakes of air became a game, a challenging game, but a game.

At one point her mask got pushed over and some water came in which meant she had to surface and clear it with some more spitting. Pete explained that there was a chemical that could be used to keep the mask clear, but it was good to know how to clear if it wasn't available. She got to talk with Suzanne at this time who also was having a great time with the snorkel.

Now Pete added to their challenge. He had them put on the wet suits and asked them to repeat the dives and snorkeling skills. Going to the bottom of the pool with a lot of scuba suit around you was a whole new experience. It was more difficult and awkward to work with the snorkel while your suit was taking in some water. He then added heavy rubber-covered bricks to the bottom of the pool, asking them to pick them up and bring them to the side of the pool.

Lisa was losing her breath a few times and had to stop and rest. She was surprised to find herself getting tired. Two of the adults had already stopped, climbed out of the pool, and asked for a few minutes break. Pete asked them to all to come out of the water, take their wet suits, snorkels, and masks off and sit around and talk about what they had just learned. Everyone felt good, comfortable, but a little exhausted. They had been in the water almost two hours and it was time to end their first lesson. Pete explained how new this all was to them and tomorrow they would be doing the same things in half the time and with greater energy.

Lisa and Suzanne showered and got dressed with continuous chatter about the wonder of it all. Saying goodbye to Pete and the others, they went back to the office where Derek and Lawrence were waiting. It was difficult to hear anyone talk since all four were talking at once.

Lawrence asked, "Did Pete tell you about the kelp?"

"No," said Suzanne.

"Well, near the shore there's a vegetation called kelp floating on the surface of the water. Most of it is dark red and it grows like a forest—thick at the top thinning down to its roots near the bottom of the ocean. If you come up from the bottom and into a mass of kelp, you can get your equipment entangled in it. If you have a knife, you can cut yourself free. The best thing to do though is to watch where you're going to surface, staying away from the kelp. I got caught in it once, but it wasn't that thick and I was able to descend again out of the mess and surface away from it. My partner wasn't so lucky though. He had to tread water until the instructor came over and cut him out of it. We laughed about it, but the instructor told us it was a good lesson to learn about looking up to the surface as you're coming up," explained Lawrence.

The girls looked at each other with eyes and mouths wide open.

"Ready for your next lesson? Tomorrow, right?" asked Derek.

"Absolutely!" said Lisa. "I want to take all the lessons my Dad can afford, including the ones from the boat."

"The fees have already been taken care of. Pete is a friend of ours, and he's arranged to give you two gals all the lessons you need to actually go way out in the ocean and down to the caves," added Derek.

"Caves?" screamed Suzanne and Lisa.

"Dad, they're fifty feet down, and I think you have to be twelve to go that deep. I didn't go down there till my second year. Cool, though, using flashlights to swim through them," said Lawrence.

"Oh, let's ask Pete if we can go down that far," said Lisa.

"No! Let's go one step at a time. We'll do whatever Pete tells us to do," warned Suzanne.

Lisa looked at her and saw a new Suzanne. One who was not so adventurous, one who was wanting to obey rules, one who wanted to go slowly and carefully. Lisa wondered if Suzanne was frightened. But she kept quiet and decided to wait and see what happened. For herself, Lisa was ready to go anywhere in the ocean, do anything that was possible. She didn't want to do anything but scuba dive!

When they got home, Rochelle wanted to hear all about it, and the two girls never stopped talking. They talked about tomorrow's lesson and how they would be learning how to put the tanks on their backs and learn to breathe with the regulators.

"Maybe we can go out in the boat by Saturday," suggested Lisa.

"Not this Saturday, girls. We're going down to Disneyland for the weekend. Dad's got Friday off from work and from rehearsal. It's our only chance to go there, and we'll have more than two days to try to see any new exhibits and of course try out any new rides," said Rochelle.

"Great!" said Suzanne.

"Yeah, that sounds great. But if we miss a lesson, will we still be in the same class?" asked Lisa.

"What's the difference, Lisa?" asked Suzanne.

"I just don't want to miss anything."

"Don't be difficult," said Suzanne. "We'll get back to scuba some day next week."

"I know. I know. And I do want to see Disneyland. I'm sorry if I sounded difficult."

"You didn't sound that way at all," said Rochelle, looking at her daughter severely. "You just happen to fall in love with a new sport. You'll be going at least three times next week"

Lisa suddenly felt terribly shy again. It was as if a wall had surrounded her and was closing in on her. She thought she had gotten over that scary feeling she first felt when she arrived in California. She had gotten used to her aunt and uncle and her cousins and felt relaxed with them. Except for that one evening when she escaped with Timmy and went home instead of walking the beach, she felt comfortable with Suzanne. Now she wanted to hide. Now she felt all tight again. Like she had done something wrong even though Rochelle had tried to make her feel comfortable. She wanted to crawl up into a little ball and roll away to a corner of the room. Looking at Lawrence who had a twinkle in his eyes didn't help her. She wished Helena had been there. From the first day there Helena had made her feel safe but Helena was visiting a friend for the day. Derek was another one that made her feel at ease but he had gone off to rehearsal. She looked to Rochelle for help but couldn't say anything. Rochelle would just have to guess that she needed a friend. Someone to push that wall back!

"Why don't you girls get dressed and help me with dinner? Derek had an early rehearsal and will be home around seven for dinner. Can you wait until then, or are you starving after all that swimming?" asked Rochelle.

"Starving!" said Suzanne. "Can we have some of that pizza we didn't finish last night?"

"Sure. Lawrence, what about you? You had a good lunch while the girls were swimming. But a piece of pizza?" asked Rochelle.

"No. I'll have some of that salad if there's any left," said Lawrence. "I have to get up to my friends and feed them soon."

"Good. Get dressed, girls, and come down for your snack. I'd like to show you some maps of Disneyland, Lisa. And you haven't been there for a while, Suzanne. You can't see everything so you can decide which rides and exhibits you're interested in. Get dressed and come down for your pizza and a coke while we go over all the literature I collected," said Rochelle.

As they went upstairs, Lisa told Suzanne what a wonderful mother she had.

"She knows just how to make people feel good."

"Yeah, most of the time," answered Suzanne.

Chapter Ten

Driving down to Los Angeles gave Lisa a chance to see the scenery surrounding Route 1 again, even though it was still rather dark. An early start would get them there just before lunch. Using a route away from the coast would have made the trip much shorter, but Derek was so proud of his state's beauty. Reaching their destination and winding through the streets of one of America's largest cities gave Lisa a chance to see crowds she had never witnessed before. She wondered where all the people had come from and how they could all live in one city. Los Angeles, the City of the Angels, was alive!

"We're almost there," said Derek, anticipating the children's questions.

"I don't remember anything. It's been so long," cried Helena.

"Well, it has been several years," her mother agreed. "What section do you want to visit, Suzanne?"

"Doesn't matter."

"I want the rides," yelled Lawrence.

"Are they scary?" asked Lisa. "I'm not very good on rides that are too scary."

"Not scary for kids. Mom and Dad won't go on them. They like the exhibits. Dull stuff, most of them. The Presidents, The History of the Wild West, stuff you learn in school."

"We'll do the rides first. Have some lunch and then a few quiet exhibits. So we can keep the food we just ate," said Rochelle. "Then maybe some quiet rides that your father and I can enjoy."

"But we stay together, remember. We don't want to lose any time looking for each other," Derek warned.

"There it is!" yelled Helena, as they reached the entrance of Disneyland.

"And it looks like there's still some parking space left. Weekends are not the best time to visit an amusement park. Especially this one," said Derek.

Lisa stared in amazement. The crowds, the colorful buildings, the balloons, the flags—a fairyland! They joined the lines to buy their tickets. Before they even went through the turnstiles, they were approached by Mickey and Minnie Mouse. Lisa laughed, then giggled when Mickey spoke to her.

The rides were waiting for them. So were the long lines. They switched a few times over to rides that had smaller lines. But the rides they really wanted—the various slides, the swings, the parachute jump—were worth the long wait. So they lined up and waited. Derek and Rochelle stopped at a coffee stand and enjoyed a post-breakfast snack. The kids didn't want anything, just the rides. Lisa was a bit befuddled. She stuck close to Suzanne who strangely was very quiet.

"You okay?" asked Lisa.

"Yeah. Just a little tired. I'll wake up. The big twisting slide will do it," she answered. "It's long and fast and dark. But not scary. Want a coke while we wait?"

"That would be good," said Lisa. "I am thirsty."

"I'll be right back," called Suzanne as she left her place and headed for her parents across the lawn.

Derek gave her a few bills and back she came. Then she and Lawrence took the orders and aimed for the soda stand which happily also sold hot dogs. They returned with arms loaded. This made waiting in line more fun.

Two hours of rides brought the six of them to a regular lunch spot where hamburgers and fries and salad and more cokes and coffee filled them up.

"Did you go on anything?" asked Lisa of Derek and Rochelle.

"One. The smaller slide. We mainly watched you all enjoying the scary rides. But now, after lunch, we do a few exhibits. I hear they have a new one that shows computerized photographs of the country. A lady was describing it to us. Said the film showing the rivers and dams and rafting was exquisite. We think even you guys will enjoy it," replied Rochelle.

"We missed a few good rides. We have time to go back later, right? They don't close up until 10:00," said Lawrence. "It's great to be back here, Dad. I'm glad you came to visit us, Lisa."

"We should come back here every few years, Mom," suggested Suzanne. "And not just when we have to bring guests." Lisa felt the closing in of shyness again and moved towards Helena.

"She's right. Every two years, how's that?" said Lawrence "You can come visit us again in two years, Lisa."

"No, I go to New York then," murmured Lisa. But she liked Lawrence coming to her rescue.

"Here she goes! When will you run out of relatives to visit?" asked Suzanne.

"When I'm fourteen," answered Lisa.

"Everyone finished?" asked Rochelle. She took Suzanne's hand as they walked out of the restaurant. But Suzanne took it back and scowled.

Lawrence sidled up to Suzanne and whispered to her, "Take it easy, kid."

"Mind your business," she snarled.

Derek called out to Lawrence, "There's a pavilion with live animals and lectures about their histories." Looking at the map of the park, he continued, "It's somewhere over to the right."

"Great!" said Lawrence as he looked at the map and where they were.

"Must we?" cried Helena.

"Yes," said Rochelle with a quick look to Derek.

As they all aimed to the right, Suzanne softly said to Lisa, "Sorry, kiddo. Guess I'm still tired. Didn't mean to be rude."

"It's okay. Guess I talk too much about my summer travels."

"You okay?"

"Yes. I'll be okay." as she took a big breath.

Walking over to the animal house, Lisa felt herself relaxing more. "Where do these strange feelings come from?" she asked herself. She reminded herself that Derek and Rochelle had invited her to spend a month with them. And Derek's mother, Isobel, had highly recommended her, telling him that Lisa was easy company, able to take care of herself for long periods while she tended her shop. She had learned to conquer the awful feeling of loneliness there in Southampton. Now she wished she just had loneliness to fight. Here in California she was never alone. There was always something to do and someone to do it with. But this new feeling of what she would call shyness was worse than loneliness. It scared her. Like everyone, especially Suzanne, was crowding her into a small box. She liked all of them. Derek and Rochelle treated her like their child, Helena was kind and thoughtful, Lawrence was a little rough but also kind, Suzanne was polite most of the time but sometimes a little cool and distant.

This bothered her. Why should someone, a girl, the same age, a cousin, make her feel "in the way"? Jealousy? No, why should Suzanne be jealous of her? Suzanne had everything, Lisa wasn't even as pretty. Suzanne was much better at tennis. (She'd been playing since she was six.) She was just as brave and energetic during the scuba lessons. (Of course, she was glad to cut them short when it came time to visit Disneyland.) Lisa had been almost willing to give up the famous amusement park if she could have continued the lessons. She had loved them more than anything. Now she would only have three more lessons because of the plans to visit San Francisco. Suzanne liked the idea of going to the big northern city, especially since Rochelle had suggested that Michael and Timmy join them. Maybe that was it! Suzanne missed Michael. Lisa was glad she didn't like anyone so much that she would become unhappy and mean without him. Once she realized it was Suzanne's problem, Lisa began to feel better. In fact, she didn't feel shy or uptight anymore. She had found a reason for Suzanne's rudeness to her. She was so deep in thought about this new idea that she walked right past the entrance to the animal house, not even hearing Lawrence calling after her.

"Where you going, Lisa?"

"Lisa, we're going in here," said Rochelle.

"I'm sorry. I was thinking about something. I was a million miles away,"

"Back home with your Dad?" asked Helena. "And Mitzi?"

"No, but I do think about them. And wonder how they are," Lisa said. "I'm sorry."

Derek bought the tickets, and they all went in to see the animals.

Chapter Eleven

"Best taste in the world, right?" chuckled Lawrence.

"I like chocolate. But I like lots of flavors," said Lisa.

"What I like, man, is the ice cream. Whatever the flavor. This is delicious," quipped Michael. "Thank you," he said to Rochelle, adding a big smile.

Suzanne was so glad that Michael was being polite and on his best behavior. She was also proud of her mother for including him and Timmy on this one-day peek at San Francisco. And she was again in a great mood. Lisa was glad about that.

"Can we go on the cable cars again, Mom?" asked Helena.

"Yeah, that would be great. They're really cool," said Michael.

"You mean *awesome*," commented Suzanne.

"What's the difference? Both mean the same thing."

"'Cool' is a bit out of it, isn't it?"

"And who made you the expert?" said Michael, laughing.

"Are you laughing at me, Michael?"

"No, silly."

Rochelle was about to say something, but Helena, the peacemaker, asked Timmy if he wanted to go on the cable cars again. He smiled and said yes. Michael cooled down as he laughed about Timmy being "the one word kid". Lisa saw how both boys were good for each other. Volatility and calmness made a good friendship. She also saw how Suzanne was heading for trouble if she kept nagging Michael. Driving up from Carmel, Suzanne was picking on him for silly things, like humming, or whistling. It was stupid of him to start making spitballs on the end of his tongue. Suzanne told him to stop, but Michael just took the challenge and doubled his efforts. Rochelle came to the res-

155

cue by pointing out some of the beauty spots of the surrounding land. Lawrence who was sitting next to her realized what she was doing and added his comments about the landscape and its history.

"And when we get into the city, you'll notice all the white houses. Historical."

"Why are they all white and what's the history?" asked Lisa.

"Don't know," blurted Lawrence. "But just look at all the houses."

Lisa laughed. "You're funny, Larry…Lawrence. Can we find out why?"

"Sure. Michael will look it up in the library. Right, Michael?"

"Don't know how to look things up, Lawrence."

"Oh, that's right, you only use the library for your social life," teased Lawrence.

"Isn't that what it's for?"

Rochelle changed the subject by pointing out the Golden Gate Bridge in the distance. And here Lawrence added some history. "They paint the bridge with an anti-rust, orange paint every year. And because the bridge is so large, the painters never run out of work. When they get to the end of the bridge, they simply carry their paint cans to the beginning of the bridge and start painting. Never have to look for another job. They just keep painting." He laughed so Lisa wasn't sure whether he was kidding or not. But his bridge story did settle Suzanne's nerves and she became pleasant again. The whole atmosphere in the car became pleasant. Lisa wondered how long Suzanne could be happy. Her grandmother on Long Island had spoken once about certain people being moody. "Not happy people, moody people, and the people around them become unhappy. Don't know what causes it. But it's something you want to avoid, Lisa," she had wisely lectured her granddaughter. Thinking about this, Lisa realized how much she missed Isobel. That was a good summer!

"Well, here we are. And do notice all the white houses," Rochelle said.

"Look at the hills! And all the cars going up and down them," yelled Lisa.

"We'll be going up and down one of them," Rochelle softly explained.

"Sorry. Didn't mean to yell like that," apologized Lisa.

"We'll park in the middle area and then take a cable car to the top. There's a lovely park up there, and you get a wonderful view of the Golden Gate and the harbor," said Rochelle.

The cable car was absolutely thrilling! As it went up the hill, it had to catch on to the cogs which kept it from sliding down to the bottom of the hill. Lisa was a bit frightened until she saw that the others were just smiling. They had all been through this before and knew the cogs would hold them. But it was still a thrill for them because the hill was so steep. When they got to the top and reached level land again, Lisa was smiling with them.

And in front of them was the most beautiful panorama, as Helena would say. The Golden Gate Bridge in its orange brilliance looked like a toy—from where they stood. As they were all admiring the beauty of the view, they heard drums beating away just behind them. They saw lots of people walk over to an area that held a wooden floor, a large curtain hung on two poles, and several people in costume holding all kinds of props. It was a show of some kind. Rochelle suggested that they walk over and see what was happening. The drums soon stopped, and a young man with a mike started talking to the crowd. Some of the people in costume were carrying signs that had "Fire Department" or "Police Department" or "Transportation" written on them.

"It's a political play," whispered Rochelle.

"What does that mean?" asked Lisa.

"They're an acting group that are unhappy about something the city is doing. And they act out their grievances. In mime. See none of them are talking. Just the announcer to get everyone's attention. They're telling a story with their actions. They're good." said Rochelle.

"Not my favorite kind of entertainment. Let's walk down the hill," said Lawrence.

"Wait a few minutes. Let Lisa see a little of it. They're famous," argued Rochelle.

"In San Francisco," chuckled Lawrence.

"Well, that's something. This city is pretty large and rather important, brother dear," said Suzanne.

"Just a few minutes, Lawrence. Let's watch just a little longer," Lisa added.

"Who are they? Do they get paid to do this? If so, who pays them?" asked Michael.

"I don't think they get paid. I believe they do this instead of marching for a cause. Saw them once before when they were fighting against the war," commented Rochelle. "It's rather exciting to see people stand up for their rights."

"That's funny: "fighting against the war". And where are our rights? Who speaks for us?" asked Michael.

"Michael, if you want to put on a play about your rights, why don't you start a group in Carmel. I'm sure you would get lots of attention. Carmel people like individuality, and they would appreciate your efforts to tell them what you believe."

"No thanks. Too much work."

"That's what I thought. But you are honest. And that's the best character trait a person can have," said Rochelle, smiling at Michael. "Let's watch for ten minutes more. Then enjoy the view and the fresh air before we have lunch."

"Lunch sounds good," Michael laughed. He appreciated Rochelle's comment about honesty and the big grin she gave him. He looked over at Suzanne, gave her a big smile, and waited for a pleasant response. And it soon came. Suzanne seemed in control again. Maybe she could learn to master these mood swings, thought Lisa.

"Where are we going to eat?" asked Helena. "I'm hungry."

"How about Chinese?" suggested Rochelle.

"Great!" everyone answered.

"Okay then, everyone to the cable car station and down we go," Rochelle responded.

Chinatown was just a few blocks wide and long but it contained the most interesting store fronts and gift shops. They went into almost all of them. Lisa bought a few trinkets and some postcards. Then they found a restaurant they all thought was a good choice. And what a meal they had. Seven people, seven dishes. And a few more to satisfy some of the appetites.

"Best meal I ever had," said Michael, as they left the restaurant. "That food is really good."

"Now back to Ghirandelli Square?" asked Lawrence.

"Yes, but I don't know how you have room for it," said Rochelle.

"Always have room for ice cream."

"We'll walk over there. That'll will help," suggested Rochelle. "I promised Lawrence. Okay with everyone?"

"Sounds good to me," said Michael. "Suzanne, some ice cream?"

"Sure," answered Suzanne, already in a better mood. Filling one's stomach helps people feel better. And ice cream always wins.

As they left Ghiradella Square, each licking his cone with enthusiasm, Rochelle pointed the direction of the parking lot where they left their car.

It was a short but wonderful day. And a long drive home to think and talk about the things they saw and did. Two more days in California! How did it ever go this fast?

Chapter Twelve

Even before they got to the highway, Helena was asleep. Except for Rochelle, everyone else was quiet and seemingly without energy. Rochelle wanted company while driving the long trip home. She started several topics of conversation but not until she spoke about the scuba lesson the next day did the car jump alive.

"I can't believe this will be my last lesson," moaned Lisa.

"Maybe you can find someone back home to teach you," suggested Michael.

"In the mid-west, without an ocean?" Lisa moaned again.

"What about rivers?"

"Do they scuba dive in rivers?" asked Lisa.

"Don't know, but you could ask," said Michael.

"We go out in the boat," Suzanne sleepily said.

"That's right! Our first real test. That's a great way to end my scuba experience."

"In California," said Michael. "This is not the end of scuba diving for you."

"How do you know?" asked Suzanne.

"From her enthusiasm for the sport. She'll pick it up somewhere. Right, Lisa?"

"Michael, you're absolutely right. Definitely next year when I visit my aunt and uncle in Charleston, South Carolina. But I hope before that."

"That's the spirit."

"My plane ticket is for Thursday morning, right, Rochelle?"

"Right. You can sleep all the way home."

"We won't be out on the boat all day, will we?"

"No, but tomorrow night we go to Derek's rehearsal," reminded Rochelle.

"Oh, I forgot about that. The last rehearsal we went to, the actors were still using their scripts. Derek said they haven't been using them for a week now. It'll be fun to see them trying to work without them. What do they do if someone forgets a line?" asked Lisa.

"I believe they can still call on the prompter. But some times the other actor gives them a hint, enough so the actor who forgot can remember. Derek said that everyone is very easy to work with, and they all help each other. He said it's the best cast he's worked with," said Rochelle.

"I'm glad I'm going to see an almost perfect play," said Lisa.

"Oh, there will still be lots of mistakes. With the costumes, a missing hat or something. Or something wrong with the props. They don't open till a week from Friday. Lots of time to straighten everything out," said Suzanne.

"Are you all going?" asked Lisa.

"Of course. We wouldn't miss Dad's performance," Suzanne said.

"Michael, will you and Timmy see it?" asked Lisa.

"Don't know. Mom and Dad will probably go. Timmy's folks, too. So we'll string along probably."

"No wonder Timmy is a one-word kid," said Suzanne. "You do all his talking."

"Say, Lawrence, you did arrange for Johnny to feed your animals, didn't you?" asked Rochelle.

"Sure did. He loves to take over that job when I can't be there. Lisa's visit will cost me a lot of money."

"Oh, no. I'm sorry, Lawrence. Can I pay you?"

"Only kidding. I don't give him money. Let him ride my new bike. Kidding. He just likes to do it. He'd like to have his own animal set-up. But no room in his house. In fact, two of the critters—the white mice—are his. He owes me money for rent. Kidding."

"I'm going to miss you and your crazy sense of humor. I love it," said Lisa.

"Going to miss me?" asked Michael.

"Yes. I'm going to miss all of you. You have all given me a wonderful summer. It'll take me months to tell Dad and Barbara everything we did.

"You've been a great guest, Lisa. So easy to do things with," Rochelle said. "I just hope we showed you enough of the West Coast. But you can always come back. You're welcome any time."

"Thank you," said Lisa as she curled up on her seat and smiled to herself. She felt very fortunate having such great relatives that gave her such great summers.

She wondered if there were other children her age that were treated so well by her or his relatives. But she knew in her own thoughts that all the attention they gave her was because of her mother's death. They were being kind. Rochelle had said that honesty was the best character trait a person could have. Lisa decided it was kindness.

The End

Book Four
Lisa in South Carolina

Chapter One

Lisa stood by the airline desk, waiting. The lady behind the desk and Lisa were both waiting for Uncle Walter to arrive, sign some papers, and take his niece home. Without him, she was not allowed to leave. This was her fourth summer to arrive by plane at a relative's hometown to be his or her or their guest for a month or more. The previous three visits were all successful, although she had had doubts in the beginning of each.

But she had always been met at the airport and promptly. Once, in Long Island, she did have to wait for a few minutes till her grandmother showed up. But never this long! The plane experience was another enjoyable trip, and she was really looking forward to meeting her father's brother and his wife. But where were they?

"Did my plane arrive early?" asked Lisa.

"No, it was right on time. Why don't you sit down over there?" said the airline clerk, eager to be rid of this polite but complaining customer.

"Thank you, but I've been sitting for a few hours already."

"Do you want to try to call them again? And it's only been about ten minutes."

"I don't think so. Maybe the phone was off the hook. Could I take a taxi to their house? I have their address."

"Not allowed. The papers that your father filled out say you are to be picked up by your uncle."

"I am twelve years old and am used to traveling around the country. I wouldn't have any problem," explained Lisa with a strong sense of authority.

"Sorry. We have our instructions. Please be patient. He'll be here shortly."

Lisa was a little annoyed, not with her, but with her uncle. Not a very good start for a month's vacation with him. Then she saw in the distance a gentleman striding towards them. He looked just like her father. A little older but definitely a family resemblance. He walked right up to her.

"Lisa, right? I am so sorry. Had to go to court this morning, and the case took longer than I thought. You weren't worried, were you?"

"Uncle Walter? I'd know you anywhere. You look just like Dad. No, I wasn't worried. Just a little impatient."

"One of your Dad's faults."

"Being impatient?"

"Yes, my sister and I somehow found our faults in other directions. But both of us are more patient than your Dad," said Uncle Walter with a laugh.

"He's always talking about taking care of that problem. Just talk, really."

"Let me sign these papers, and we'll be off," Uncle Walter said. "Are you hungry?"

"No. Had a snack on the plane. That's the first question I always get asked when I arrive for a 'relative vacation'."

"A relative vacation? What's that?"

"First vacation, when I was nine, was with your mother and father. Next one was with my mother's mother. Then last year when I was 11, I visited her son in California. Now that I am the 'grand old age' of 12, I have come down and over to Charleston, South Carolina, to visit you."

"Let's go and get your luggage. Aunt Mary Joan will be waiting. Doesn't know I was held up in court."

"What kind of a lawyer are you? Criminal? Real Estate?"

"Taxes. Do you pay yours, young lady?" asked Uncle Walter.

"Funny. Are you in a company or on your own?"

"A gal with a lot of questions. Well, that's a good way to learn."

"Dad prepares me for these vacations. Told me all about different kinds of law. I might be a lawyer."

"Good for you. I'll have you look over the office and give you some pointers. I have my own business. Used to be with a fine company but find it more profitable to be on my own."

The conversation dwindled as they searched the revolving machine for her suitcase. Once retrieved, they walked out into the hot sun to the parking lot. Uncle Walter's car was beautiful, one that obviously cost of lot of money, Lisa decided. And its strong air-conditioning felt so good. Driving through Charleston was different from the rest of her vacation adventures. Here were lots of highways, some way up high. When they finally got to the houses, Lisa was pleased to see such pretty ones, all separate from each other. Each had a driveway and each was very skinny. And many had open porches on one side of the house. She would later find out the skinny ones were called "single houses", having only one room in the front as well as all the way to the back because of taxes. Seems that in the olden days, the taxes were based on how wide the house was. There were lots of "single houses" in Charleston. And the porches were called piazzas and they faced the east so the breezes from the ocean would cool anyone using them. Of course these were built before air-conditioning.

"Here we are," said Uncle Walter. And they drove up a driveway right next to a "single house."

Aunt Mary Joan stepped from the open porch and down the steps to greet them. She had a sweet smile and a delicate look about her.

"Hello, Lisa, and welcome to Charleston," she said as Lisa got out of the car.

"Lisa, your Aunt Mary Joan," said Uncle Walter.

"Hi. I mean, Hey, Aunt Mary Joan. That's what my father told me to use instead of Hi. Seems that's the way you say hello in the south. When I reminded him that he had always taught me that hay was for horses, he told me that wasn't true below the Mason-Dixon line—the line dividing the south from the north."

"Your father is a good teacher. Yes, we greet people with Hey. Don't know when it started, but you are going to learn a lot of new expressions down here," Uncle Walter said as he brought Lisa's suitcase onto the porch, then into the house.

"Lisa, would you like something to drink? Iced tea? Lemonade?" asked Mary Joan. And you may call me Mary Joan, without the aunt. Seems a little long that way. Most of us have double names down here so a lot of us drop the "aunt and uncle." Of course the men don't have double names. But still....we want to be consistent. So how about 'Mary Joan and Walter'?"

"I'm used to that. In California, I called my aunt and uncle Derek and Rochelle. But that was because they were hippies, in a way."

"Lemonade?"

"Yes, thank you. I am thirsty," answered Lisa, looking around. "What a pretty porch. The tables and the chairs and all the flowers."

"It's called a piazza. I'll get you your lemonade," said Mary Joan as she disappeared into the house.

Coming back, Walter said in a low voice, "Piazza is another word that's new to you, Lisa. Not that "porch" is not used. Just piazza is more popular. More southern. I had to learn a lot of new ways and new expressions when I came to Charleston."

"I like learning new words. Seems that each section of the country has different words for the same things," said Lisa. "I like traveling. Some day I'm going to go to Europe, even though I don't have any relatives over there."

"You might. Do some research. You might have a few aunts and uncles and cousins sprinkled about."

"That would be fun. Great idea. I have one more relative over here. Next summer I go to New York City to visit Aunt Sally. Then in a few years I'll be old enough to travel to other countries," said Lisa.

At that point Mary Joan brought out a tray of pretty glasses filled with liquids of various colors. She was having a coke and Walter, a beer.

"What's this? Traveling abroad? You haven't seen Charleston yet. What shall we do this afternoon, Walter?"

"Let's have lunch first. Then Lisa can look at all the maps and folders and decide what she would like to do," suggested Walter.

"See Charleston!" said Lisa, with a laugh.

Chapter Two

"So, this is your ocean. It looks different than Isobel's ocean and the beaches are very different. Her beaches were white. And when you walked on them, the sands were soft and loose," said Lisa.

"Oh, don't think this is the beach. We're looking at the harbor where a lot of boats travel. The sand here is really muck from the bottom. Nobody swims here. We'll take you out to Sullivan's Island for a walk on the beach and a good swim," Mary Joan said.

"Don't forget Folly Beach. They have a good beach and even a more exciting ocean," said Walter.

"Why is it more exciting?" asked Lisa.

"It's open to the ocean while Sullivan's has a sandbar protecting the beach. There are more waves and turbulence at Folly."

"I'd like that. I was in Florida a couple of years ago, and the ocean is called the Gulf. And it is calm! But I was nine years old then and only a beginner. So it was perfect. Now I'm an advanced swimmer. I race. And win medals."

"Well, then, we'll be sure to go to Folly," said Walter.

"Sullivan's Island has more class," suggested Mary Joan quietly.

"Island? Did you say island? I've never been on an island," screamed Lisa.

"It's not a real island, surrounded completely by water. Might have been at one point, when they named it. Do you know, Mary Joan?"

"No, I don't. We called it Sullivan's Island even when I went out there as a child. It might be because when you sit on the beach or go for a swim, you just feel separated from the rest of the world. Like your own little universe. You'll love it, Lisa."

169

"Can I try both of them?" asked Lisa. "Can we go to one of them now?"

"Not a bad idea," suggested Walter. "Let's go to Folly. Then tomorrow you can take her to Sullivan's while I'm at the office."

"Sullivan's Island! Don't forget the Island," said Lisa.

"We didn't show her Charleston yet. But it is warm, and I would enjoy a swim. You do have to go to work tomorrow."

Lisa was thrilled although she did want to see the city one of these days. But to swim in an ocean that is open and rough. What could be more perfect. She felt at ease with her aunt and uncle, more with her uncle. Perhaps because he was her father's brother. But also because he seemed more direct. Mary Joan seemed polite and uncertain. Meeting all of her relatives was giving her an edge on character analysis.

Chapter Three

Mary Joan and Lisa spent a few days seeing the sights in the town of Charleston: the old dungeon where the British kept their prisoners during the Revolutionary War; the slave market where men, women, and children from Africa were sold as house servants or farm workers; the Dock Street Theatre which claimed to be the first house for live performances in America; St. Michael's church where George Washington once worshiped; the original pillars of the old Charleston museum; the new museum which had in its outside entrance, a replica of the Hunley, America's first submarine. There was so much to see, and Lisa was trying to remember the story behind each historic sight.

"I believe you need a rest from history, Lisa," suggested Mary Joan the following morning, after a delicious breakfast of eggs, bacon, and grits. At first, Lisa thought grits were some kind of hot cereal and concentrated on the eggs. But she soon began to enjoy the grits and ate them first. "Let's spend a leisurely day at a plantation," Mary Joan continued.

"Okay. But what is a plantation?"

"Before the War Between the States, known to you as the Civil War, there were many plantations, many acres of farmland as well as a large house, outside of a city. They grew cotton or rice or tobacco which were the main products of the south. They required many workers to plant and then to harvest. After the war there were hardly any workers and a lot of the plantations had to close down. Today there are a few still open to visit and see how the old south lived. Of course, they are not working plantations. Just places of beauty and history. I believe you'll enjoy seeing Middleton Place, one of our prettiest. And they have a lovely restaurant for lunch."

"I have so many questions, I don't know where to start."

"I'll try to answer them, but there will be some guides out there to help you. Wear something comfortable, even shorts and a sleeveless top. It's in the country so you won't have to wear a dress."

"I liked wearing the dresses you bought me. I liked feeling 'dressed up' because Charleston is a city and not the seashore or the country. It makes Charleston seem important. I do have a nice pair of shorts and a shirt though. I have one big question about what you said. Why were there so few workers after the war? Were they all killed?"

"No. The workers were slaves. And when the south lost the war, the slaves were free to go where they wanted to."

"Why didn't they just stay and work on the plantation? Weren't they happy with their jobs?"

"Well, they were free and they wanted to be paid for their work."

"Weren't they paid before the war?" asked Lisa with a scowl on her face.

"No, Lisa, they were bought and owned by the owners of the plantation. They were given houses to live in and a certain amount of food. But not a salary as we know today. The owners could never have afforded to pay the many workers it took to run a working plantation. You'll understand more when you see it. The guides will help."

"I don't understand," said Lisa. "Can I ask them some questions?"

"Yes, but be gentle. And if you don't agree with them, just let it pass. And you can talk with Walter about everything at dinner tonight. He has a wonderful way of expressing himself about these things. He's direct but very understanding."

"Shall I change into my shorts now?"

"Yes, and do wear comfortable shoes," suggested Mary Joan.

"You're very nice to take me on all these little trips. And we're not even related."

"And tomorrow I thought we'd go to Sullivan's Island. It's going to be very hot, and we should have a day of just relaxing on the beach. We're to have a busy weekend, with Walter not having to go to the office."

"Swimming! Yippie! And Sullivan's Island where we'll be in our own universe."

Chapter Four

As they walked the various paths of Middleton Plantation, Lisa asked a million questions. How did the slaves become slaves? Where did they come from? Why didn't they escape? Who gave the owners the right to buy a slave?

Mary Joan did her best in trying to satisfy Lisa, but being brought up in the south gave her a different viewpoint from what Lisa was trying to figure out. She just thought it was unfair that someone could buy you and then claim they owned you. And could tell you what to do. She was glad she wasn't a slave. And with her newly found brazen ways of speaking out whenever she felt something was wrong and had to be corrected, she would probably be punished like the slaves that were tied to the whipping posts she saw earlier at the old slave market. She did ask the guide about those posts but he just said that only disobedient slaves were tied up there. Yep, she thought, she surely would have been whipped.

"Now let's get off the slave discussion and go through the house from those early days. It's filled with antiques, and the guide will tell us a lot of history. Or do you want to have lunch first?" asked Mary Joan.

"Lunch. I am hungry. Aren't you hungry? Been a few hours since breakfast."

"Yes, I can eat. We'll do the house after," answered Mary Joan.

They entered a quaint building that looked as if it could have been a stable. A waitress led them to a corner table where they could see a good part of the plantation before them Looking over the menu, Lisa announced that she would like a hamburger.

While they waited for their food, Lisa opened up a sensitive conversation.

"My Dad told me you had a baby and it died. Would you rather not talk about it? It was a boy, he said. He would have been my cousin so I'm interested."

"I don't mind talking about it. It was several years ago so I'm not sad any longer. But the sadness is that I've been told not to try to have any more babies. Seems I just can't carry them. Walter is upset about that as much as I am. He wanted a family. He even thought he would have liked to have a large family. Five or six children. I wasn't so keen about that. But I did want one or two. The room you're using was painted for the baby's room, white so we could add lots of colorful toys. I'm glad it's white now, for our guests."

"What about adopting a baby? I know someone back home who adopted three children and they're all happy kids. Have you ever thought of that?" asked Lisa.

"Yes, in a way. I'm more for it than Walter. But he loves me enough not to want to get a new wife."

"Of course not! He wouldn't do that. Oh, this world is crazy, isn't it?"

The food came and the conversation ended quietly.

"You're only 12 years old and I feel like I'm talking to one of my good friends. You're really quite mature," remarked Mary Joan.

"It's a good idea. Adopting a baby. I heard somewhere that there's a lot of children that need to be adopted, from all over the world."

"Well, yes. We have our name down for one at the Adoption Bureau, but they tell us that there is long list. There are babies, like you said, that need homes, but the system is not very good. True they have to check everything about us and our home, but it still seems too long to wait."

"And too unfair. Specially for the babies," cried Lisa.

"Maybe they think we might change our minds. And we have from time to time. We're so happy right now, we wouldn't want to disrupt our lives."

"A baby wouldn't disrupt. He, or she, would be perfect. And to get a mother and father like you two! Oh, think about it some more. And get them to move faster.

"I don't know what Walter will think about my telling you all this. He's a private person, kind of. Don't share all this with your father, please."

"No, I won't. But let's discuss it with Walter tonight. Okay? He won't really mind my knowing about it, will he?" asked Lisa.

"No. I think he might want to discuss the slavery question instead. But let's see how the conversation goes. Walter is a serious man and does like to discuss heavy subjects. When I first met him, I thought he was too serious, not light like my other boyfriends. But we did have lots of fun when he wasn't talking about justice and fairness in the legal business. And, well, I fell in love.

"And he did too."

"Yes. We have a very good marriage. We just would like to have children. Your enthusiasm might tip the scale," said Mary Joan.

As they left the restaurant, Lisa noticed a beautiful swan in the lake below. She had never seen a live swan before and asked if they could walk down the hill.

"Of course. And that's right on the way to the path that leads to the Butterfly Lakes. We can stretch our legs and walk up the hill a little later to go through the house. Okay?"

"Yes. Yes. First the swan. Then the Butterfly Lakes. Are there really butterflies there?"

"No, the shapes of the lakes are in the form of a butterfly. You'll see."

"This is a beautiful plantation, Mary Joan. Do you come here a lot?"

"About once a month. Some of my friends enjoy it as much as I do. And we enjoy the restaurant. Makes a lovely day."

At the bottom of the hill, they sat on the lawn and watched not one swan but four of them swim around and under a small bridge as if to entertain Lisa. She loved it. As she "talked" to her new friends, Mary Joan thought about the adoption situation. She found herself getting excited over the idea as she once did. Maybe Lisa would be a good influence with Walter. Maybe….

"Time to walk down to the lakes and then up to the house," she said.

"Okay. I'm ready. I could come here every day."

"Well, we'll come back. We will go to the beach tomorrow though, right?"

"Yes. To Sullivan's Island."

After walking around the magnificent Butterfly Lakes, they climbed the hill to the house. Lisa thoroughly enjoyed the house tour. She asked good questions and got good answers. She made sure she didn't ask difficult questions about slavery or the Civil War. But she was surprised to hear the guide talk only about The War Between the States. She had forgotten. Looking at Mary Joan for an answer, she whispered, "What war was that?" Mary Joan whispered back, "The Civil War."

"How come it has two names?" asked Lisa.

"Don't know really. Ask Walter at dinner."

"I have a lot of questions for him tonight."

Chapter Five

"I just don't understand. How could that be legal?" asked Lisa.

"Before the Civil War, it was legal. Each state had the right to make its own laws regarding slavery. Called States' Rights. And because the southern states were agricultural and needed many workers which they could never afford to pay, they allowed slavery," said Walter quietly.

"Was it legal in northern states?" asked Lisa.

"I understand that there were some slaves in the north. But the northern states were manufacturing states, not agricultural. The southerners didn't own slaves because it was fun to own people. They had to in order to run their farms, whether they were growing rice, cotton, or tobacco. In the beginning owning slaves probably didn't seem right to them either. But as generations passed and children became adults and then the owners of the plantations, they simply became slaveholders as part of their economy. Two hundred years of doing something can become a habit, even if it is a nasty habit. The average southerner probably never thought about his owning people as property. He just did what his father did. Some day, Lisa, you'll study economics and you'll understand much better."

"Walter, that's the best explanation I've heard you give on the awful subject of slavery," said Mary Joan.

"I still think it's unfair and should have been illegal," cried Lisa.

"Well, it's illegal today. The Civil War decided that. Tomorrow we're going to visit Ft. Sumter and Ft. Moultrie. Ft. Sumter is famous because of the Civil War. Ft. Moultrie goes back to the Revolutionary War. You'll enjoy both," explained Walter.

"And they have lots of guides there to answer your questions. But again, be gentle. The guides are no doubt southerners, and you don't want to hurt their feelings. They were brought up to believe the South was right and the North was wrong. And children usually believe their parents. Or they should," said Mary Joan.

"But don't the southerners see now how wrong their families were?"

"Not really, because they know that in those days it was the right of the state to permit the owning of slaves for the reasons I told you. Now I think we've discussed this subject long enough. You'll learn a lot tomorrow, Lisa, and we can discuss what you still don't understand tomorrow at dinner. Okay?" asked Walter.

"Yes. But you said something about obeying parents, and that reminded me that we have another topic to discuss."

"Now let me get the dessert before you get into that one," said Mary Joan as she cleared the table and left the dining room.

"Let me help," said Walter, getting up from the table.

"Thanks. Lisa, do you want more milk?" asked Mary Joan from the kitchen.

"No, thank you. Can I bring in some plates?"

"No, thank you. We're almost cleared."

As Mary Joan brought in the ice cream and cookies, Walter settled down again. He was a little exhausted from the office and from his long explanation of slavery. He hoped the next discussion was of a lighter nature.

"All right, my favorite niece, my only niece, what is your next subject?"

"Your adopting a couple of kids."

"What?! Where did this come from?" Walter asked.

"Walter, I hope you don't mind, I told Lisa that we wanted a baby so much and when the doctors said I couldn't carry another, we thought about adoption. And that we had kind of applied. But now we weren't so sure."

"No, I don't mind. But it is a rather adult subject for a child of twelve to understand."

"I understand. And I'm all for it. I was telling Mary Joan that I know some adopted kids and they love their new family."

"And the family loves them?" asked Walter with a wise smile.

"Sure. Of course. I don't know any of the details but it's a happy family. The youngest is in my class."

"Well, Lisa, it's a big decision for us. Once you choose a baby, you can't just turn him in any time you're not satisfied. And you never really know how they'll grow up, what they'll look, and so forth," said Walter.

"You can take one that's a little older. Then you'll know."

"But we would want to bring him up according to our ways and practices. You take an older child and you don't know what he has already learned from other people."

"That's true, but you can always re-train him. Jeff, the oldest of the three that were adopted in my town, was 9 years old. Whatever he learned from others, he learned a lot in his new family. He's now, let's see, he must be sixteen by now. He's one of the best basketball players we have and he's real smart in all his classes."

"You two keep talking about "he" and "him". What about *she* and *her*?" asked Mary Joan.

"Right on. Choose a girl!" exclaimed Lisa. "And don't choose one that looks like you, blond hair and blue eyes. It won't be like she was being born to you, so you can have her in any shape or color."

"Lisa, you're taking this too far. Why don't we drop this subject also," remarked Walter rather strongly.

"Yes, Lisa, we know you want to help and we appreciate that. But we must stick to the color of our race," said Mary Joan.

"Why?"

"Because race is very important, Lisa. This country is made up of many different races, and they're all fine and good people, but we do want to keep them separate," Walter said sternly.

"My teacher told us that there is only one race. The human race."

"You're not shy with your ideas, are you? Go right to the bone, you do," added Walter.

"She has a point, Walter. But, Lisa, in this town, it would be wiser to stay within your own race," Mary Joan quietly said. "More ice cream, anybody?"

Lisa noticed that there were tears welling up in Mary Joan's eyes and she wondered why. Had she said something that made her aunt feel badly?

Walter was quiet for a moment, then spoke up, "Do you think the child of a different race would be happy here?"

"Better than living in an orphanage."

"Oh, Lisa, you make me want to cry. You uncomplicate things so easily. I can't keep up with you," Mary Joan said softly.

"That's it. No more, Lisa. Let's go for a walk along the Battery without any discussion at all. Just walk and enjoy the cool breezes and the moon on the ocean. We'll do the dishes later, Mary Joan. Lisa, you'll need a sweater or a light jacket." Then he noticed that he had another woman or girl with tears in her eyes. Women!

The three of them left the houses quietly and walked slowly along the harbor's edge. No one spoke but all admired the moon on the water and were glad to be cooled by the breezes. A friend of Mary Joan's was out walking her dog, and the two women chatted about their quilting club and the next meeting. This gave Walter a chance to talk with Lisa, privately.

"Lisa, I know you don't mean to be abrupt but I believe you hurt Mary Joan's feelings. I don't know where you get your ideas from, but they're rather radical, and we're not ready for them. May I ask you to go easy. At least easier. I've been told you were independent and I guess that's to be expected what with you losing your mother the way you did and your father spoiling you, letting you have your own ideas about everything. Just cool it for awhile, okay?"

"Yes, Uncle Walter. I'm sorry. I'll be quiet," promised Lisa. Her voice cracked, and she had to blow her nose. Walter gave her his handkerchief and gently hugged her.

"You're a bright girl, Lisa, and will no doubt make a fine lawyer but for now, play the part of a 12 year old. And I promise you, I will seriously consider everything you said about adoption. I know Mary Joan's heart aches for a child and your comments brought it all up to the surface. That's okay. But no more, okay? Let her settle down and let me do some more thinking."

"Yes," whispered Lisa.

"Now, let me tell you a little bit about tomorrow's excursions. First, we'll do the Fort Sumter trip. We go out by boat. You'll enjoy that. About a 20 minute ride and you get a great view of the city of Charleston."

"Oh, I'll love going by boat," exclaimed Lisa, drying her last tear. "How come it's a fort and you need a boat to get to it?"

"There's a taped explanation on the boat, telling a lot about the fort. But I can begin by telling you that it was specifically built at the entrance of the harbor. The southerners wanted to keep any and all northern ships from getting into the harbor."

"Then this is going to be about the Civil War?"

"Definitely. You're going to learn a lot, my young lady. And here's your aunt ready to join us again."

"Well, we settled on the restaurant for our next meeting. She's the president so I'm sure what we decided will be it. And what have you two been chatting about?"

"Fort Sumter," answered Lisa.

Chapter Six

"1861? That's a long time ago," said Lisa, as she sipped from her can of coke. She was so glad Mary Joan liked coke as much as she did. It was her idea to have one now.

"More than one hundred years ago. Keep listening," said Walter. The tape continued with lots of history about Fort Sumter as the boat chugged along the waters of the harbor. It was true—it gave you a wonderful view of the city.

"We've done this trip a dozen times with our out-of-town guests, and I enjoy it each time," Mary Joan softly said.

The boat docked next to a long ramp, upon which the tourists walked to get to the entrance of the fort. Inside the guides told them many stories about the capture of the fort from the Federal troops and how the fort was almost destroyed by the fighting between the two sides. They showed them so many artifacts from that now-famous episode of American history that before Lisa could ask any questions, it was time to return to the boat. She had plenty for the guide on the boat. But there was more tape to listen to, and Lisa listened carefully.

"I'd like to do this again, can we? There was so much to see inside the fort, and I loved the monuments around the fort. And all the flags this country had! Could we come again?" asked Lisa.

"We'll see. Maybe toward the end of the month. That way you'll be all filled up with Charleston history, and you can entice your father to come down for a visit. I've been trying to get him here for years now. And we'd like to meet Barbara. I'm so glad Josh found someone to fill that awful hole," said Walter.

"That's a funny way to put it, but you're right, there was a hole. And Barbara's pretty nice. Dad doesn't give me too much attention now, but he seems a lot happier these days. So that's good."

"We're going to have lunch in a fun restaurant, Lisa. You like seafood?" asked Walter.

"Like it? I love it."

"It's over in Mt. Pleasant. A little shanty of a place with delicious food. And almost on the ocean. Then we're off to visit Fort Moultrie."

"Another fort? They needed two forts to keep the north out?" asked Lisa.

"This fort was built back in the days of the American Revolution, to keep the British out."

"Charleston has been very busy keeping everybody out."

"Not everybody. Just the enemy," said Walter.

"Right. It didn't keep me out!"

Chapter Seven

Lisa lay in bed a little longer. They had such a full weekend that Mary Joan suggested that the two of them have a quiet Monday. Perhaps they could take a carriage ride through the city later in the day, but otherwise do nothing. Mary Joan had a few errands and maybe Lisa could read on the piazza, which she wanted to do ever since she had arrived in Charleston.

Lying in bed, but fully awake, gave her moments by herself to think about all that was happening. She certainly was having a good time. She wasn't either being left alone for long periods as she was on Long Island or she wasn't being constantly surrounded by others as she was in California. Both her uncle and aunt were kind, generous, and fun to be with. Of course, her uncle was a little stern with her about how she blurted out her ideas on slavery and adoption. It was the last topic that worried her now. Did she really say too much? She certainly didn't mean to hurt Mary Joan's feelings. Maybe her aunt was just a bit over sensitive and her uncle a bit too concerned about his wife's feelings.

She decided that she didn't like growing up all that much. Everyone watched her and corrected whatever she said. She knew she had a "big mouth" but there were times she was proud of that. Times when people congratulated her for speaking up. Then there were times when these same people told her she had said too much. "Life is too confusing" she said out loud as she rolled over for a look out the window from her bunched-up pillow.

She wished she could call her father tonight. That would help. They had talked for a few minutes the day she arrived, but that was only to sat hello and that everything was okay. Now, of course he was in Europe. Kind of a honeymoon, he said. But now she was a little homesick and needed to hear his voice.

She was suddenly hungry. The clock said 8:25. She thought she better get dressed first in case Walter was still at home. Pants, shorts, or a dress? She chose a clean pair of shorts and an almost clean shirt. Maybe she could do her laundry again.

Brushing her teeth and splashing water on her face, she heard Walter's car pulling out of the driveway. He was a nice man, even if he was a little cross now and then. She combed her hair, put her sneakers on, and looked for her watch. Where did she leave it? Not on the bureau; not on the desk; not in the bathroom.

Jumping down two steps at a time, she called out, "Mary Joan, do you know where my watch is?"

"Good morning, Lisa," answered her aunt. "No, I haven't seen it. You had it last evening during supper so I am sure it is in the house somewhere."

"Good morning, Mary Joan. It's not in my room or the bathroom. Let me check the dining room."

She dashed into the large room off the kitchen where Mary Joan was standing and sipping some coffee. The watch wasn't on the table or on the floor beneath it. She was trying not to get upset, but where was it?

"Let's not look for it. It'll turn up. My mother always told me that when you lose something, stop looking for it. Go about your activities and it will suddenly appear," said Mary Joan.

"Is that magic? I don't believe in magic," said Lisa with authority.

Mary Joan laughed. "My, you sound so serious. No, I don't mean using magic. It's just that when you look too hard for something, you're apt to overlook what you're looking for. No magic."

"Oh, okay. Can we have breakfast? Or can I have breakfast? And I'll forget about the watch for awhile."

"Good. Now, grits and scrambled eggs again? Or pancakes? We can use that marvelous peach jam my neighbor brought in yesterday. Every summer she buys dozens of peaches and spends evenings making peach jam. Most of it she saves to give away at Christmas, but I always get a jar right away. How about it? Pancakes?"

"Yes. Sounds great. We're going to hang around today, right? Think I'll do some writing. Those postcards I bought the other day."

"Good idea. And some reading, yes? Both of us on the piazza. Then we'll go for the carriage ride around 5 when it's cooler. Walter has to work late this evening so dinner won't be till 8. Not too late for you? We'll have an early lunch and then some tea sandwiches around 3. And lots of coke or iced tea all day."

"Sounds like a fun day. I'd like reading on the piazza—if it's not too hot out there. But you have fans all over the place."

"And there might be a breeze. Come and help me fix breakfast."

"Great. I'm really hungry. I'm not looking, but no watch yet!"

"You have to stop worrying about it, too."

"Oh, I didn't do that. I'll forget about it altogether now. On to the kitchen!"

After another delicious breakfast, Lisa sat down at a table on the piazza and wrote several postcards: to her father and Barbara; to her grandparents in Florida; her grandmother on Long Island; her friend Francesca; her friend Abby; her aunt and uncle and cousins in California. She was collecting quite a group of correspondents. Most of them responded throughout the year with a phone call or a short note. Or the new way of keeping friends: E-MAIL! But postcards showed everyone what she was enjoying at the moment. Lisa was pleased with her relatives and friends around the country. Of course, she also sent postcards to two of her best friends back home.

When she stamped them and placed them in the outgoing basket near the front door, she went to the kitchen to get a coke. There were always plenty of them in the fridge.

She climbed the stairs to her room to get the book she wanted to read on the piazza which she had found was not too hot for relaxing. There was a slight breeze from the ocean which mixed with the breezes from the ceiling fans. As she reached for her book, there was her watch! Just sitting quietly between the bed lamp and her book. She remembered that when she had finished reading the night before, she saw that she had forgotten to take off her watch. So she had simply slipped it off and laid it next to the book which she had carefully placed on the small table next to the bed. It was there all the time, but in her hurry or excitement to find it, she never thought of her book. So she never remembered where she took the watch off. Lisa thought how right Mary Joan was with her advice. "Stop worrying about it and stop looking for it. It'll turn up," Lisa took it another step: it was never really lost! Putting it on, she raced down to the piazza with her book and the coke to tell her aunt her good news.

Mary Joan was delighted of course and gave Lisa a knowing smile. Lisa thought about her early opinion of her aunt—how quiet she was, how polite, how warm but a little distant. Now she saw her as quiet, polite, and warm but not at all distant. All of her relatives were friendly after she got to know them but all friendly in different ways. People were nice. She wasn't feeling so confused anymore. It was fun being who she was and fun meeting so many good people. She settled down to her book and coke. She no longer read just horse stories although she still loved horses. Now she was reading stories about young girls and boys growing up with the new occupation of dating. Suzanne, her California cousin, started her on such books. Lisa turned down a few of them after reading a chapter or two, feeling they were too nasty in their descriptions of how the characters talked to each other. But she enjoyed many of them just as much as Suzanne did. At Christmas time the two of them exchanged some that they had discovered in the aisles of the libraries they used. New ones, of course. Lisa always put a note inside the book instead of writing on the title page, in case Suzanne had already read it. That way she could give it to someone else. Barbara had taught her that.

Mary Joan served an early lunch and then an afternoon tea with cucumber sandwiches. That was Lisa's first experience with fancy sandwiches without crusts and without peanut butter or ham and cheese. She didn't like them too much but managed to get down three of them, enough to hold her till dinner.

They rested a little longer before setting out for their carriage ride. It was still a little warm at 5, and Lisa felt sorry for the horse that pulled her carriage. She complained that it wasn't right to keep horses out on the hot streets. Mary Joan explained that there were laws about when horses couldn't be used because of the heat and therefore their horse must have been cleared for the weather. Lisa had a strong streak of justice from where nobody knew, and she let everyone know when something had to be corrected. She was trying to curb her outbursts of indignation. Her friends kept telling her to relax and have some fun and stop worrying about everything around her. These friends helped, but it was Lisa that had to do the changing and quieting down. Not easy.

The ride through the city was quite pleasant. Easier than walking. The man who held the reins of the horse was also their guide, and he told them many funny stories about the city as well as giving them some good historic facts. Charleston was a pretty place.

This reminded Lisa of the license plates of South Carolina: SMILING FACES. BEAUTIFUL PLACES. When she first saw those words on her uncle's car, she thought they sounded a little silly. She meant to ask him what they stood for. And now after almost a week in Charleston, she figured out that they told the truth. Everybody was happy and nice to her, and she certainly was seeing beautiful places.

Chapter Eight

Walter took a day off from work so that he could take Lisa back to Folly Beach. He decided Mary Joan needed some rest, too. Even if she came with them, she would have someone to share Lisa's questions with and the pressure of watching a child all day needed to be taken off her. Mary Joan chose to stay at home and catch up on her own activities dealing with the three clubs she belonged to.

Lisa liked Mary Joan but she glad to have a full day just with Walter. They went to the County Park so they didn't have to pack a lunch. Hot dogs and potato chips were yours for the buying. And soda, of course. Walter and his niece enjoyed a great swim in a turbulent sea, ducking or riding each wave that came along. Walter never took his eyes off Lisa. She laughed at him, the way he worried about her. He still watched her.

"Let's go get some food," suggested Walter after a big wave carried them toward shore.

"Good idea. Can we bring it back to the blanket or do we eat it up there?"

"Your choice."

"Let's eat on the beach."

As they munched through their food, Lisa started asking questions. About everything! The carriage horses, the dungeon she visited, the plantation, the slaves back in the old days, and finally, the topic of adoption.

"You don't do this to Mary Joan, do you? Try to make her a walking encyclopedia?"

"Not really. But she knows a lot and doesn't seem to mind my asking about things."

Walter took another potato chip and looked seriously at Lisa before he asked a question.

"Why are you so interested in adoption? Are you planning to adopt a child? Afraid you'll have to wait a few years. Besides you'll have your own some day and won't have to adopt."

"I think that even if I have my own children, I would like to adopt."

"Why?"

"I guess I would just like to have one from every country around the world."

"There are hundreds of countries, Lisa."

"Well, you know what I mean. Five or six, but children different than me. My teacher taught us about the U.N., the United Nations. I'd like a house full of children from all over the world. Is that strange?"

"Yes, I mean for a child of 12, yes, it is. She must have been some teacher."

"He. Mr. Watkins had maps all around the room and about three globes. It's a small world but lots of people. Mr. Watkins used to work for the Peace Corps. I'd like to do that."

"Okay. That's a good ambition. Better than having your own United Nations running through your house. Imagine trying to feed all those children. Besides, Lisa, you would have to be rich to have even just five or six. It's expensive to have a large house and think of all the clothes you'd have to buy. You'd have to marry a millionaire. Nothing wrong with that, of course. But do marry a man you love."

"Of course, but he could make a lot of money."

"Adoption is not as easy as you may think, Lisa. Lots of legal work has to be done. It can be very complicated."

"But you're a lawyer! You could solve all the problems. Oh, Walter, it would be so wonderful for you and Mary Joan to have kids. You would be a great father. And Mary Joan a great mother. And you don't have to try to find the perfect baby. It might be fun to take home a child who's two or three. Even seven or eight."

"Now why would we want a child that old? He or she would already have learned a lot of habits we might not agree with. That would be rough for both us and the child."

"But think how wonderful it would be for him, or her, to finally get a mother and a father. I heard that some children grow up, all the way, without parents."

"Another teacher? Or Mr. Watkins again?"

"Mrs. Beecham. She teaches music and has us listen to a lot of songs from all over the world. She told us about some children who grow up with only other children. They have grown-ups in charge of course. But sometimes there are twenty or thirty children in one group. She showed us some pictures of children from the age of one all the way up to fifteen who had spent their whole lives with each other. No real parents. They must be lonesome. She said they never got tucked into bed the way we are. Daddy always used to tuck me into bed and then read me a good story. He stopped doing that a couple years ago. Found out I liked to read in bed before going to sleep. So now he just kisses me good night and up the stairs I go. But these kids around the world, I don't think they get kissed good night, do you? Well, maybe they do. She said some of the people who work with lots of children are very kind and try to be like parents. Still, she said, none of them has his own parents to kiss them good night. I think that's sad."

"That's some teacher you have. She's probably good friends with Mr. Watkins and they both contribute to UNICEF."

"You know about UNICEF? She had lots of pictures and folders about children from all over. You could take one of those children."

"Lisa, you're so worked up about this. Suppose the child were to come all the way over to Charleston from a foreign country. Wouldn't he miss all his friends? That would be awful."

"Not as bad as not having your own parents."

"Boy, she really brainwashed you kids. Do all your friends feel the way you do?"

"Not really. A few do but most of my friends just want to play all day."

"And why not? You're all children."

"But there are other children, Walter. Maybe right here in Charleston. You won't have to go around the world. Maybe there's someone right here who would love to have some parents. Then he wouldn't miss anyone. He could visit his friends, right? Once in a while."

"Good lunch. I'm going to take a few moments of sleep. You can read or sleep some. See you later." He rolled over, closed his eyes, and smiled.

Lisa took out her book. And smiled. She liked her uncle.

When Walter woke up, he quickly told Lisa about Mary Joan's idea of having Lisa take some art lessons at the Gibbs Art Museum. They have a couple of classes for children, Monday through Friday.

"Do you have art in your school?" he asked.

"A little. But it's not really my thing."

"Well, we can go down and see what the classes offer. I know one of them has the class drawing little animals. Live animals—in cages of course. Would that interest you?"

"Okay, I guess."

"They're both in the morning. From 9 to 11. I think you would enjoy it, where you could meet other kids."

"Are you trying to get rid of me for part of the day?"

"Lisa, I really believe you would find it fun. And it has been a little tiring for Mary Joan, having you all day long. She really likes you and says you're fun to take around the city. But we have almost three weeks left and you two could run out of conversation. Come on, give it a chance. Let's go there tomorrow morning and see if we can register. They say both classes run all summer, and you can go for a week or two. Just start in whenever. And you bring your lunch and you all eat in the back gardens. It would be fun to talk with other children, Lisa."

"Okay. I'll try it. As long as it's not arts and crafts. Drawing animals might be fun. I have a cousin in California, Lawrence, who just loves little animals. I'll send him some of my drawings."

"And we have some more ideas. We thought you might enjoy a trip to Beaufort, a small town south of here. It's also on the coast and has some beautiful old homes. We could try their beach, and I hear they have some great restaurants. How about Saturday?"

"Sure. I'd love to go to the beach. And, Walter, I really think I would enjoy those art lessons. It might be fun to meet some southern kids. Hear their accents."

"Mary Joan also wants to take you to one of the historical houses. She thinks you would enjoy the Nathaniel Russell House. Or the Edmondston-Alston House. Both are beautiful and have lots of history. And you definitely have to go over to Mt. Pleasant again to see and visit the aircraft carrier, the Yorktown. We were over that way when we visited Ft. Moultrie. The Yorktown was in service during our more recent wars and you can see how planes actually landed on the ship's runway. Fascinating."

"Do they land now?"

"No. But they've kept some planes on board for you to examine, and there are films on how they landed."

"When do I go to the art museum?"

"Tomorrow morning, okay? You're an easy guest, Lisa. We were a little concerned when your father first mentioned it. But when Mom and Dad raved about your visit with them, we felt sure it would be a great experience for all of us. We originally thought two weeks, but when your father said that he and Barbara were going to Europe for a month, we signed up. And we're glad we did. But I do think the art lessons will help Mary Joan and be a lot of fun for you. You should have some children to communicate with. You must miss your friends at home."

"A little. I'd like to meet some kids."

"How about another swim, young lady?"

"Beat you down there. Last one in is a rotten egg."

Chapter Nine

Mary Joan came a little early to pick up Lisa from her first art lesson. She had given herself an easy morning and was hoping Walter was right about Lisa enjoying the lessons enough to keep her going to them for at least this week, and maybe the next. She hadn't realized that taking care of children could be so exhausting.

Lisa was the first one out of the class and she was smiling!

"It's great," she said with more enthusiasm than usual.

"Terrific," said Mary Joan.

"Could I bring my lunch tomorrow? Most of the kids eat in the garden after class. Looks like fun."

"Sure. Tell me what you like for sandwiches, and we'll send you off each morning with your favorite. Now tell me about the class."

"Well, first, the teacher is great. She introduced me to everyone and gave me a little more attention in the beginning. But when she saw that I already knew some of the basics, she just included me with her introduction to the week's work. And guess what it was? Sketching a baby gerbil! Just like my cousin's gerbil. Adorable. He was moving around a lot until she gave him some food. Then we all started to sketch him from where we sat. When he started moving again, we all laughed and took time to look at each other drawings. Ms. Jenkins explained a lot about how to use the pencil and how to shadow light and dark. And the two hours were up. So fast. Then some of the kids came over to my chair and introduced themselves. Some of them live right on your street."

"What are their names?"

"There's Ann Johnson. And Minerva Wallis. And Colin Jacoby. And Billy something."

"I know the Johnson's. And I think the Wallis family just moved in last month."

"Minerva looks like fun. Ann seems a bit snobbish, but I can take care of that. Billy, can't think of his last name, he's funny. And a good artist. His gerbil was a riot."

Mary Joan suggested that they eat out. Knowing how much Lisa loved hamburgers, she drove to a small place down by the river. They were early for lunch so had no problem finding a parking place. And no problem getting a booth in front of the window so they could watch the yachts and sailboats going up and down the river.

"Do you go in those kind of boats?" asked Lisa. She didn't know what all of them were called. She had seen some of the ones with large white sails on a lake near her home but wondered if their name were simply sailboats. During the recess that day the kids in class called them that. But kids don't know everything.

"You mean the sailboats? And the yachts? Walter and I don't own any boats, but we do go sailing once in a while with some friends. I was hoping we would be asked to go while you were here. I don't want to be pushy. We have almost two more weeks for them to think about it. But the yachts. No, we don't know anyone that well to get asked onto a yacht. Pretty though, aren't they? After lunch we can drive over to the boat basin, where they "park" their boats, and walk around the docks and get a good look at them."

"Good. I hope your friends remember to ask us to go on their sailboat. That would be a blast."

The waiter came, took their order and Lisa continued telling Mary Joan about the funny antics of Billy and some of the other boys. This was interrupted by the delivery of their hamburgers. After finishing up with some banana cream pie, they headed for the boat basin.

They walked up and down connected docks that brought them past large yachts, very large sailboats, as well as small vessels of all shapes. Lisa was more than thrilled. She made another decision. When she was her own grown-up person, she would live by the sea. The Gulf in the south, the Atlantic, or the Pacific. For now, she was glad all her relatives lived next to water.

When they passed by an empty bench, Mary Joan suggested that they sit there for awhile and watch some of the boats go out and new ones come in. For the first time Lisa wasn't asking questions. She just sat there and watched the people and the boat activity all around her. Her aunt wondered if her silence had anything to do with Walter's talk, which of course he had later shared with his wife. She just accepted the silence and enjoyed the boat scene along with Lisa.

Chapter Ten

"You're acting like a five-year old!" said Lisa to the girl sitting in front of her.

"And what are you acting like?" asked Ann with much malice in her voice.

"Well, I'm not bragging about how wealthy I am or how many servants I have or how clever my mother is. Minerva just moved here. You are giving her a GREAT impression of Charleston."

"You don't even live here. Who are you to talk?" Ann came back defensively.

"You're nothing but a snob. A real snob! You've been bragging ever since I got here and you're mean, too. Telling Minerva that anybody who's anybody in Charleston has to have hired servants. How dare you! That women who did their own housework shouldn't live downtown! What nerve!"

"Forget it, Lisa. I don't care what Ann says. I've been picked on before and like my mother says, "You just keep getting thicker skin, darling. They soon learn you're not the one to pick on." Leave her alone, Lisa. We have an assignment to do. Let it go," pleaded Minerva.

"No I won't. She's just a skinny jerk who has nothing but money to brag about. I'm tired of it. She told you the other day that you'll never be a Charlestonian just because you weren't born here. Didn't that make you mad?"

"No, Lisa, it didn't. Leave her alone."

"Aall right, daarling, I'll leave her alown. Do I sound like her? With that fake southern accent? Just who does she think she is? I guess she believes she's "the belle of the ball". She's not even pretty.

Stringy hair and a long jaw. All she's got are the pretty clothes she wears," cooed Lisa as she strutted around her table.

"Lisa, Ms. Jenkins is looking over here. Better be quiet," whispered Minerva.

"I don't care what she thinks," Lisa pouted.

"Lisa, may I see you outside?" asked Ms. Jenkins coming down the aisle.

Lisa stopped in her tracks and nodded as she made her way to the door. The two of them stepped out into the hallway, and Ms. Jenkins quietly closed the door behind them.

"Lisa, why are you being so mean? You've been picking on Ann for a couple of days now, and it has got to stop."

"It's a private matter."

"No it's not. Everyone in the class can hear you. Our class was, and still is, such a lovely class. But these past few days you've been saying such awful things to Ann. What has she done to you?"

"Nothing." Lisa shuffled her feet as she leaned against the wall.

"Stand up, Lisa. I can't allow such arguments in our class. Can you tell me what the problem is? Did Ann do anything to you? She has always been nice to all the kids. I can't imagine her doing anything nasty to you."

"All she talks about is how wonderful her mother is. And how rich they are. It gets on my nerves."

"And making fun of her accent. Why it's a true Charleston accent. I have it. So do most of the kids."

"Well, on her it sounds fake."

"Well, it's not. Now there's no need to cry," as she saw some tears slide down Lisa's cheek. "Whatever it is, it's just a silly girl fight. Being 12 years old is not easy, for either of you. But you have to learn to control it. You simply cannot insult anyone without a good reason. And I don't see any reason."

"I just don't like her."

"That's not a reason. I want to share something with you, Lisa. Ann has had a lot of problems this year. Her father walked out on the family a few months ago and left her mother terribly upset. Ann also. She loved her father, and her whole world turned upside down when he left. And there was a bit of a scandal with it all. That had a terrible effect on Ann. I knew her from last summer and I saw the awful change in her when she came back to class this year. Everyone, except Minerva, knows all about what had happened. Everyone has been especially kind to her. Then you joined the class and within a few days, you're going after her. Why? Did she do anything to you?"

"I told you. She never stops bragging about her mother. And about all the money she has. Telling Minerva she has to get a servant if she wants to live downtown. She's the one who's mean!"

"She shouldn't have told Minerva that, you're right. But it's not that serious. Not to cause such a fight like you had. Now, Lisa, I have to go back to the class. Dry your eyes and wash your face in the bathroom and come in as soon as you can."

Ms, Jenkins left Lisa standing there with her head down and her feet still shuffling. Lisa walked into the bathroom and cried some more when she was alone. She had a good cry. And felt very sorry for herself as she threw lots of water in her face. Her heart was thumping and her hands were shaking. She was so confused. She knew Ann was wrong but she didn't know about her father and his leaving her family.

She was glad her mother had not walked out of her life. Or had she?

Lisa dried her face and hands and walked slowly back to the classroom. Having no idea what was going to happen next, she simply slid into her seat, took her pencil and made more marks on the paper that already had half of a mouse. She looked over at Ann and then at Minerva. Ann did nothing; Minerva smiled. Ms. Jenkins went on with the lesson and for a good half hour, all was peaceful. Then they broke for a recess and had a chance to see other student's drawings. Lisa walked over to Ann.

"I'm sorry for yelling at you, Ann. I've been upset this week – with a family problem – I shouldn't have yelled at you."

"No servant at your aunt's house?" Ann commented with a smirk.

Lisa was ready to pounce right back but she held herself close to her heart and her thinking. She told herself Ann also has a problem and she better leave her alone. She walked over to Minerva and they chatted about their drawings.

"What did Ms. Jenkins say to you?" asked Minerva.

"Not much. Just to stop yelling at Ann."

199

Billy made a joke about his mouse, and Lisa got to laughing. She liked Billy who always made her laugh, even when he wasn't funny. It was just his way of expressing himself that pleased her. She then walked over to his table and made some remarks about his drawing. They both had a good laugh.

Minerva said quietly to Lisa when she returned to her table, "Billy defended you before, when you were outside with Ms. Jenkins."

"How did he do that?" asked Lisa.

"Just said he knew you had a real problem. His father is a good friend of your uncle. They go fishing together. Anyway, his father told him that your mother committed suicide a few years ago, and he decided that all of us should know that. He guessed that was your problem, why you were so angry with Ann always talking about her mother," offered Minerva.

Jason, one of Billy's friends whispered, "Ms. Jenkins was shocked when Billy made that announcement. She told the class that some people have problems that cannot be shared and that sometimes these problems make people so sad that they do things that are not very nice, or something like that."

"Gosh, everyone was talking about me? That's awful."

"I was glad to hear Billy tell us that. It helped," said Ann.

"Helped? How could my mother's suicide help you?" asked Lisa who really felt like punching Ann. But somehow, she didn't punch her. She didn't even want to punch her after a few seconds. She just wanted to get out of the classroom and away from everybody.

It was almost time for lunch. Ms. Jenkins perched herself on the corner of her table and sat looking at the kids for a long minute before talking. Then she quietly and kindly said, "Well, we had a good drawing lesson and we had a good lesson today on how to deal with other people. It's not always an easy thing to do, but you all did it quite well. Thanks to Billy and Jason and Minerva and Ann and Lisa. See you in the garden." She hopped off the table, grabbed her bag of lunch, and was the first one at the picnic table. The kids filled the rest of the table and two of the other tables. They were all laughing and joking around. And soon everyone was busy eating.

As Lisa passed by Billy already munching his sandwich, she gave him a high sign which really said "Thank you." He just smiled back and returned the high sign.

Ann put her bag of lunch on the place next to Lisa. As she sat down, she asked, "Okay?"

"Okay." was Lisa's answer.

Chapter Eleven

"Sorry I missed that trip to the zoo. I just couldn't get away. Glad I could do it today though," said Walter.

"And I'm glad we're out fishing. I did some fishing in Florida but this is the first time fishing from a boat," said Lisa with a laugh. "I'm glad you can take these days off from work. If you weren't in your own business, if you were working for a company, could you take so many days off to be with me?"

"No way. That is one of the joys of owning your own company. You set the schedule. This time of year is slow so I'm taking advantage of that. Just had to teach you how to put a worm on a hook," Walter said as he handed her another worm. "Let's see you do this one by yourself."

"I have a cousin, in California, who says "yuk" all the time. And now I'm going to say it. Yuk! Give it to me. I'll do it."

Walter handed her the can of worms and watched as Lisa gingerly pulled one out. He laughed and encouraged her, "Go on, catch a fish. They must be hungry. I've caught four already. And I'm a better golfer than a fisherman."

"I wish Mary Joan was with us now. She told me she doesn't like putting worms on hooks either. Think it's a boy's, I mean man's, thing?"

"Maybe. But Mary Joan is good at it. She just had too many things to do today. How was the art class? Only two more days left to catch up with Picasso."

"I'm going to miss it. I've made some good friends there. Billy and Minerva and Ann. And Ms. Jenkins. And I learned a lot about drawing. My teacher at home will be surprised when I show her my pictures. I have eight to show her. Two of them are too awful to take home."

"Have I seen them all?"

"Think so. Oh, I just had a nibble. But no fish."

"Still have the worm?"

"Yes. Yuk!"

"I have plenty more if you lose him," said Walter with a teasing laugh.

There was a long silence. Both man and girl were thinking. Then Lisa said, "Walter, Billy Williamson said his father goes fishing with you."

"Yes m'am. Good ole Joe Williamson. We've been fishing for about eight years. He's good. Of course he doesn't catch as many as I do. But he's good. What's his boy like?"

"Billy?" She took a beat before continuing. "He's one of my best friends there. He's a very funny boy." She took another beat. "And a very kind boy."

"That doesn't surprise me. His father's the same way. Very funny and a very kind person," assured Walter.

Lisa didn't want to say anymore about Billy. She was glad Walter liked his father. She wondered if she were like her father. Guess you're like the people who bring you up.

"You should have a son. Or a daughter." said Lisa.

"Where did that come from?" asked Walter.

"Thinking about Billy being like his father. You and Mary Joan would be like your son. Or daughter. Or they would be like you. Wouldn't that be nice?"

"No. Lisa, don't push. You've already given me much to think about. No more, okay? Are you ready for Myrtle Beach this weekend? They got lots of rides and fun stuff to do. And great little places to eat. We can have Frogmore Stew."

"What's that?"

"Sausage, shrimp, and slices of corn on the cob. Delicious. And the shrimp have to be peeled. By you. They're served with the shells still on. Messy but so good."

"You're making me hungry."

"Okay. How about a sandwich? Check the line first to be sure there's no fish on it." Walter said as he opened the lunch box.

"The line's empty. The fish are probably having their lunch somewhere else. They'll come back later. Is there a peanut butter there?" asked Lisa.

"Sure is and it's all yours."

"And some soda?"

"More? You just finished one."

"I'll split one with you," suggested Lisa.

"No, I'm having a beer. You can have another but let it last for awhile."

"Your father used to split cans of soda with me. Guess he doesn't drink beer."

"No, he doesn't. Never did. Your line's jumping!" yelled Walter.

"I'll get it." She pulled the line up. No fish. She laughed and decided to eat her sandwich. "I'll fish later."

Chapter Twelve

"Check your closets? And the bathroom? And under the bed? I don't want to send anything, like shoes," said Mary Joan.

"Checked and double checked everything. Got it all," Lisa answered as she climbed into the car. "I don't like leaving, you know."

"And we don't like seeing you leave," chirped Walter.

As they drove through downtown Charleston, Lisa waved goodbye to the houses and the gardens that she loved to walked through. It was a terrific month. A few problems but they were all solved. As problems usually are. She learned a lot but she would think about them later, if she thought of them at all. The past is the past, someone had said to her. The future is in the future. What's important is the present. What's going on right now. Well, right now she was content to sit back and watch the scenery go by.

"You will write to us, Lisa. won't you? We want to hear all about your new classes and if you decided to join the newspaper staff," asked Mary Joan.

"I'll write. Will you write back?

"Of course." Mary Joan continued her questioning. "What was your favorite happening? What did you enjoy doing the most?"

"Everything. I don't know if I can pick out one thing. I loved the zoo. And I had a ball at Myrtle Beach. And of course I loved swimming in your ocean. And the art classes were great. I have some new friends now. Besides you. I'm sorry we didn't get to do some scuba diving, but you explained to me why we couldn't."

"You're young, my friend. Plenty of time to do a lot of scuba diving," said Walter.

"I know. I just really wanted to find out how it was like to dive without all those rubber clothes on. And to see schools of colorful fish. But you're right. I got plenty of time. I wish I could talk Daddy into trying it out. Barbara, too."

"Talking about your father, hope you're going to talk him into coming down here on his next vacation. After Europe, we might seem a little dull. But you come with him and you can show him the town," Walter added.

"What would you show him, Lisa?" asked Mary Joan.

"Definitely Middleton Plantation. Definitely the carriage ride. And definitely Fort Sumter. I'd give him two days there."

"I'm sorry, Lisa. We just didn't have the time, and I couldn't take any more days off. But when you come down with your father and Barbara, we'll spend three days there. My brother is a history nut. He might even want a week out there."

They got close to the airport and everyone went silent. Goodbyes are sometimes very difficult. Especially when a child is involved. The next time Walter and Mary Joan would see Lisa, she no doubt would be a young lady.

Going as far as they could because of security, Lisa's aunt and uncle both gave her a strong hug as her suitcase was being searched. Lisa was so fascinated watching the woman look through her things that she hardly said goodbye. But after walking past the electric eye, she turned and gave them a big wave. She took her suitcase, turned it so the wheels were on the ground and rolling, and blew Walter and Mary Joan a big kiss. In fact, she blew them a few kisses.

Chapter Thirteen

Settling into her seat by the window, she felt so happy. She was sorry she wasn't going to see them soon. She really enjoyed herself with them. They were so good to her. In spite of some of the problems she had. "Nice people," she thought.

As she opened her book to read about the adventures of knights in shining armor, Mary Joan and Walter talked about her all the way home.

"It was a great month, Walter. She's a lovely child. She won't be a child much longer. Maybe the next time we see her will be at her wedding."

"Her wedding! Come on, Mary Joan, she's only twelve."

"They marry young these days."

"I hope not that young. Let her find out about life first. Let her go the Europe, to the Orient. To Africa. Let her explore the world. Then she'll be ready to find the one she wants to spend the rest of her life with."

"In a little white cottage with a path to the garden gate? That's not Lisa, if I got to know her at all," said Mary Joan.

"Doesn't have to be a little white cottage. We didn't have one. We fell in love and took an apartment."

"You're right. She just needs to fall in love. And want to spend her life with him."

"Okay. Just remember Lisa is only twelve! Good kid. But still a kid."

The End

Book Five

Lisa in New York

Chapter One

The plane kept flying over the city, over the ocean, over land that was not populated. Lisa wasn't worried but she did wonder why the pilot came on the loudspeaker every few minutes to tell everyone that they would be landing in just a few minutes. Seems that Newark Airport had too many planes coming in that day and at that moment, so Lisa's plane would have to circle the airport until permission was granted to land.

Funny, Lisa thought, that she had to land in Newark, New Jersey, in order to visit her Aunt Sally who lived in New York. Her father had explained to her that New York City was not very large a place for building airports but had millions of people living there that needed airport service. Thus an airport was built on the other side of the Hudson River and on New Jersey property and called Newark Airport as it was right next to the city of Newark. People from both New York City and New Jersey used the same airport. All day, every day. And now every minute! Lisa figured they had been circling the airport for over an hour. Actually, it was only ten minutes. But Lisa was thinking about her aunt down there, worrying where she was and why didn't she come down to earth.

The steward appeared at her side with comforting words. "Any minute now and we'll be on the ground."

Lisa gave him a big smile. "I hope my aunt is still waiting for me."

"Of course she is. In the middle of a busy day like this, we often have to circle around until there's room for us. She'll be waiting."

Lisa gave him another big smile.

Maybe she would be an airline stewardess. They meet all kinds of people and fly in and out of many different cities. Great way to travel! Last summer she wanted to be a lawyer, the summer before, an actress. As she was still only thirteen, she had plenty of time to make her final decision. The aunt she was visiting this summer was an elementary school principal. Would she want to be a principal or maybe even a teacher? She didn't think so, but 3 weeks with Aunt Sally might change that. She also wanted to write but she had found out that a lot of writers near starved to death. She was on the newspaper staff at her school and loved it. Maybe a reporter. Travel the world and write about what she sees and hears!

As she daydreamed about her future life, the plane straightened out and came down for a landing. She loved flying. Maybe she could be a pilot.

Walking out of the plane and up the ramp to the terminal, she spotted Aunt Sally standing right in front of a crowd of smiling faces. She, too, was wearing a smile. Everyone was glad the plane had finally landed even if twenty minutes late.

Lisa recognized Aunt Sally from the photos her Dad had. She didn't look like either her father or her uncle, Walter. She was short, thin and bony, had very blue eyes separated by a long nose. She was smiling but in an officious way. Lisa returned her smile.

"Hello, Aunt Sally. Sorry we're late."

"Not your fault, Lisa. Come, let's get your suitcase," her aunt directed.

Nothing was said until they collected Lisa's belongings. Then they headed for the exit door where they waited for a bus to take them into New York City.

"It's warm for June. Warmer than home," said Lisa.

"Believe we're going to have a hot summer. You brought light clothing, didn't you? What you have on is too heavy for New York."

"I have some cotton skirts and blouses. And two cotton dresses."

"We can always go to Macy's if you want more. I live in the Village where there are lovely dress shops, but they are a bit expensive. Macy's has large selections of clothing," said Aunt Sally with assurance.

"I've heard of it. Also Lord & Taylor's and Sak's Fifth Avenue."

"Too expensive. For children."

"Is this our bus?" asked Lisa as a long line started to move forward toward a very large bus.

Her aunt did not answer her but simply guided Lisa up the few steps after leaving her suitcase for the bus driver to store into the belly of the bus.

"Sit down here," Aunt Sally pointed to the two front seats. Lisa started to tell her about having the same seats in the jitney out at Kennedy Airport. But decided not to. She didn't know her aunt well enough to judge her reaction to a lot of talking. She would remain quiet, and let her aunt start the conversations. This was her fifth summer of visiting relatives around the country, and she was almost an expert in sizing up people. Getting to this point though cost her some difficult moments. She would stay quiet.

"Now there's a sight, Lisa. The New York skyline. It was one of the features that attracted me here. Thirty years ago. I just knew it was the city for me," sighed Aunt Sally.

"So many tall buildings and so close together. Which one is the Empire State Building?" asked Lisa.

"A little over to the right of the center, to the right of that other very tall building. You can't see the street below but it's on 34 Street, the same street as Macy's."

"We can go there, right? Up to the top?"

"Yes, of course. And lots of other buildings. We'll visit the Lincoln Center complex, Rockefeller City, the United Nations. Unfortunately, they took the World Trade Buildings away from us. You know about the terrorist attack in 2001," remarked Aunt Sally with some anger mixed with sadness.

"Yes, I remember. My father explained it to me. He bought me a book filled with photographs from that day."

"My brother, thank heavens, is good at that sort of thing. Keeps himself informed and anyone else who is willing to listen and learn. Our father was like that, too."

"I love your father. Grandfather, Grandy. He taught me so much when I visited them in Florida. I was only 9 then but he treated me like I was older. My grandmother, your mother, was also teaching me all the time. It was my first summer away from Dad. I had such a good time with them."

"Yes, they told me. In fact, it was their enthusiasm that convinced me to take you on this summer. Three weeks is a long time but I had decided anyway not to take any courses. I have lots of work at my school, but most of it can wait until August when you're gone. The days I must be at school these next few weeks, I figure I can take you with me. In between seeing New York, you can learn something about our education system in the elementary schools. Would that interest you?"

"Oh, I'd love to see your school. I could even help you with some of your work. I'm good at figures if they're not too complicated. And I can file papers, alphabetically."

Their bus took a long, slow curve around and into a tunnel. Lisa had never seen such heavy traffic and was never in a tunnel. A little scary yet thrilling to think about being under a river for almost ten minutes. Coming out on the other side and into a terminal filled with hundreds of buses and thousands of people kept Lisa quiet without trying.

Her aunt carried the suitcase and bustling through the crowds almost left Lisa behind.

"Keep walking, Lisa. Follow me," Aunt Sally bellowed.

They finally made it to the sidewalk and found other crowds moving up and down the street. And a lot of taxicabs along the curbs.

"With this suitcase, we'll take a taxi," said Aunt Sally as she arranged for the suitcase to go into the trunk of the next cab and stepped back to give Lisa room to get into the back seat. When Lisa tried to let Aunt Sally get in first, she was rebuffed with "You do the sliding over." They headed downtown and soon found themselves outside a tall brick building. Aunt Sally collected the suitcase and led them up two steps and into a well-lighted foyer. She opened a door with a large key. An elevator took them to the fourth floor, and they walked down the hallway to the door marked 4C. Aunt Sally used the other key on a fancy key ring to open the door and walked straight in, simply expecting Lisa to follow. She did. But then she waited for the next command. She had already learned that Aunt Sally was in charge.

She stood in the middle of a large, pleasant room while her aunt disappeared into what had to be the kitchen, mumbling, "I'm having a cup of tea. Would you rather have iced tea?"

"Do you have any soda?" asked Lisa.

"Soda is not good for you. Iced tea?"

"Okay."

"Your bedroom is the small one on your left. Why don't you start unpacking?" said Aunt Sally without a question in her voice.

"Sure." Lisa took her suitcase into a room just wide enough for a window. A bed, a chair, and a tiny table for a bedside lamp did not discourage Lisa. She was grateful to have a room by herself. And a window. Looking out, she saw the rooftops of a lot of buildings. This allowed her to look beyond the street beneath and over several streets. There were children running around and that pleased Lisa. None of them were over six years old, but she would look for some teenagers when she took a walk. She was definitely going to take a walk and be alone with her thoughts. She started unpacking but saw there were no hangers in the closet, either for skirts and pants or for shirts. There was also no chest of drawers. She went back into the living room and asked Aunt Sally through the doorless kitchen if there were any hangers she could have.

"How many do you need?"

"Oh, five or six would do. And are there any skirt hangers?"

"I'll get some from my room," her aunt shouted. "Sit down and relax for a few minutes. Sit," she said as if a command.

Lisa sat. She thought of a funny joke her uncle in South Carolina had told her but decided Aunt Sally would probably not enjoy it. This might be a difficult summer, she thought. But she had had so many discouraging beginnings of her summer travels which turned eventually into wonderful vacations. Patience!

Her aunt came in with a tray of drinks and some cookies and also sat.

"Well, my dear, you're in New York. Welcome. What would you like to do this afternoon? We have about four hours before dinner. You do like roast chicken, don't you?"

"Sure." And took a cookie with her iced tea. She was hungrier than she thought.

"Would you enjoy walking around Greenwich Village? We're so different from the rest of Manhattan . No skyscrapers down here. It was settled, you see, much before uptown. Actually, Manhattan was first settled down by the battery. Several miles downtown. Where we are now was all farmland at first. Fourteenth Street was considered uptown. Perhaps we should start your sightseeing with the battery. And some day we'll take one of the boats down there over to Staten Island, although I don't know why. There's nothing to see over there. Why don't you change your clothes to more comfortable shoes and a lighter skirt and blouse. Have you finished unpacking yet?"

"Could I have some hangers?"

"Oh, yes. I forgot. I'll get some from my closet."

They stood up, each going to her own room. Lisa peeked into her aunt's room as she passed it and saw that it was large, had two windows and lots of furniture. She didn't care. As long as she had a door she could close and a window she could open.

Aunt Sally brought in four blouse hangers and two skirt hangers.

"Here you are. You can double up on a few of them. There's no room here for a chest of drawers, but you can keep a lot of your things in your suitcase under the bed. I took this apartment because of the living room and the large bedroom. I figured any guest I might have would soon tire of her small room and leave after a few days. I'm not much for company. But you're not company, you're family. Now let me show you the bathroom and where you can put your things."

Walking into another small room off the living room, Aunt Sally gave Lisa a shelf of her own for her toiletries.

"I like showers and I have a good shower. But if you prefer a tub, just be careful to use the bathmat. Here's a hook for your towel and facecloth. The supply of towels are right here behind the door. Take what you need. Well, now I'll let you freshen up and get some cooler clothes on. Do wear more comfortable shoes. We'll be doing some walking and our sidewalks are made of the hardest cement."

There were so many instructions and so much to get used to that Lisa didn't have the energy to ask her aunt why the cement in New York was harder than at home.

"I'll get changed," said Lisa as she left the bathroom. But after closing her door, she plopped down on the bed, exhausted. Aunt Sally was nothing like her father, her uncle, or her grandparents. She had brought a diary and she wanted to describe her initial thoughts, but she was too tired. Later.

She must have dozed off because the single knock on her door startled her. She sat up but had no idea where she was. Her aunt called out.

"Lisa, are you ready?"

"Yes. Almost. Be right out."

She quickly changed her clothes, combed her hair, grabbed her shoulder bag. She would hang up her clothes later. When she opened the door, there stood her aunt.

"You didn't change your shoes."

"I forgot. They're right here."

Slipping on her sandals, she hurried out to the living room. She gave up the idea of brushing her teeth when she saw her aunt standing by the open front door.

"They don't look very comfortable," commented Aunt Sally looking at Lisa's shoes. As she rang for the elevator, she gave Lisa a business card.

"Here, put this in your bag. My address and telephone number in case we get separated. This is a big city, and you should know how to get home. You're too young to have a key to the apartment. Just sit on the step outside and wait for me. But do try to keep me in sight. If you lose me, take a taxi. You do have some money with you, right? I'll pay you back."

A block from the apartment building, they got on a bus marked "Staten Island Ferry". Lisa enjoyed the ride down to the battery. There was no conversation for which Lisa was grateful. At the last stop, they had a choice of a boat to Staten Island or take a walk through Battery Park. They walked and talked. Aunt Sally relaxed or it seemed so to Lisa and their conversation was mainly about the harbor, some of the more famous buildings, and some history of what was known as lower Manhattan.

They then walked along a river until they came to what was known as South Street Seaport.

"Why don't we walk up this hill a few blocks and you can see where the World Trade Buildings were. It's still a hole in the ground."

"Yes, I'd like that. You're a good walker, Aunt Sally. And you were right. The cement is hard."

"We'll get you more comfortable shoes tomorrow."

As they climbed the cement hill, they passed many small shops. Lisa was tempted to buy some things, but Aunt Sally suggested she wait a few days before spending her money.

They stared at the big hole and some of the construction going on. The men in the trucks looked as small as ants. Lisa was duly impressed, and her aunt scored another point for bringing her there.

"Do you think I could ask that man inside the barricade some questions? Looks like he works here. Sort of an interview for my school paper?" asked Lisa.

"You may try. But do make it short. He's resting and might not want to be bothered."

Lisa took out her small notebook (which she always carried) and approached the man who was now leaning on the barricade and staring into the hole known as Ground Zero, she later found out.

"Excuse me, sir. I'm on the staff of my high school newspaper. May I ask you a few questions about the work you do?"

"Such as."

"I'm not from New York. But everyone in the country knows what happened last September. And I know my classmates will want to know about the work you do and….how ….you feel about working here."

"School newspaper, eh? Kids, eh? Well, I feel pretty proud about my work here. I don't make important decisions. I do what I'm told. You see those big machines, that move all that dirt? I drive one of those. I'm on a break now. It's hard work but I feel good about helping everyone here to clean this mess up."

Lisa wrote as fast as she could. "Have you been working here long?"

"Since day one. Since those rotten guys hit us. You understand what happened?"

"Not really. I have a book of photographs of that day, and it was awful. But I really don't understand it, what happened. And why."

"Well, sweetheart, we live in a great country. The best. We're free over here. And a lot of people are jealous of us. And I guess afraid of us. Cause we're so big and powerful. Nothing to be afraid of. Cause we're good people. We don't mean no harm to anybody. We'd like everyone to be like us. Happy and free. It's a great world, don't you think? But you can't keep hating. Can't be happy if you hate. You tell those kids back home that all this happened because of hate. Teaches a good lesson, right?"

Lisa kept writing but murmured, "Yes." She thanked him. Quite profusely. Then she went back to her aunt who was patiently standing by.

On the way down hill to get a bus that would bring them back to the Village, Aunt Sally suggested, not commanded, that they save the chicken for tomorrow night and have a seafood dinner in the South Street Seaport complex, as long as they were there.

"That's a wonderful idea, Aunt Sally. I adore seafood, simply adore it."

"Settled."

They walked around to choose a restaurant and found just what they wanted, right on the river's edge. After a delicious dinner, they walked around some more and then gladly headed for the bus. The ride home was filled with Lisa going through her notes of the interview with the worker at Ground Zero and with Aunt Sally answering all her questions.

Chapter Two

While Aunt Sally was taking her shower, Lisa decided to start her diary. Curling as best as she could on her bed, she wrote in large letters: LISA IN NEW YORK. She thought for a few minutes, then filled the page with her opinions of her aunt:

> I met my Aunt Sally, the last relative to visit during my summers. She lives in a small apartment in a section of New York called Greenwich Village. This is my first time in an apartment. They're nice but only made for one person. The room I sleep in is really a den – TINY! Aunt Sally's bedroom is nice though. And her bathroom would be nice if I didn't have to share it with her. So far she seems ok. Very strict like a lot of teachers. But I think she likes me. She kept checking my shoes when we were walking in the park down by the battery. My feet started to hurt, and she knew it. Didn't say anything but that we would buy some comfortable shoes tomorrow. We ate in a restaurant in a place called the South Street Seaport and had shrimp and a plate of clams. She likes seafood, too. I think she's nicer than she thinks she is. She let me talk a lot on the way home. I hope this is going to be a good month. I'm going to ask for some iced tea and then I'll write about all the things I saw today, especially where the World Trade Center was. And the man I interviewed.

"Aunt Sally, could I have an iced tea?" Lisa called into the bathroom.
"I'll be out in a minute."
Coming out into the living room and wearing a good-looking navy blue bathrobe, Aunt Sally headed for the kitchen. "I'll have one, too. Are you going to take a shower now? I left the lights on."

"I'd like to take one in the morning. Okay?"

"As you wish. Then turn off the lights, please. Now let's relax with a long and cold iced tea. Tell me about your father, Lisa. Is he happy with Barbara, his new wife? I suppose that's a foolish question. He was so unhappy these past few years. Do you like Barbara?" asked Aunt Sally as she adjusted the air-conditioning and sat lengthwise on the sofa.

This left the large chair by the window or the smaller chair facing the television. She plopped in the large chair, too tired to watch any T.V. Sipping her iced tea, she told her aunt about Barbara and Kevin, her half brother, who was born last year. Aunt Sally was a good listener. Although she did ask lots of questions.

"Do you enjoy your school work? What subject do you enjoy most? Do you have difficulty with any one in particular?"

"Not so fast," Lisa answered kindly. "Yes, I like school and I like English best. And I do have difficulty with science. And a little with math. Algebra, ugh!"

"Perhaps I can help you a little," her aunt said. "But not tonight. It's been a busy day for both of us. Tomorrow we'll start off in Macy's for some shoes. Then we can go right up the street to the Empire State Building. Then perhaps a leisurely walk up Fifth Avenue. Have some lunch in Lord & Taylor's where there is a very nice soup bar."

"What's a soup bar?" asked Lisa.

"You sit in a high stool at a bar that mainly serves soup. In the winter, it's vegetable barley or tomato. In the summer, it's cold fruit soup or hot vegetable barley."

"That last soup must be good if they have it all the time."

"Yes, it is. But you might like to try the cold soup. Have you ever had cold soup?"

"Sure, lots of time. Barbara makes cold peach soup. I love it."

"Oh, good. After lunch, we can continue walking up to Rockefeller Plaza. Unfortunately they don't have ice-skating this time of the year. But it's a place I think you'll enjoy seeing. Now let's think about going to bed. A little early but you can read in bed if you'd like. There's a good lamp near your head."

"I love reading in bed. And I have a great book."

"Well, Lisa, let me turn off the lights in here and lock up. Don't open your window with the air-conditioning. You can knock on my door if there's anything you need."

"Thank you, Aunt Sally. It was a wonderful day and I'm awfully glad I'm here. See you in the morning."

"Goodnight, dear."

Chapter Three

"A few more minutes here and we'll head up to Central Park," suggested Aunt Sally.

"Central Park! Wow. Gram and Grandy told me all about Central Park, how they have Shakespeare plays for free and how a lot of people bring their picnic and blankets on the line waiting to get in. Could we do that? Not now of course. But some day?"

"Yes, that would be fun. I usually do it once or twice a year. But today we'll just walk around the lower park where they have what they still call a zoo. Years ago it was a fine zoo with all kinds of animals but evidently some animal protection groups complained and most of the animals are gone now. Of course, they were caged up in small areas, and I suppose it was a little cruel. But most of them were born in the cages so they wouldn't know the difference. Anyway they rebuilt the area and made special places for some polar bears and penguins and a few sea lions. Would you like to see them?"

"Yes, I would. But no lions or tigers or elephants? That's not a zoo. I thought New York would have a great zoo."

"Well, we do have the Bronx Zoo but it's quite a trip to get there. They do have all the animals you would want in a zoo, and a lot of them roam freely in fields that are surrounded by moats. You know what a moat is?"

"Water wide enough to keep the enemy out. Those moats must be to keep the animals in the field," said Lisa.

"Yes. You are a well informed child. Your father has done a good job."

"Could we sit on one of these benches for a few minutes before leaving?"

"Lisa, are those new shoes comfortable?"

"Yes, Aunt Sally. I just want to sit for a minute. My father told me you would be "a good walker." It's the hard cement I'm not used to." Lisa laughed as she got up to join her aunt.

"I suggested these kind of shoes," said Aunt Sally as she thrust her left

220

foot forward. "The thick soles are the answer. But you wanted something more stylish."

"My feet are fine. Come on, let's go. To the zoo!" Lisa said with a big smile.

The walk to 59th Street where Central Park started was filled with beautiful shops for both Aunt Sally and Lisa to walk in and out of. Lisa spotted some clothes that she thought she would like, but the prices were astronomical! She couldn't believe them.

"How could they be that expensive? They must be made of gold. Who could pay such prices?"

"Lots of people. A lot of very wealthy people live in New York City. And a lot of very poor people. We have them all."

"How do people get so much money?"

"Business people, artists, writers. They work hard and most of them deserve to make a lot of money. Of course I work hard but I don't make a lot of money. Have you had any economic courses?"

"Not really. But Walter, your brother, told me I would learn a lot about the problems in the world when I got into economics."

"He's another smart brother. The problems we see every day—in person, in the papers, on television—can be figured out mostly by studying economics."

"I was born into a very smart family," said Lisa.

"You were born into a family that had good habits. We were given books at an early age, taken to museums, discussed topics of the day at the dinner table. I understand that today most families don't even sit down together. Each child has a different schedule for his or her sport and if the mother works, which most mothers do, she doesn't spend a lot of time preparing dinner. So there's really no time for a discussion. Books they can still give out to the children and most of them do. Trips to the library or a museum can still be taken on the weekend. But lots of children tell me their parents are usually too tired for that. They love going to museums on a class trip during the week. Too bad, but this is what they do today."

They walked to 57th Street, admired the Plaza Hotel, then crossed the two short streets to 59th where they entered Central Park.

"Let's sit on this bench for a few minutes and get our breath before entering the zoo," suggested Aunt Sally.

"We don't always eat dinner together. Barbara is home with the baby and she does make good dinners. Dad comes home most of the time at 6 o'clock. It's me who's not always there to eat. I have swimming two afternoons a week till 6:30 and the newspaper gets put together on Thursdays until 7 or 8. Those nights I get warmed-up dinners. So we only have two nights for discussions. On the weekends, never. Me, again. I'm with my friends. Or a soccer game." Lisa laughed. "But I do read. A lot. And my mother had a lot to do with that. Did you know my mother?"

"Not really. Met her a few times but I do know your father was crazy about her. Had to be. She was so different."

"Because she was black?" asked Lisa.

"I don't know. She was a smart woman. Clever with her hands. Studied design and got her masters. Had a good job, too. Don't know what disturbed her. I do know that your father was utterly upset for a long time. Couldn't seem to shake it."

"What does that mean?" Lisa asked.

"Just that most people who lose their partners get over it in a year or so. Your father mourned, and I mean mourned, for over two years. Do you remember her fairly well? She was a sweet person. Good to your father and to you."

"I remember her very well. I was only 7 but we were very close. We were friends. I still miss her. Always will." Lisa took some deep breaths. " It was her illness that made her commit suicide. The doctors just couldn't help her."

"They tried, Lisa. She had lots of good care that last year. The best doctors, the best hospitals. Nobody could help her. And she suffered so much. Your father told me how much pain she had. Did you talk about it at all with her mother, your grandmother on Long Island?"

"We cried about it. I don't remember too much but I liked the things she said about her. She missed her, too. Probably like me, still misses her. I like Barbara, but I'll always love my mother."

A few moments of silence came upon them. There was nothing really left to say. They watched the people walking across the entrance to the park, coming and going. People are always fun to watch. Now it filled the silence.

Finally, Aunt Sally got up and motioned to Lisa. "Time for the zoo or would you like a cold drink. I'd like a hot cup of tea."

"On a hot day? I'll take a cold drink."

They walked a few feet to a open-air restaurant and found a table quite close to entrance to the zoo. No waiter, and then they realized they had to go to the counter for any beverage. Aunt Sally got her hot tea and Lisa, a cold root beer. Her aunt still didn't like to give her soda but on a hot day and after a long walk, she gave in. Lisa smiled in victory. She was truly beginning to like her Aunt Sally. Like she had said to herself: Patience!

They drank, they rested, they finally got up and entered the zoo. As they stood and watched the penguins walk in and out of all kinds of rock formations, Lisa was fascinated. She had seen pictures of these seabirds that couldn't fly and always liked their waiter-like appearance, but she loved the way they strutted around. So dignified, so full of importance. They made her laugh.

They moved to the sea lions and polar bears and again she was fascinated with the way they moved around their rock habitat. A few monkeys kept them busy watching and laughing. Lisa thought that anybody who was sad or depressed should come to the zoo. It would cheer them up.

Aunt Sally decided it was time to go home. She was more gentle about her decision but she certainly didn't ask Lisa. They walked out to Fifth Avenue and took the next bus that was marked Greenwich Village.

"There's the Rockefeller Plaza! And some of the shops we went into. It's fun seeing everything again from a bus. There's the library with those huge lions. You can see them better from here. Are they stone all the way through? They must weigh a ton. Look at all the people. Hundreds of them. There's where we had lunch, Lord & Taylor's. That was good soup. And here's the Empire State Building! What a view you get from up there. I've only been here two days and I've seen so much. What's on for tomorrow?"

"I thought we might go to my school tomorrow. I could start my ordering for next year. That all right with you?"

"Sure. Look, we're already back in the Village. These buses are fast."

"Because it's not rush hour. In a half hour they will creep along because of everyone coming out of work. I try to avoid that," said Aunt Sally with a look of self-satisfaction.

"Smart."

As they left the bus and walked down the street, Aunt Sally gave out a few directions. "I'll put the chicken on. You can make the salad. I have tomatoes, lettuce, and onions. Just be careful slicing the onion. The knife is not too sharp but still be careful. You can also set the table. Use the good dishes. They're your grandmother's, and I only use them for company. Be careful with them. And use the glasses from the same china closet. The napkins are in the linen closet, second drawer, on the left."

By the time they reached the apartment, Lisa forgot everything she was supposed to do. But she was sure her aunt would remind her.

After a successful dinner and a quick clean-up, Lisa got into her bedclothes while Aunt Sally took her shower. She brought her diary out to the living room and started describing her day. She was tired and she was hoping to go to bed soon, but it was still early and she couldn't walk out on her aunt. Maybe her aunt would also be tired. She doubted it though. Aunt Sally was made of steel, at least her feet were. It was those thick soles. But those shoes were a little on the ugly side. Not for Lisa. She would rather have her feet a little sore than wear those thick soles.

"My, you're ready for bed. I'm almost ready, too. A little television first. I always tape the evening news and then watch it after my shower. Do you watch the news, Lisa? You should, you know. Know what's going on in the world. You're only thirteen but you should be aware of what's going on. You can't vote for another five years, but it's good to know who does what and where and when. Get some ideas for your opinions later on."

"I have to watch the news for my Social Studies class. It's not bad. But do you mind if I do some writing now. Want to remember all the things we did, and how I feel about it all."

"No, go ahead. Will the television bother you? Your concentration? I'll keep it low. Or you can go in your room," suggested Aunt Sally strongly.

"Okay. Think I will." As she gathered herself and went into her bedroom, she called out softly, "Thank you, Aunt Sally, for such a great day."

"You're welcome, Lisa. I enjoyed it also. Have a good sleep. See you for breakfast around 8 o'clock."

Aunt Sally settled into the smaller chair to watch her daily news program. She liked her niece, thank heavens.

Chapter Four

The school was smaller than Lisa was used to. It did have four floors though. Lisa's schools were both one-floor buildings and were spread out in three or four wings. Her aunt's school was similar to her apartment building. Squeezed between other tall buildings. All the buildings were brick and not very new. Old, dirty brick with old, dirty windows.

"Come along, Lisa. We'll go to my office first. Then I'll show you around. Meet some of the teachers who are working here today."

They climbed a long flight of stairs which were also old and dirty. Aunt Sally's office was right off the staircase and although the outside of the door was dark wood and looked a little dirty, the office itself was full of light and quite cheerful. Two large windows with shining, clean panes were surrounded with white material that looked like flannel. On the material along the sides were charts with clear, large black letters giving the names of the students in each classroom. Lisa was attracted to them and began reading the names. The chart under each class was the schedule of each day.

"I do that so I can immediately find a child or a teacher. A fire drill last month proved their value. We lost one of the classes at first and knew just how to locate it."

"Wow! That's really organized. Barbara would love to have something like that. She's a school secretary. She's not working this year but hopes to go back soon when she can find a good day-care center. She's always complaining that her desk and the principal's desk are covered with lists of children, lists of class schedules, lists of teachers' duties. Are the red notes the duties?"

"Right. It took a while to get it all in order. Of course it will be all done over in September. But the set-up will be the same. Leaves my desk clean for reports and so forth. I sit right here between the windows and just swivel to one or the other. A lot easier than the old days. Now, Lisa, how about some alphabetizing. I'll get started on the ordering. Here are the cards for the new students and the lists where they go. I'll do a few for you to give you an idea.

And do ask if you have any questions rather than assume. My secretary won't be in till tomorrow. She'll appreciate whatever you can do."

Lisa sat down next to her aunt's desk and waited for the cards and the lists. As she waited for Aunt Sally to settle down, a tall, middle-aged woman came into the office.

"Good morning, Sally. I see you brought your niece with you this morning. You must be Lisa. Oh, don't get up." she said as Lisa was half out of her chair. "I'm not that old."

Aunt Sally quickly introduced Lisa to Ms. Jackson, one of her fourth grade teachers. "Glad you're here today, Betty. When Lisa gets through with these lists, can she come up and help you with something?"

"I'm just cleaning and putting books away. But sure. If you want, Lisa, I could use your help," said Ms. Jackson, with a nice smile.

Lisa just smiled back.

"Here are my order sheets, Sally. Come up whenever, Lisa. Room 402. Up the stairs and turn left. And call out if you're not sure."

Ms. Jackson put the papers on Sally's desk and left. "See you later, funny alligator. Or funny bunny."

"Don't mind her. Ms. Jackson is our comedian. Or at least she thinks so. And she's a bit behind the times. She's a good teacher. The children love her, and their test results are very high. So I put up with her jokes and silly comments. Now, here we go. Remember, ask before doing anything you're not sure of."

Lisa came out of the whirlwind of conversation and directions with the patience that she was working on this past year. She finished the lists Aunt Sally had given her and stood up for a stretch.

"Why don't you go on up to Ms. Jackson and see how you can help her? In an hour or so, it'll be time for lunch. Ask her if she wants to join us. A hamburger okay for you? We have a small café around the corner that serves good food. Also fast and reasonable. We'll leave a little before 11:45."

"I love hamburgers. Okay, see you later. Room 402, right?"

Lisa climbed the stairs and found Ms. Jackson standing on the top step of a ladder, reaching for old and heavy books.

"You came just in time. Here, take these to the table. Lisa, right? I should know your name. Your aunt has been speaking about you for the past month."

"Pile them any which way?"

"Let me show you. We have to copy the inside numbers so it's easier to stack them flat. So how do you like staying with your aunt? Is she more relaxed at home? She's a real dynamo and a strict boss here at school. But we love her. She gets things done. Even if she loses her temper now and then."

"Oh, I haven't seen her lose her temper," said Lisa.

"She has one to lose and she can lose it. Can't find it sometimes."

"I've only known her for a few days, but she seems to be in such control that I can't imagine her losing it. But we do have a teacher back home that is usually very much in control, all stiff and proper. We call her the "washboard." I don't even know what a washboard is but that's her nickname. She's been around for generations, taught my father and his father. It might have come from then. Anyway even though she's stiff and proper, if she should find something terribly wrong with what you've done, she blows up like a tornado. I've never been the cause but I've seen it happen. But I still can't imagine Aunt Sally blowing up."

"It happens with her more than she would like to acknowledge. Last week when the kids were cleaning up to go home for the summer, she came into my room and when she saw that some of the kids were balling their papers and throwing them at each other, she kicked the half-full basket by the door clear across the room. Yelling, "that is what the basket is for" and other stuff that wasn't so nice. Fortunately, the basket didn't hit anybody, but when a lot of its paper and stuff came out as it flew over their heads, the kids started to laugh. It was funny. But that was not the time to laugh. She said a few parting words, then slammed the door as she left."

"Good heavens, I can hardly believe that."

"Well, don't you tell her I told you. I shouldn't have told you. I'm sorry, Lisa. But I'm laughing about it. Your aunt is a great principal and the kids like her, as do the teachers. She's a real educator. Just has, what they say, "a short fuse.""

"Good heavens. I hope I don't upset her."

"Now, young lady, let me hand you some more books. I have to clean out all these shelves by 2 o'clock."

"Ms. Jackson, Aunt Sally wants to know if you would like to join us for lunch. At 11:45. She says there's a good café around the corner."

"Love to. But we mustn't laugh or mention the wastebasket. Here, take these and put them on one of the desks if there's no room on the table."

They counted and listed the numbers for all the books from the open shelves. It was soon time for lunch, and they both had to clean up before going down to Aunt Sally's office.

After a satisfactory lunch, Aunt Sally asked Lisa if she would like to help with her ordering supplies. Lisa promptly sat down next to her aunt's desk and waited for instructions.

They started with ordering small equipment for the science classes. Aunt Sally called out the item—bells, wire, chemicals, litmus paper—Lisa checked them off.

"Be very careful, Lisa. If I'm going too fast, tell me. Each item must match the order sheet. Last year I didn't have anyone to help me, and a terribly error was made. I still don't think it was my error. I believe someone down at the warehouse simply read it incorrectly. I had ordered 40 test tubes and the warehouse send 400! Can you imagine?"

"When you sent them back, did they admit their mistake?"

"I didn't send them back. My dear, if I had sent them back, I would never have received my original order. If I had subtracted 40 from the lot, and sent back 360 test tubes, I would have confused them so that I probably would have received another 360, if not 400," said Aunt Sally with a laugh. "That warehouse is not run very efficiently."

"What did you do with the 400 test tubes?"

"Stored them in the basement. I'll never have to order more test tubes."

"Oh, Aunt Sally, that's awful. Three hundred and sixty test tubes just sitting down there. Doing nothing."

"Now don't you judge me, young lady. I made the best decision considering all of the circumstances."

"I'm not judging you, Aunt Sally. Sorry if it sounded that way. I just feel it's a terrible waste."

"Well, it is judging me, my dear. You don't realize the responsibilities of this job. I have to make final decisions all the time. Most of the time, correcting other people's mistakes. Now let's get back to work. And be sure when I call out a number that it is correctly noted."

"Yes, Aunt Sally. And I'm sorry I sounded like you said I sounded."

"It's all right. Now, 20 burners. Be sure it's 20."

Chapter Five

Finished with her ordering, Aunt Sally asked Lisa if she would mind coming back to school the next day to check the list of reading scores with the master list. She had done the many class lists and was ready to send it on to headquarters. But she always checked everything before headquarters could find any errors.

The following day Lisa sat in the same chair. She was happy to spend another day at the school and to help her aunt.

The lists her aunt gave to Lisa were attached to the reading tests that the children had taken. Her aunt had the master list. As they worked, Lisa became curious about the tests attached the class list. During a few phone calls that her aunt was busy with, she looked over the tests and was pleased to see that she would have answered the questions the same way. But when she looked at the tests under a 4th grade list, she saw that some of the scores did not match the scores on the list. She had time to carefully check each student's reading score and realize that some 6 or 7 of them did not match. When her aunt got off the phone and was ready to continue her work, Lisa mentioned this discrepancy.

"Oh, it's all right. We had to change some of the scores. Just go by the list on top of the tests. Ready?"

"Why don't they match? It says here Philip somebody got 2.6 on the test, yet the list says he got 3.5."

"Lisa, it's all right." She looked at her niece carefully and then quietly said that if they sent in 2.6 for Philip, and anything below 2.9 for any of the other students, her school would lose a lot of Federal money, and she wouldn't be able to have special reading classes to help these students catch up with their skills.

"I don't understand, Aunt Sally."

"Lisa, it's quite simple. The law says that a child cannot be promoted if he is more than two years behind. We are now at the 9th month which is 4.9

for the fourth grade. Philip and a few others would have to repeat fourth grade and could not enter a special reading class. This way, with a score of 3.5, he can go on to the fifth grade and because he is below 5.1, he can be included in a special class for reading help. I know it sounds confusing, but I do want these children with reading problems to have extra help."

"If he was in the fourth grade again, wouldn't he get special help anyway, being below 4.1. And maybe he would learn more by repeating that class."

"No. Lisa, you're judging me again. I know it sounds complicated but believe me, the child will do much better in the fifth grade along with that special class. The rules are crazy, not me. His teacher agrees with me, and we changed the scores together. Headquarters doesn't know these children and really doesn't care what grade they are in. Do you know how embarrassing it is to be left behind as the rest of the class goes on to the next grade? You have to consider the child."

"Is it judging you by saying that it's wrong to change someone's reading score? I don't know about any rules and regulations, but to change someone's test score seems wrong to me," said Lisa very quietly and carefully.

"Yes, it is judging me. You're a child and don't understand that certain rules are wrong, and to try to fight it at headquarters where they make the rules, is impossible. I used to try to fix things that way and I always failed. Let me tell you another strange story. When I was principal in a Brooklyn school, that's still in the New York system, there was a test for students who mainly spoke and read in their native language. Some organization insisted that if a child failed the test because he did not fully understand English, he should graduate anyway. That's when I had a middle school. Anyway, if he passed the test but with a low score, under 75% I believe, he would not get a diploma, only a certificate. Well, we had a student, Pablo, who had worked very hard during the year in his special reading class but only scored 72%. This meant that although he would graduate with his class he would not be called up to the platform to receive his diploma. He would get his certificate in the mail. I couldn't do that to him. It so happened that the rest of his class had failed this test. But because English was not their native tongue, they would all march up to the platform and receive their diplomas."

Lisa gasped. "Let me finish, Lisa. The teacher of that reading class was furious. She came to me and tried to fight the rules. She told me that Pablo had worked harder that year than any other student. That he deserved a diploma. She couldn't let his classmates, who didn't work as he had, go home with diplomas and he only get a certificate. We both felt awful. She finally devised a way to solve it. She cleared it with me first. I took a chance but I felt so deeply about justice being done in Pablo's case, that I went along with it. We obtained another blank test and she spoke to the child. She explained the whole thing to him and told him to deliberately fail the test. Because his native tongue was not English, he would receive a diploma. He was nervous about doing it and did ask his teacher what he should do when it came to the oral part. She told him to speak the truth and give the correct answers. She couldn't ask him to lie in person. But on the written part, he was to give all the wrong answers. She explained that not only would his family feel better the day of graduation, watching him go up to the platform and receive his diploma, but that for the rest of his life, he would be proud to show his friends and his future children, his diploma from middle school. This did it. He agreed to do as she had suggested. He gave honest answers to the questioner in the oral part and he wrote down all the wrong answers in the written part. He failed the test and he marched up to get his diploma. That teacher and I had tears in our eyes on graduation day. Neither of us have any idea how he is doing today, but we feel sure we did the right thing."

"You make me want to cry now. You did the right thing. But, Aunt Sally, didn't that teach the boy that cheating and lying was okay. I've been taught at home, and with my relatives, that cheating and lying were wrong."

"I forgot that part. This teacher, who I still see now and then, told the child in no uncertain terms that what she and he were about to do was wrong! Yes, it was wrong to lie and cheat, and he was never to do it again unless a similar situation came up again. We three were fighting a stupid rule, a rule that would have hurt him and his family. He seemed to understand what she was saying. A brave teacher and a brave student."

"What about a brave principal? I see now what you mean. It would have been awful for Pablo to just get a certificate, especially when he had worked the hardest in his class. Just awful. I'm sorry, Aunt Sally, for thinking you were wrong about changing the reading scores. Why are there such stupid rules?"

"I don't know. But I do know that we have about an hour left to finish these lists. We're having lunch with Grace and Betty today. You might go up to their rooms to remind them to be down here by 11:30 if we want to get a seat at the café. But come right back as I do want to send the master list off today with the noon pick-up."

Lisa put her papers down and got up. As she left the room, she turned back to her aunt and softly said, "Thanks for telling me that story, Aunt Sally."

"Haven't told that story for many years now. It was the right time to tell it again."

Chapter Six

It was Saturday and Aunt Sally decided that it was time to visit the United Nations. The ride up First Avenue gave Lisa a good view of the East River. The buildings of the U.N. loomed large in comparison to the surrounding structures. The entrance fee was not too much, but Lisa thought about all the entrance fees her aunt had paid that first week and a half. And for places she had already seen, probably many times. She was a good person in spite of some of her strange ways. Like always, Lisa was learning patience with her relatives' habits and behavior. And learning to like them.

The large entrance hall and staircases were impressive. The quiet atmosphere pleased Lisa. A holy feeling like a church. They signed up for a tour and their guide was more than pleasant and informative. He allowed them to listen on earphones to English translations of foreign diplomats as they discussed the issues of the day. Lisa had read about the U.N. in school but she really didn't understand what it was all about. When they finished the tour, she understood a lot more.

They visited some special exhibits, saw a lot of photographs, a lot of flags, and a lot of maps. Maybe she could work for the U.N. some day.

When they left the building and walked around the vast plaza, Aunt Sally asked Lisa if she were hungry and would she like a hot dog. Of course, she was and of course she would love a hot dog. They walked across the plaza to a hot dog stand, got their food, and walked over to the railing that separated them from the East River. Sitting on a bench which faced the river, they ate their lunch as they watched small boats go up and down. It was a glorious day and both ladies were fully enjoying themselves.

"I'm glad you came to New York, Lisa. I'm seeing things that I haven't seen in such a long time. And you're good company. I should do this more often, maybe get one of my friends to join me. But I don't have many friends who would like this sort of thing. I don't have many friends. The ones I do have like to play bridge or go to the theatre. That's all. Of course they all have husbands to go home to and fuss over. Making dinner and so forth. I do get lonely once in a while. Especially in the evening. I don't mean to tell you my problems but somehow you seem to be a good listener. Do you mind?"

"Of course not. But, Aunt Sally, you did choose to be single. My father told me you were engaged once. But he turned out to be fortune hunter. Not that you had a lot of money Dad said. So you broke the engagement and Dad said you concentrated on your career. Is all that true?"

"Yes, it is. He was a lovely man in the beginning because he was fooling me. I fell for it and him. I'm not sorry now to have had that experience. But I am sorry that I don't have any children. But I have a niece, and that's just fine. And isn't it wonderful that my brother has adopted a little boy. Walter and Mary Joan will make wonderful parents and there are so many children in this world who don't have parents."

"I had something to do with that. Last summer when I was down in South Carolina, I talked and talked about their adopting. And they finally did it. And they didn't take a new-born like some do. Freddie was perfect. Two years old and full of the devil, they tell me. And they already love him to pieces."

"You do manage to work yourself into tight places. Your grandmother on Long Island told me you practically arranged the marriage of one of her friends."

"I like to see people I like happy and making other people happy."

"There's a great play called THE MATCHMAKER just about such a person. It was turned into a musical called HELLO DOLLY. I saw the play a few years ago at the Shakespeare theatre in Central Park. Oh, yes, our play in the park. A friend of mine saw their production of ROMEO AND JULIET last week and loved it. Would you be interested in that? Have you read it or studied it in school?"

"No, but Barbara was telling me about it when our class was studying JULIUS CAESAR. It has some beautiful speeches. She read some of it to me. I'd love to see it, Aunt Sally. When can we go?"

"Either tomorrow night or next Wednesday."

"It's free, right?"

"Yes it is."

"Do you think we could take Rosie? She lives across the street from you. The girl I met in the park a couple of days ago. I told you about her."

"The girl with the dog. From what you said, she seems quite nice. Do you think her parents would let her come with us? We won't get home till 11 or so."

"Let's ask her. See what she says. It won't cost you anything. Oh, we'd have to make her a sandwich for the picnic before hand."

"We'll see," said Aunt Sally. Lisa laughed. Aunt Sally asked what was so funny and Lisa told her that that's what all grown-ups ever say when asked a difficult question.

"Well, we'll see. Come on, let's go home. We can take the Second Avenue bus before it gets too crowded."

Lisa didn't want to leave but grown-ups made the decisions.

Chapter Seven

"Hello, Lisa. Going to the park?"

Lisa turned around to find out who called her. And there was Rosie coming down her front steps.

"Just going for a short walk. Come with me. Where's your dog?"

"Herbie, that's my brother, he has him. Think he took him to the river."

"I didn't know you had a brother."

They walked down the street, or as Rosie called it, the block, and continued their new friendship.

"Little brother? But old enough to take your dog for a walk," asked Lisa.

"Seventeen. Last year in high school and thinks he's a big shot. But he plays a mean game of Monopoly."

"Monopoly? Isn't that just for kids? I haven't played that for years."

"Not if you're interested in money and real estate like Herbie is. He tells everybody he's going to live on Park Avenue some day and be a very rich man.

"Is he going to college next year? To learn about Real Estate?"

"I don't know. If it doesn't cost too much. He's not rich yet!

The girls laughed and continued their walk into the small park. Rosie introduced Lisa to some girls they met and they all decided to sit on the benches and talk *girl talk*. This was new for Lisa. She had been introduced to it by her cousin, Suzanne, in California. Her own friends at home talked mainly about swimming meets and the school newspaper. Boys were boys and girls were girls. What's the big deal? thought Lisa. But now she was hearing all about who was dating whom and where did they go and what time did they come home? They talked about some of the fights their friends had and how they 'broke up' with whomever. Lisa didn't open her mouth. She really didn't contribute anything and she didn't want to comment on what she was hearing. This was unusual for Lisa, not commenting. But she was learning of late to keep a lot of her opinions to herself. Life was simpler that way.

"Looks who walking to us!" cried one of the girls.

"It's Herbie," Rosie explained to Lisa. "He's coming back early. Snowball had hardly any time to play. Maybe there's a baseball game on T.V."

"He's so cute, Rosie," exclaimed one of the girls. "He's not going out with Mirabel anymore, I hear. Did they have a fight?"

"Not really. He just lost interest. She talked too much."

"I don't talk much," said Louise.

"You do too!" cried the rest of the girls.

"Well, I could learn to shut up if that's what he wants," Louise offered quietly.

"Herbie, come on over." called one of the girls.

Rosie explained to Lisa, "He's a little shy. Herbie, I want you to meet Lisa. I told you about her, remember? From out west, visiting her Aunt Sally, the school principal across the street."

"Oh, yeah. Hi, Lisa. Nice to meet you. This here is Snowball. And he doesn't melt even on hot days like this."

"Hi. I used to have a dog, Mitzi. She died last year. She wasn't sick. Just 14 years old. I still miss her." Lisa shut her mouth and thought how she had promised herself to be quiet. She couldn't have made a very good impression with Herbie. He smiled at her but kept walking along with Snowball.

"Herbie," yelled Rosie, "Mom wants you to go to the store."

"What's wrong with you going? I got a game to watch."

"Too heavy for me. Dog food's on sale."

"Come with me and we'll split it," Herbie yelled back.

"What about your game?"

"We'll run."

"Come on, Herbie, you can run with all the cans. Get going."

The girls continued with their girl talk for another hour. Then they split up, leaving Rosie and Lisa sitting on the bench by themselves.

"Rosie, Aunt Sally and I are going to Central Park tomorrow night to see some Shakespeare play. ROMEO AND JULIET I think. Would you like to come with us? We take a picnic supper to eat while we wait on the line to get in. It's free. The play. And we can make a sandwich for you."

"At night? What time do we get home? Mom won't let me stay out after 10 o'clock."

"Oh, it'll probably be about 11 before we get home, but Aunt Sally will be with us. We could take Herbie with us if that would help."

"Get him to go to a Shakespeare play? Are you kidding?"

"Ask him. He might say yes. Then ask your mother. We could have such a good time. They say it's beautiful, the scenery and all. And we wear dungarees since we sit on the ground to eat. Herbie would like that, wouldn't he? And he could help us carry the food. Ask him."

"Okay. Let's go now. I'll go to the store with him and help run back and I'll ask him on the way back."

"He seems like a nice kid. Is he a good brother? I'm an only child, no brothers, no sisters. But I have a few friends who have brothers and a lot of them say they're pests."

"He's pest sometimes. But most of the time he's a good kid. He liked you. I could tell the way he looked at you. He doesn't like any of my friends. Says girls talk too much."

"He was only here for a minute and I talked too much, especially about Mitzi, my dog."

They reached their houses and Rosie crossed the street, yelling from the other side, "See you later."

Lisa went upstairs, deciding to spend the rest of the afternoon writing in her diary. She didn't know what she would say about Herbie except that she thought he was cute and nice. She wondered what Aunt Sally would say about him joining them for the play. If he was going to join them. She certainly hoped so.

Chapter Eight

Herbie joined them, promising his mother to never leave Rosie's side. His mother also made some salad for their picnic in the park and gave Herbie a blanket for Aunt Sally to sit on. Aunt Sally was a little skeptical about taking Herbie, not knowing him at all and wondering what a 17-year old youngster would be like. She had read enough to know that a lot of them were incorrigible. But Lisa, then Rosie whom she did know from the neighborhood, both convinced her that Herbie was a gentleman. His mother said he was, and Aunt Sally decided to take a chance.

It was a most successful evening. They all got along quite well, and the food was delicious. Lots of olives and pepper in the salad. And Herbie had carried most everything. When he spread out the blanket, Aunt Sally was impressed and made room for the others to at least have a corner of it. They all loved the play. Lisa was in sheer heaven. Knowing a bit of the story gave her a head start and she went with the romance, the sadness, the tragedy.

They got home a little after 11 but Rosie's mother was pleased to see them still all together and laughing and singing. She thanked Aunt Sally so much for taking care of her children. And Aunt Sally thanked her for the delicious salad. And for the blanket.

A couple of days later Aunt Sally and Lisa went to the Metropolitan Museum of Art. Lisa had wanted to include Rosie and Herbie but Aunt Sally thought not, having found out that neither of them had ever been to an art museum. She remembered when one of her teachers had a student who loved to draw and did quite well with all his pictures. She thought the child was especially talented and so got permission from his parents to take him to the Metropolitan Museum of Art on a Saturday afternoon. The child, an eight year old, was dressed for the occasion in a black suit, white shirt, and red tie and scrubbed clean to almost shining. He was quiet all the way to the museum and walking through the galleries, never said a word until he got to the Rembrandt collection. There he said quite loudly, "I can do that!" in front of

237

every portrait. The teacher was a little embarrassed and explained to the child that he shouldn't talk so loudly. That didn't deter him. He stuck to his one and only statement. When she brought him home, he didn't thank her, just said goodbye and went in the apartment building. The next week he never said a word about his excursion to the art museum. He just kept on with his habits of no homework, no passing tests, and drawing pictures all day.

Aunt Sally told Lisa this story with the conviction that Rosie and Herbie would not enjoy the museum. Lisa's only comments were, "Maybe that boy would grow up to be an artist. Maybe Rosie and Herbie would like to see all the pictures." But as Lisa knew, adults got their way, and she and her aunt went by themselves.

Lisa enjoyed the museum, all its paintings and statuary. She and Aunt Sally discussed the following few days left of her vacation. They would go to the Bronx Zoo and if time permitted, they would visit Chinatown where Lisa could buy some gifts for home and sample some of New York's best cooking. If they had time they would also visit the Museum of the City of New York where they had a fabulous display of doll houses. Aunt Sally kept forgetting Lisa was 13 and probably not into that. But with the conversations they've been having, how could she forget?

Chapter Nine

Both of them loved every minute of the Bronx Zoo. Lisa wasn't so sure that one of the lions wasn't going to leap across the moat and finish her off.

"This is really wild!" she said as they continued on to the giraffes.

During lunch, Lisa asked Aunt Sally if she could go with Herbie to a baseball game in Central Park.

"In Central Park! There's a team he's been following and they play their next game in the Park," explained Lisa.

"I don't know. Let me think about it."

The expression 'we'll see' was more positive than 'I don't know' so Lisa tried again.

"It's in the daytime. One o'clock. And there'll be lots of people there. He says it's always crowded. I would love to see a baseball game in New York, even if it's only kids playing.

"I should have taken you to Yankee Stadium to see a real game. How did your visit go by so quickly? I was afraid I wouldn't be able to find enough for you to enjoy. But you're easy to have around. Mother and Dad said the same thing. We'll no doubt have a long phone conversation about all the things we did do. A few phone conversations. I won't remember everything at once. Let me think about Herbie's invitation. You wouldn't be foolish and go anywhere else. I'll call your father and get his opinion."

"He'll say yes, I know he will."

"We'll see," murmured Aunt Sally.

That expression gave Lisa more hope.

"We have three more days," said Lisa sadly. "Did you want to go back to your school?"

"You don't have to go. If your father agrees, I can go to the school when you go to the game. When did he say it was?"

"Tomorrow."

"Oh, we have to move fast. We'll call tonight. Then the next day I think we should have lunch in Chinatown and then take the Staten Island ferry so you can see the Statue of Liberty even closer than from Battery Park. On Thursday I take you to the airport."

"And you can go home and "put your feet up." That's what my Dad always says. You've been so good to me, Aunt Sally. I'll never forget this trip. And I'll never forget you."

"What will you do next summer? I'm the last of the relatives, right?"

"Maybe go down to your parents again. Or I might just hang out around home. It might be nice to spend the summer with the kids. And of course Barbara will be there. If she doesn't have a job. If she does, maybe I can take care of the baby."

"You don't want to spend the whole summer taking care of a toddler. You're a good traveler by now. You're a better traveler than I am. Maybe go away to a camp. This country has thousands of camps, each offering something different. Why don't you do some research this winter and see what is available. Maybe be a counselor. Although Mother and Dad would love to have you visit them again."

"Why didn't you travel a lot? So many summers off, all these years. You could have gone around the world."

"I studied. Got my Masters, then my Doctorate. And by that time I was a principal and spent a good deal of the summer working at the school. And taking courses. We have quite a few colleges in the city, and I've been to them all. Wonderful schools. And as I said, I had lots of work at school. During the school year, there's no time for study or heavy planning. I've enjoyed my life. When I retire in five years, I hope to start traveling. But not in the summer. That's when all the teachers and young people travel. Spring and fall is the time to go. I'd like to go to Russia. China. Australia. And of course Europe."

"That sounds great. Some day I'll travel out of the country. I enjoy traveling. Who knows? I've got years to decide. Maybe we could go somewhere together. That would be fun. I'd have my own money by then and you wouldn't have to pay for everything. Aunt Sally, you're been very generous with me this summer. I really appreciate it."

"You're very nice to say that, Lisa. So many children today have no manners. Take everything for granted. I've enjoyed these weeks as much as you did, Lisa, and I thank you for giving me such a good time. Now let's see some more of the zoo. Elephants interest you?"

Chapter Ten

Lisa went to the baseball game with Herbie. Her dad thought it was a great idea. So did her grandfather. That was where he used to play with the company baseball team before retiring. He loved New York. Oh, he loved Florida, but his heart belonged to New York, he told Lisa.

Lisa had a good time with Herbie. He had watched her more than the game. She wasn't used to being looked at. Her cousin, Suzanne, told her how she loved it when Michael looked at her. Lisa wasn't sure. She wondered if her hair was a mess. Did she get mustard from the hot dog on her chin? So she asked him.

"Do I have mustard on my chin?"

"No. Why?"

"You keep looking at me, at my face. I just wondered."

"You're pretty. That's why I'm looking at you," Herbie said softly.

"No, I'm not. I'm not pretty like the other girls in my class."

Herbie laughed. "I don't know them so I can't compare. But you're pretty to me. Okay?"

"Okay."

And Lisa suddenly felt a strange feeling in her body. She was never really aware of her body before. Now even her heart started pounding. She remembered when Suzanne told her how her blouse would move when her heart pounded. Lisa looked down to see if her blouse was moving. Not really, but her heart still did a few flips. Strange feeling.

The rest of that afternoon, Lisa and Herbie had great conversations about the game, the Park, New York, Lisa's home town, her father and new mother, her brother. Lisa found Herbie so easy to talk with. And laugh with. They walked all the way home.

They walked and talked all the way home. It was hard to say goodbye when they got back to Greenwich Village. She wanted to swing on the swings, to bounce on the seesaw, to run through the grass of the little park next to her aunt's building. She did not want to go upstairs. Not yet.

241

"Are we very late? I mean do you eat now? Guess it's time for me to go up. Aunt Sally will be cooking dinner. But I don't want to. Could we just walk through the park for a few minutes?"

"Sure. It's still early. Want to swing?"

They each grabbed a swing and both of them went flying through the air. Laughing and swinging.

"I haven't done this for years now. What fun!" Herbie yelled.

"This is so silly and such fun. I'm so glad I met you, Herbie. And that you asked me to the baseball game."

"Me, too. You make me feel like a kid. And free. I feel so free. The swings make me feel free. No, it's you. You make me feel free."

"I feel free, too. Oh, I wish I didn't have to go up. Aunt Sally will worry, I know she will. And I should care. But I want to swing some more."

Herbie let his swing wind down. Then he got off and reached over and slowed Lisa's swing down. "You better go up. It's getting late."

He walked her slowly to the front door and said good night.

"Good night, Herbie. Thanks for everything."

Lisa walked to the elevator and traveled to the fourth floor as if in a stupor. She had to shake this feeling before seeing Aunt Sally. Knocking on the door with a burst of energy, Lisa called out a big hello.

"Where have you been?" her aunt asked as she opened the door. "Did the game last this late? I called the Park Department and they thought it was over hours ago. Did you go somewhere else? I asked you not to. Come in. Are you hungry? I couldn't wait so I had my dinner. Tell me, Lisa, why are you late?"

"I don't know, Aunt Sally. I'm sorry I'm late. I'm sorry you had to eat alone. It's so silly. We walked home from the Park. And I guess that's what took so long."

"You walked from 62 Street to Greenwich Village?"

"Before that we went on the carousel. I'm sorry. I really am. It just looked like so much fun. And it was. We were on it for a long time. Herbie spent a lot of money on me. But it was wonderful. Then we walked down Fifth Avenue. The same street you and I walked on. There were some buses, but we felt like walking. And talking. Herbie's a nice boy, Aunt Sally. He's a real gentleman. He felt awful when we realized how late we were. But it wasn't his fault. I was the one who wanted to walk home. He's very nice. Very funny. We had such a good time. But I didn't mean to worry you. You didn't worry, did you? I'm so sorry."

"I don't believe this. You went on the carousel. You walked a few miles. And you look so alive. And you're feet probably don't hurt. If you were sixteen, I'd say you were in love. But not at 13, and not under my watch. Oh, Lisa, I'm not angry but I am disappointed. Of course it's still light out. But you should have thought about me, waiting here for you. Worrying where

242

you were. That wasn't very considerate. And we better not tell your father. I don't know what he would say."

"He won't be angry. He trusts me. We just walked and walked. We thought we would get a bus but we were home before we knew what we did. I'm so sorry. I didn't mean to worry you. New York is a wonderful city. You live in a terrific city. There's so much to see. I would miss our parks and our fields all around us, but we don't have any of the things you have. It's so exciting."

"Are you thinking of moving here?"

"Oh, Aunt Sally, of course not. I am only 13 as you said and I did a very silly thing. But we didn't do anything bad. We didn't hurt anybody or anything. We just walked and talked and did a lot of laughing. He's a very nice boy."

"I'm glad you know you're only 13. That's a relief. Now, Lisa, you must be hungry. Or did you stop for any food?"

"No. And I am hungry."

"Okay. Let me heat your dinner. You can take a shower if you'd like. To cool off. To relax. Some iced tea? Tomorrow we have a big day, that is if you feel like it. We'll go to Chinatown and then over to Staten Island and that should wrap up your visit, Friday morning we take a cab to the Port of Authority and then a bus to the airport. Can you manage all that? You had better pack tomorrow morning while you have some energy."

Aunt Sally turned and went into the kitchen. Lisa just stood there for a minute, not knowing what to do. Yes, she thought. She would take a shower. No, she thought again. After dinner, she would just like to get into bed and think about her wonderful day. And the wonderful boy from across the street. "My heavens, he's Rosie's brother!" she said out loud.

"May I eat in my pajamas, Aunt Sally?"

"Yes, you may. Shower tomorrow morning? Okay. Your dinner's almost ready. Get comfortable. I'll take my shower while you're eating. Do you mind? Then I'll watch the news while you hop into bed, exhausted from your three-mile walk It's okay, Lisa. You're okay and for that I am grateful. A little silly but I'm sure I was silly when I was 13, too. We'll have a simple day tomorrow. Chinatown and the Staten Island Ferry. Would you like to *walk* down to the battery? There's a nice park down there, remember? But no carousel. Go on. Get into your pajamas." Aunt Sally smiled. Then laughed a little.

"No, I do not want to walk to the battery. But thanks for the offer," said Lisa with a smile also.

Lisa liked Aunt Sally even more now. Oh, she thought, what a terrific world I live in.

Chapter Eleven

The day before leaving was a quiet but colorful day. They walked up and down all the crowded streets of Chinatown. Lisa bought several gifts for her family back home, and they had a fabulous lunch, very much like the lunch Lisa had in San Francisco. She was now addicted to Chinese food.

They relaxed on the ferry that went to Staten Island. The Statue of Liberty majestically towered over everything else as they went by. In fact, the ride was so delightful that they decided to take the return ferry right away. Aunt Sally said there wasn't much to see on the Island anyway. And they both loved the ferry ride as it chugged back to Manhattan.

As they rode up to the fourth floor and Aunt Sally's apartment, what to have for dinner was the conversation. Lisa was still full from lunch and still a little excited about the past two days. She said she wasn't hungry.

"I'll roast the chicken anyway and whatever you don't eat, I'll have for the weekend. Just chicken and a salad."

"I'll make the salad again. And set the table. You make a great chicken so I'm bound to eat something. It was a great day, Aunt Sally. Really great. I'm glad we went back right away on the ferry. And that Statue of Liberty is awesome! Too bad you can't go up into it now. 9/11 sure put a crimp on things to see in New York. On my next visit. Okay?"

"Okay," said Aunt Sally as she took the chicken out. "Why don't you finish up your packing? I'll call you when it's time to toss the salad."

Lisa did just that. Sadly she checked the closet and under the bed. She decided to take her shower now so she could pack most of her bathroom stuff.

There was small talk during dinner. Aunt Sally mentioned a couple of times that they had to be on their way by 9 o'clock. She would call for a taxi in the morning. Lisa started to tear up a little but her aunt ignored it. She didn't know if the tears were for her, for leaving New York, or for leaving Herbie. And she didn't want to know.

They watched the news and went to bed before 10 o'clock.

There wasn't time for sadness in the morning as they both rushed around, collecting and checking. The taxi was on time, and they were off.

The Port of Authority was still crowded. Aunt Sally was less authoritative, and they both walked briskly to their bus. Lisa looked back to see the Empire State Building and sighed.

When they got to the airport, there was too much to do and too many people to avoid to let sadness take over. Lisa went through the security check, and Aunt Sally was smiling and waving. Lisa threw a final kiss and walked to the plane.

After settling down in her window seat, Lisa took out her prepared writing paper and pen, pulled down the tray, and started writing.

"Dear Herbie,"

The End